THE
WAYFARERS

*To Sheree
Best wishes*

*Howard H. Effman
Dec. 6, 1999*

THE WAYFARERS

Howard N. Ellman

Our motto – *In order that a good story may be told* –
reflects our belief that tomorrow's literary heritage depends on investment in today's writers.

First published in Great Britain 2000 by
The Malvern Publishing Company Limited
32, Old Street, Upton-upon-Severn,
Worcestershire, WR8 0HW, England

http://www.malvernfirst.com

USA Sales, Distribution and Rights
The British Book Company, Inc.
149 Palos Verdes Boulevard, Suite B
Redondo Beach, California 90277
USA

British Library Cataloguing in Publication Data
A catalogue record for this book is available
From the British Library

ISBN 0 947993 93 2

Printed in Malta by Interprint Limited

To my wife Betsy,
who endured the long periods of distance
while I was possessed by my characters.

To my daughters, Stephanie and Janet,
who cheered me on.

To my agent and friend Hilary Zelman Katersky,
whose encouragement helped me traverse
those bleak intervals when inspiration failed.

CHAPTER ONE

I found my way to Blackfriars Abbey in the summer of 1221, anno Domini, at eleven years of age, orphaned by my mother's death in childbirth and my father's at the hand of brigands on the high road from York to Oxford. I had been born on Christmas day, 1210 and christened John Wheelwright. My name befit my station — John, the most common and ordinary name in all of Christendom, and Wheelwright, no name at all but the description of my father's lowly trade — well beneath that of blacksmith, armorer, carpenter or stonemason.

We lived in a one room hut with a dirt floor, walls of stone, timbers, mud and a roof of grass thatch. My father plied his trade outside against the south wall of the hut under an extended roof held up by two poles so that he could remain dry during periods of rain or snow. His work area included a stone fireplace so that he could heat and bend the stays that he fashioned into wheels.

I was the second of four brothers. None but I survived past age six. I will not linger over tales of my own childhood. It was as unexceptional as my name. I speak of it only to explain how I came to Blackfriars.

When my parents died, I had nowhere to go. My father's brothers quickly came and, telling me that he owed them money, took everything from our house, including my tools. No one stopped them. As the last remaining son, I supposedly had rights to my parents' property, such as it was. But the house and ground belonged to our Lord the Duke of York, with my father having no more than a life tenure on condition of paying a land rent that I, with no trade or means of livelihood, could not. My uncles also claimed that I was obliged to work for them to pay off the rest of my father's debt.

At eleven years of age, I lacked the power to contest them. But when they commenced to quarrel over me as though I were some sort of chattel slave, I ran to the Abbey to seek refuge. Brother Wilfred persuaded the Abbot to take me in. The custom of the time allowed a monastery to keep a fleeing serf against the claims of those who pursued him by placing a bell rope around his neck. I gladly accepted the rope in preference to the tender mercies of my uncles.

The Abbey being under straitened circumstances, my sustenance came from Brother Wilfred's share. There being no quarters for apprentices or trainees, he had to make room for me in his cramped cell when I could not stay in a corner of the dining hall or next to the cook's fire. He obtained the Abbot's permission to take me under his care as an apprentice in the art of illumination. When my uncles came to reclaim me for their service, he showed them the rope and further dissuaded them with most un-Christian threats and demonstrations.

Four years passed before Brother Wilfred explained why he had performed his kindness for me. As we lay in the chill dark one winter's evening on the shelf that served as a bed in his cell, I asked, as I had done on several previous occasions. Whereas in the past he had made a joke or refused to answer, this time he paused, and I could tell that he weighed my question seriously for the first time.

"I will tell you now, Johnnie. You're old enough to know and be trusted with the knowledge. I saw myself in you, Johnnie-lad. I truly did. Not too many years ago, I came here myself needing shelter and a refuge."

"Did you have uncles demanding that you be their indentured servant to work off a debt?" I asked.

He laughed quietly. "I suppose you could say that — in a manner of speaking."

"What happened? Please tell me."

He took hold of my shoulder and shook me, not hard but firmly, his face close, eyes holding mine. "You must swear on the blood of Christ never to reveal what I tell you. Swear it." His tone startled me.

"I swear it."

He said nothing more for a moment. When he spoke, his calm tone had returned. "Think hard on it, Johnnie-lad. A mortal secret sworn on the blood of Christ is a weighty thing to carry. Do you want that burden?

10

There are certain things you do not need to know in order to function as a servant of the Lord in this life and the next."

I did not hesitate. Curiosity consumed me. "I swear again, Brother Wilfred. Please tell."

He spoke after a short pause as though choosing words with care. His voice remained casual as before, out of keeping with his statement. "I killed a Sheriff up north, in the Lake Country, near to the land of the Scots. Brained him with my axe when he tried to arrest me while I was gathering wood. The wood belonged to an Earl who would rather have his tenants die of cold than share with them the bounty of his lands, even the dead limbs and fallen trunks.

"So I, too, had a debt to pay. Only in my case, drawing and quartering was the form of payment required. Not being of a mind to have my guts spilled and my body sliced into rough fourths while I remained alive and of such a young age, I left. By the time the Sheriff's successor came looking for me, I had demonstrated my value in temporal ways both to the Abbot and the Duke who conspired together to preserve my secret."

He paused for a moment, then continued. "Understand Johnnie-lad, they do not know of my guilt. Only you know, beside myself. They suspect, but they do not wish to give me over to the authorities for fear that they will lose what I give them. So now my debt runs to them. I do their work. They preserve me to do it. The arrangement will last so long as it suits the convenience of all and not a moment longer. A man who renounces all earthly possessions in the service of Christ, as I have done, can never be a cynic. But I am no fool and I know these things to be true."

So my earthly savior, teacher and protector, the only true family left to me in all the world, was a trespasser, a thief, a murderer, a fugitive. Being a mere lad of fifteen, I found this exciting rather than disturbing. His already formidable stature seemed to grow as I thought of it.

Brother Wilfred was thirteen years my senior, of medium height and slender build, rather dark of complexion. He had wide-set dark eyes with thick eyebrows and a broad nose that gave his face a fierce and powerful look. His eyes seemed unusually large and filled with the fire of his unique vitality. Quick and graceful in movement, he was much stronger than he appeared, able to hew timber for the fireplace with a two-handed axe all day long without rest. Although hardened by constant labor, his hands

11

were well shaped with long and graceful fingers. Regarding his hands, one was not surprised to discover his artistry in script and as an illuminator. The surprise lay in how rapidly he had learned these skills, merely six years an apprentice.

Brother Wilfred seemed a devout and pious monk. Yet, several of his skills and practices were incongruous with the normal rhythms of monastic piety. For one thing, he was skilled with the longbow, spending many hours in the Abbey yard and the fields beyond, sending arrow after arrow into targets placed against mats of hay. His right shoulder showed the heavy musculature typical of a longbowman. When questioned, he stated that the skill of archery required a quiet and reverent mind, and was therefore akin to prayer even if not prayer itself. The Abbot rolled his eyes and crossed himself when he heard such assertions, but he did not forbid the activity.

Many years ago, so I am told, the Pope decreed that monks should not spill the blood of humankind. Monks did not cease fighting in the myriad wars of the times. Instead, they went to war carrying clubs rather than swords or daggers. The Pope's decree was interpreted in practice to mean that a monk could bash in a man's head but he could not sever it, as the latter let blood and the former presumably would not.

By some vague interpretation beyond the ken of one so simple as myself, various exceptions arose over time. The Knights of the Hospital Of St. John of Jerusalem were a monastic order who fought the Saracens, wearing the white Maltese cross on their armor. The Templars, equally fierce and equally monastic captured and then defended the King Solomon's Temple in the First Crusade and thereafter, displaying ornate red crosses on their chests and banners. The Holy Order of Teutonic Knights participated in these and other battles. All of these knight/monks used swords, lances, studded maces, daggers, in short all the tools of the armed and armored man. All of them went into battle with the blessing of the Holy Father. With these precedents, Brother Wilfred believed that his use of the longbow fell within the realm of the permissible. I never heard anyone gainsay him on the point.

When tilling the garden, Wilfred often lapsed into reveries contemplating a flower or a blade of grass. Reverence for the work of God, he would call these interludes. I never saw him exhibit the same degree of reverence when contemplating the cross or other symbols of the faith.

He wrote short couplets of verse on secular subjects with no religious theme whatsoever, sometimes interrupting his illumination of a sacred text to write down a thought that had diverted him. Sometimes these thoughts seemed base and vulgar — even carnal, sometimes frivolous, sometimes comic.

Innocuous as these incongruities may seem, they were unique behavior for a follower of Francis of Assisi. But Wilfred was allowed them because he compensated with a level of productive work around the Abbey unequaled by any of the others. When I came to the Abbey, he drove me mercilessly as I assisted him in these tasks, a burden I bore to earn his protection and tutelage. And I probably needed his protection as much as I desired both his tutelage and approval. He often told me in apparent jest that if it were not for him, Brother Bradwin and Brother Andrew would have their knobs shoved up my arse in the commission of mortal sin nightly, whether I consented or not. After a time, I began to suspect that he was right. I received certain ambiguous overtures, certain veiled suggestions from time to time; and I observed the two of them engaged in strange and suspicious behavior.

As for Wilfred himself, nothing of the sort ever occurred, though we often shared a bed or a robe in the Abbey and in our travels. If Wilfred sinned in that fashion — he did it with women.

The life of the monastery was an austere but comfortable monotony, suiting my nature perfectly — prayers, meals, work. The seasons came and went without serious incident beyond the petty quarrels of the brothers, the ebb and flow of sickness and health, feast days and fast days, occasional news from beyond the walls as to events occurring in the world near and far, none relevant to our lives. Only on occasion did we venture forth in an effort to perform a charitable task. More frequently, we provided a refuge for wretched victims of some calamity or other. We neither enjoyed abundance nor suffered want.

As I advanced in my apprenticeship, I expected to spend the rest of my days within the gentle rhythms of Blackfriars in the status of lay brother. Stone blind, I could have found my way to every nook and cranny of the place. Our church with a long nave for processions stood at

13

the north side of the complex, with the sanctuary to the southeast to face Jerusalem. On the south, protected from the winds, stood the rectangular cloister, an enclosed yard for prayer, meditation and exercise. Illumination and writing took place in the work stalls, located in the bays between the pillars of the cloister. The chapter house, dormitory and enclosed scriptorium opened onto the cloister with the Abbot's house and infirmary a short distance beyond the walls.

All of the buildings had been constructed of the dark gray stone native to the region, with thatch, wood and tile roof on various parts. A small but boisterous creek flowed just beyond the walls, providing us with fresh water and power for our mill. I had grown to love the place, despite its austerity and idiosyncrasies.

Then in February of 1228, just two short years after the death of our beloved patron, Francis of Assisi, the sweet harmony of my life as a youthful lay brother at Blackfriars took a radical turn. The Abbot asked Wilfred to accompany an emissary of the Archbishop of Canterbury on a trip to the Apostolic See to be led by the Archbishop's assistant, Bishop Michael. The Archbishop sought Papal guidance on a number of Church matters and wished to press a case for dispensations requested by various landed nobility in good standing with the King.

In short, a routine mission. The Archbishop sent and received similar missions perhaps once or twice a year. There was no reason to suspect that this one would differ from any of the others. If all went well, the Archbishop's emissaries would return in six months' time and life would resume as before.

CHAPTER TWO

Rome lies 1,200 miles southeast of Canterbury. Fast couriers had been known to cover the distance in as little as 25 days with important news such as word of a papal election, a papal bull or encyclical. The typical mounted convoy required 60 days to cover the distance, particularly in winter when the roads could be rendered impassable for days at a time by inclement weather.

This trip would face the problems of the season. It would also face the need to circumnavigate the towns, estates and provinces caught up in the turmoil of the Albigensian Crusades, the war conducted by an alliance of the Pope and King Philip of France against the Waldensian and Cathari heretics throughout Toulouse, Provence and Aquitaine.

These impediments compounded the difficulties. The threat of winter storms eliminated the possibility of making the entire journey by way of sea voyage and also denied us any route through the Alps. The embassy could travel from Calais to Paris and then southeast to the Valley of the Rhone, through Lyon to the port of Marseille and thence along the Mediterranean Coast Road through Nice, Genoa, Livorno and Civitavecchio to Rome. Such a route avoided mountainous country, but it traversed the eastern reaches of Provence, currently racked by the Crusades.

Despite the salutary and Godly purpose, the Crusades created a climate of lawlessness, dangerous to travellers. That climate disrupted commerce and hence discouraged innkeepers and others who normally provided food, shelter and mounts. Faced with the choice between the violence of nature and the violence of men, they chose to risk the latter. They apparently believed that neither heretics nor brigands would attack travellers to Rome on official Church business. They hoped that the Crusaders would respect such travellers, despite their free-ranging Papal charter granted to Christ's warriors to plunder, subdue and wreak havoc. Whatever their thinking, they ordained that the embassy follow the Rhone Valley route and the Coast Road to Rome. But they also believed that the embassy should take certain precautions.

The Archbishop selected Wilfred to be a member of the embassy for two reasons. Followers of Francis of Assisi stood high in Papal esteem at the moment. Wilfred would thus add credibility to the quality of English piety in the eyes of the Papal Court. And then, of course, his longbowman's skills commended him for a journey that might have more than a normal element of danger. The community of the devout was not so large that a man of such unusual skill would go unremarked.

The Archbishop intended to hire a platoon of footsoldiers to accompany the mission. So much the better if a member of the mission itself could help defend the party. And even more the better that this defender used a longbow. The French held that weapon in awe, particularly in the hands of an Englishman.

I protested mightily when it appeared that Wilfred might join the embassy without me, even though I had every reason to believe that he would be back within a few months. As I had proved myself a diligent and resourceful worker, the Abbot and then the Archbishop reluctantly consented to my going. If they had not, I would have left Blackfriars and followed along anyway, a stowaway on the boat to Calais and a furtive straggler thereafter if necessary. I believed that I would have no life worth a brass farthing without Wilfred to protect and guide me.

*   *   *   *

I will not tarry long over our progress to Rome. It is a journey often made. We had much wintry weather as one would expect. In places, the wet snow and rain transformed the roads into tiresome quagmires. The inns were crowded, dark, smoky and unpleasant — but not unusually so. We had prepared ourselves for all these obstacles.

The Crusades caused us no inconvenience despite our concern. We saw evidence of struggle when we approached the Mediterranean Coast of France. Here and there, a burned out structure, a damaged castle, the ruins of a Cathari house or gathering place. While we were in the town of Aix-en-Provence, the Inquisition burned five Cathari heretics at the stake in the town square — three women, a man and a mere boy of twelve. Most of our party went to watch along with a majority of the townsfolk. I did not.

In my heart, I did not abhor the burning of heretics. To the contrary, I considered such punishment appropriate to purge society of cancerous elements and to appease God. I stayed away for a more mundane and personal reason that I shared with no one. I was squeamish at the prospect of burning human flesh and feared that I might disgrace myself.

Whenever we travelled through open country, Wilfred used his longbow to provide meat for the dinner pot. He quickly learned that Bishop Michael adored fresh-killed hare, roasted over an open fire, wrapped with strips of salt pork and stuffed with an onion. The Bishop's gustatorial enthusiasm caused him to watch Wilfred closely as he walked along the side of the road with his bow at the ready. Thus, the Bishop observed at first hand several shots that anchored hares on the run. And then one mild sunny day, Wilfred dropped a white-fronted goose that flew low over our party. The fat bird thudded to earth no more than ten feet in front of the Bishop's horse. These extraordinary feats of bowmanship together with Wilfred's energetic competence in repairing our baggage wagon, managing the horses and dealing with arrogant innkeepers earned the Bishop's admiration.

In any case, we made good time without incident through much wind and rain down the Italian west coast road to Rome. We entered that ancient city and proceeded to the Pope's Palace, where we were housed in monastic quarters while Bishop Michael performed the duties of his embassy.

Here again, I will not add undue length to this tale by describing Rome, a task that countless others have performed far better than I have the skill to do. Suffice it to say that Rome is a City of both beauty and ruin, rich and decrepit, with elegant antiquities, where marvelous architecture mingles with the most banal, where incredible wealth mingles with extreme poverty. It seemed vital to me despite the ravages it had repeatedly suffered over the last several centuries. A City of browns and pinks — where most of the buildings had a tawny cast in the sunlight and a pinkish glow at dawn and dusk, all perched and jumbled on its hills under rakish and irregular roofs and gables, cupolas and towers.

We had little to do there except rest for the purpose of preparing for our return journey.

CHAPTER THREE

We entered the great hall as part of a crowd, Cardinals, Bishops, ordinary priests, monks and their retainers. Of low birth and rank, we waited until most of the others had entered. Wilfred signaled to me that I should take a seat in the back row as he moved further up to stay close to Bishop Michael. The events of our journey had elevated Brother Wilfred in Bishop Michael's eyes. This was not the first time that the Bishop had accorded to him a privilege above his station.

We had come to hear a monk of the Pope's retinue, one Fra Cipriani, tell of his journey into the lands beyond the Black Sea in an effort to make contact with Prester John. The monk had disappeared without a trace into those vast lands for four full years, returning only recently, long after the Pope had given him up for dead.

As rumors of the news he brought circulated throughout the Papal See, curiosity grew by leaps and bounds. For if what he said held any truth at all, a vast power had developed in the East to bedevil the infidels, hew them down, destroy their cities, their shrines and seats of learning. But a mysterious power it was, destroying but not truly occupying, ebbing and flowing like the tides of some restless sea. And in the service of what God did these people wreak such devastation? Warriors for Christ? Who could say, even as they did the work that the most Christian of kings could not accomplish in his name.

The gathering took place in a great vaulted hall in the castle where the Pope held court. Whitewashed walls stretched upward to ornate, wooden joists, carved with religious symbols, decorated with icons. Alcoves with sacred texts, paintings and icons were built into the walls at regular intervals. Colored glazing at the high windows — quite rare and costly in those times — illuminated the most solemn of scenes, Calvary, the Sermon

19

On The Mount, the Resurrection, the Last Supper and others. The ceiling was decorated with an elaborate mural, vivid in the richness of its colors. Priceless tapestries adorned the walls, in dark hues of gold, blue, blood red. We sat on wooden benches carved of the same material as the ceiling joists, a dark hardwood with prominent grain, facing a raised dais with an enormous, ornate crucifix on the wall behind.

To my eye, it appeared that the hall could accommodate two hundred. Slightly less than that number had filed in when Fra Cipriani appeared and was assisted to a chair on the dais. A priest of the Papal Staff sat with him to act as interlocutor. As Fra Cipriani would speak in Italian and Latin, a few priests who could act as interpreters positioned themselves around the room to provide whispered assistance to those who might need it.

I, of course, had only fragments of the language required to understand Fra Cipriani's story, nor was I close enough to the interpreter assigned to assist Bishop Michael to hear translation of more than snatches of the narrative as delivered. So, in large part, I recount now what I was told after the event by Brother Wilfred and others of our embassy. But I suffer no such disability in describing Fra Cipriani, the most startling figure of a man not yet dead that I had seen in all my life to that point.

He shuffled in, bent nearly double at the waist, using two gnarled canes to assist him. With obvious effort, he held his head up and cocked to the left so that he could see at least partially to the front — and not merely stare at the ground he traversed — out of his right eye, the only functional eye left to him. He had hair the color of snow, irregularly sprouting in patches from a skull that looked more like a livid, blotchy death mask than that of the head of a living man. His skin, indeed his entire aspect, looked as though he had been boiled in oil and then baked in the sun for weeks on end.

He wore a grey, hooded robe that appeared several sizes too large for him, bound round the waist with a belt of coarse rope. The leather sandals he wore were black with age, cracked and nearly worn through. In all my life, I have never seen a living face so riven with chasms, running at random in a complexion darker than any Goth or Sicilian, marred with irregular dark places as though he were afflicted by some dread disease.

When he finally took his seat and turned toward the audience, the stark white of his left eye socket seemed to dominate his face, as though it had retained its original size while the rest of his head had shrunk along with his body. The inward collapse of his thin, cracked lips bespoke a mouth without teeth. When he sought to begin his tale, he spoke in a reedy voice, barely audible yet enormously irritating.

Try as I might, I could not muster the sense of Christian compassion required of me in the presence of such a martyr as this. I made a mental note of my failing for the Confessional. I will recount his story as I came to understand it, trying to leave out nothing of importance, while avoiding his epic, self-serving verbosity and the servile effluvium he directed at the Holy Father.

It seems that Pope Gregory VIII sent Fra Cipriani off on his embassy in the Spring of 1223. Ignorant of the nature and extent of the lands he would traverse, Fra Cipriani took few supplies. He planned to provision his expedition in Constantinople where he expected to find people with more pertinent information. He set sail from Venice in a transport galley and dropped anchor in the Golden Horn some fifty days later after a rough but uneventful passage down the Adriatic and through the Eastern Mediterranean and Aegean Seas.

By treaty with the Byzantines, the Venetians had established an extra-territorial enclave at Constantinople that was treated in legal terms as part of the Republic of Venice. The Venetians were the most powerful and far-flung seafaring nation of all of Mediterranean Christendom. It was from their enclave that Fra Cipriani set sail through the Sea of Marmara and the Bosphorus, heading for Sebastopolis, a Greek city on the eastern shore of the Black Sea. The Venetians resident in Constantinople knew somewhat more of the land he was to traverse than was known in Rome. They had provisioned him.

At Sebastopolis, Fra Cipriani purchased a place in a caravan organized by Greeks to trade for silks and spices with rulers of eastern nations. Beyond the Caspian Sea, the caravan travelled through country that seemed drastically underpopulated. He saw cities built for thousands and tens of thousands inhabited by a few hundred. He saw abandoned farms, fields overgrown with prairie grass, the remnants of viaducts for irrigation lying in disrepair. He saw the ruins of cities that had been burnt

21

to the ground, walls breached and knocked down, with piles of bleached human bones scattered about at shattered main gates.

When the caravan stood five days out from Bukhara, Fra Cipriani was seized by an especially violent form of the flux. He was unable to continue — as he could no longer sit astride a camel and the only other choice was to walk, for which he was even less suited. Over his protests, the caravan leader left him with a small group of nomadic herdsmen, tending flocks of sheep and small shaggy horses, who lived in round tents made of felt and animal skins that they could strike or pitch in under an hour.

Over a period of two years, spanning winters of unspeakable ferocity and inhuman cold, the nomads travelled with their flocks to seek fresh grasslands, nursing him cheerfully and attentively as they went. They showed no sign of Christian faith that he could perceive, nor could he understand their speech. He lived in mortal terror that he would die without absolution as he saw no one throughout his entire sojourn with the power to administer Extreme Unction.

During these months, Fra Cipriani saw from the litter in which the nomads placed him the ruins of Balck, Herat and Merv, formerly great cities, seats of Islamic power, now nothing but windswept stone remnants inhabited by ghosts. At Balck, a great wall is all that remains. It stands like a tomb against the incessant winds that sweep across hundreds of miles of featureless grasslands. In Fra Cipriani's words, contemplating what is left of Balck in the dead of winter, one feels the presence of the Anti-Christ. And yet the nomads who cared for him with tenderness and concern showed no interest in the ruins or the souls of those slaughtered there when the city was destroyed.

Eventually Fra Cipriani recovered enough of his health to leave his caretakers and make his way to Bukhara where he encountered a Greek trader with whom he could converse to some degree. The trader explained to Fra Cipriani the significance of what he had seen.

It seems that all of the country from north of the Black Sea in the west to Lake Balkash in the east, from the north shore of the Caspian Sea to the head of the Persian Gulf in the south had been the Empire of the Khwarazm Shah and his son Jalal al-Din, Persians who claimed direct descent from the ancient Empire of Darius I. The empire encompassed more territory and riches than all of European Christendom. The

Khwarazm Shah maintained his capital at Bukhara, a City known throughout the region as the cupola of Islam, renowned for its seats of Islamic learning, its places of worship.

In March of 1220, a force of one hundred thousand nomadic horsemen had ridden out of a desert to the northeast of the City, a desert considered impassable by the residents, particularly in wintertime. Alarmed, the garrison of Bukhara went to meet the nomads and was annihilated. The invaders then entered the City, their leader stabling his horses in the Grand Mosque while destroying all the Koranic texts stored there. He summoned the terrified citizens to the building, mounted the pulpit and told them: "I am the punishment of God. If you had not committed great sins, He would not have visited upon you a punishment such as I." He then ordered his soldiers to loot the City and put it to the torch, but not to kill the citizens. They were ordered to leave, taking nothing with them so that all property would remain for the conquerors to plunder. The evicted citizens of Bukhara ran to the four winds spreading tales of terror, demoralizing the Khwarazm Shah's Empire.

None of the other cities of the Khwarazm Shah received such merciful treatment as Bukhara. Balck, Herat and Merv, among others, were destroyed as well as looted, all male citizens killed, the women raped with those that survived the ordeal enslaved along with the children. Small armies relentlessly pursued the Khwarazm Shah and Jalal al-Din to their deaths. Immense wagon trains of booty and long lines of shackled slaves made slowly off to the east, headed purposefully somewhere unknown.

The nomads showed little interest in preserving the centers of urban civilization for their own benefit, as part of an empire, although they maintained sway over the territories their armies had pacified. It seemed that they had no concept of governance that could accommodate or use permanent settlements.

By the time Fra Cipriani reached Bukhara in 1226, a small portion of it had been rebuilt. The grand mosque remained a stable, although it seemed that several different religions had places of worship scattered about that the authorities tolerated. The Greeks had their church, Moslems a mosque complete with minarets, priests of exotic Asiatic creeds had modest centers for the practice of their beliefs. Notwithstanding the proximity of these places each to the other, peace reigned. The authorities would not have countenanced any hint of discord.

Fra Cipriani paused at this point in his tale to wet his mouth with wine. He mopped his face with a napkin to prevent the dribblings from staining his robe. One of the higher ranking officials in the hall asked him whether he thought the conquerors were Christians. He replied: "I saw no manifestation of Christian faith from any of them."

The official persisted. "But what of the leader's statement in the grand mosque? Doesn't the notion of God's punishment for unbelief comport with the behavior of a Christian conqueror?" More than one in the hall recalled the sack of Jerusalem by the victorious Christian soldiers of the First Crusade where the most Christian knights boasted of slaughtering infidels until the floors of the Temple of Solomon ran knee deep in blood. The similarities seemed striking, albeit uncomfortable for those in the room who revered human life and the possible salvation of all human souls.

Fra Cipriani thought for a moment, his brow knitted as though the effort dug deeply into his limited reserves of energy. Then he shook his head. "No. These people do not worship Christ. I believe that they are ignorant of Him and would worship Him as we do if they but knew Him. For they have His goodness in them when they feel free to express it. They showed me great kindness and solicitude in my long agony."

He struggled slowly to his feet. With much labor he stood, almost erect, wavering before us, both his good eye and the dead one seeming to transfix the audience, more potent for the contrast between them. He raised his hand, extending a skeletal finger toward the ceiling, shaking as though daring a thunderbolt to strike him, white hair wild in all directions. He was a most arresting and horrifying sight, I can tell you. His voice rose in volume at its most irritable pitch, attacking the senses of his listeners like a knife. "It is our earthly duty to bring Christ to them, these noble pagans." he shouted.

I knew enough of his language to get the full meaning of that statement. It fired the room with an outpouring of messianic zeal, shouts of approbation, many signs of the cross and invocation of God's help in the task that lay ahead, bringing Christ to the hosts of Prester John or whoever these people might be. For no one could doubt that such a challenge must be taken up by any right-thinking man of sound mind and body. Where else on earth could Christendom find allies such as these? Their like did not exist anywhere as warriors. And now they controlled the Silk Road over which the wealth of the East must pass to enrich European royalty — and incidentally, the Church.

In our cell later, we discussed Fra Cipriani's story well into the night. Wilfred seemed of two minds, fascinated by the notion of a great invincible host inhabiting vast reaches of land unknown to us. But at the same time, he doubted that they hungered for Christianity. Efforts to convert them might prove unwelcome. As this seemed inconceivable to me at such an impressionable and ignorant age, I pressed him.

He thought for a moment before responding, choosing his words with care.

"I see two problems, Johnnie. First, the Church divides the world into but two camps. 'The enemy of my enemy is my friend.' That's what we believe. But the world is not black and white. It is multiple shades of gray. What if these people know nothing of Islam as they know nothing of Christianity? What if they attack and destroy whoever happens to be within reach? If that be true, we would do well to stay beyond reach."

He paused, then continued. "Please forgive me an impious thought, Johnnie. The Pope sees himself as Christ's Vicar on earth, as you know. The Church espouses that belief. Now tell me lad, do you see a leader who walks into a grand mosque at the center of a great and powerful Moslem empire at the head of a host of conquerors and proclaims himself `God's punishment,' ever bending the knee and acknowledging the higher authority of a Roman Pope with an insignificant army in a City thousands of miles away? Do you see a warrior such as has just been described to us taking up the worship of a Prince of Peace whose teachings include renunciation, charity and mercy? Not likely, I say. I say that on the day such as that occurs, swine will take wing and we will suffer a deluge of pigshit."

Despite his imagery, thoughts of this sort troubled me. I did not question Church teachings or examine them closely. All my life, I had accepted them in the form received.

"Please, Wilfred. The power of our Lord will intervene to assist. After all, didn't St. Paul convert heathens and barbarians? Did not the Roman Empire become Christian at the very height of its power by decree of a powerful Emperor?"

25

He smiled and nodded. "Aye, Johnnie. And pray, did you happen to spy a St. Paul in that room this evening among all those bishops? Did you happen to mark a man fit to be a Confessor to the Emperor Constantine or anyone of his power? I did not, despite careful study. Nor have I encountered any such a man in all of our weeks here among the Romans."

I was puzzled for a moment. Of course, St. Paul had not been in the room tonight, nor the Confessor to Constantine who decreed that Rome adopt Christianity as the religion of state in 326 Anno Domini. Then Wilfred's meaning struck me. St. Paul, the Apostle to the Gentiles, brought Christ to pagan barbarians. He could only have done so with the aid of great personal charisma, energy and the reckless bravery of one sure of salvation and thus totally lacking fear of death. The priests who taught and then converted Constantine must have had the same qualities to have impressed a man of such absolute power and conviction. Wilfred saw his point slowly sink in.

"You see, Johnnie, the men in that room tonight are functionaries, scholars, men of books, not men of deeds. Mother Church has fallen into soft hands that lack the strength to carry the word of God to infidels. Instead the Church bribes knights to carry the name of the Prince of Peace on the point of a lance, as a part-time diversion from their more accustomed pursuits of rape and plunder." He paused, cast his eyes heavenward briefly and made a quick sign of the cross before continuing. "I, for one, believe that somewhere in the great heavens, St. Paul looks down in disgust, if he does not avert his eyes altogether."

He smiled broadly, took me by the shoulders and shook me in his characteristic gesture. "I trust you to keep my thoughts in confidence, Johnnie. If you ever let them be known, I would be roasted for a heretic." He paused, more serious than before. "You see, I believe this man who states that he is the punishment of God is as likely to be the Anti-Christ as he is Prester John. All these soft churchmen who go out to try to convert him or enlist him in some new Crusade are more likely to be turned into carrion than save a soul for Christ."

I was startled. "Why do you say such a thing, Wilfred?"

He shook his head slowly. "Our view of the world is far too simple, Johnnie. But nothing is truly simple, except that we live until we die and we never know when that will be. Just because we see the enemy now as

26

the Saracens does not mean that they are the only enemy. It is hard for a man or a king or a Church to know all the enemies that might be out there to take up arms at some point. Just think of how many times the Thracians have switched sides in the last fifteen years. And they are Christians who fight Christians, always claiming to be better Christians than their enemy of the moment."

I knew not of Thracians, but I did not argue. He got up and paced the small cell slowly, right hand stroking his chin. After a minute or two, he spoke without looking at me. I could tell that he had something important to report. Even so, I was unready.

"I have told Bishop Michael that if the Holy See mounts an embassy to the one who describes himself as `the punishment of God,' I offer my services. I have a variety of skills that could be of use on such a journey. Bishop Michael has recommended me to the Holy Father and I intend to go."

I was stunned, and then terrified. "But Brother Wilfred, what will I do? Who will protect me? Who will I serve? You yourself have often said that you are all that stands between me and having Brother Bradwin and Brother Andrew trying to stick their pricks up my arse." I spoke that latter part in jest, but I was truly distraught at the thought of Wilfred's leaving. I was just a servant boy, not a true acolyte. In a time of austerity, the Abbot might throw me out. I had no place to go. No prospects whatever.

He waved his hand at me, dismissing the problem. "You'll be fine. You've proven your worth. They need you. Keep them needing you and you will always have a place there. You may even sin a little with that village girl who fancies you so long as you avoid getting caught."

Despite his words, I found the prospect of his departure increasingly unacceptable. If he would not respond to my need, perhaps I could shake his resolve. "But why would you seek to go on an expedition that you yourself say is doomed to failure? You yourself say that the `punishment of God' is either the Anti-Christ or a man too powerful for our bishops to convert. If he is the Anti-Christ, you will likely be killed. If we lack the conviction to convert him, why bother? Why take such risks for nothing?"

Wilfred sat down next to me on the shelf we used for a bed and engaged my eyes. "I truly do not know how to answer you. I feel the need to do it, that's all." He thought for a moment, then nodded, as though to acknowledge an additional secret, ready for revelation. "And I've had a premonition, a warning that I should not return to Blackfriars. I still fear arraignment for the murder I have done. After all, it was a Sheriff with powerful patrons. The Abbot or the Duke might turn me in for some favor."

He stood up to face me now with more conviction than before, more resolve. "But the real reason is that I long to see the limits of the world and the people who inhabit it. I lie restless at Blackfriars. I pray daily for respite from my unease to no avail. I pray daily for the ability to lose myself totally in the illumination of sacred texts and earn immortality by embellishing the word of God. All to no avail. I itch to move — and when I cannot slake the itch, I grow irritable. My work suffers. My faith weakens; and I cannot expect another chance like this to come my way ever again in this life."

A single tear streaked his face from the corner of his right eye. The yearning in his aspect nearly broke my heart. It took me four hours of fast talk and much begging before he consented to have me go with him. I pray forgiveness for my rich use of guilt as a weapon in the pleading of my wretched cause.

CHAPTER FOUR

Our little party trudged slowly northward from Rome toward Venice where we would take ship for Constantinople. Pope Gregory had already sent a messenger by fast horse ahead to the Doge, the leader of the Venetian Republic, to secure our passage. In all, we were twenty in number, Cardinal Pellegrino the Papal emissary, Fra Enrico Dandolo, grandson and namesake of perhaps the most famous Doge in Venetian history as his chief assistant, and a number of lowly retainers such as Brother Wilfred and me.

The Cardinal and Fra Dandolo rode decrepit horses. A single outrider rode a more serviceable and energetic horse in front of our party. The rest of us walked. Two wagons carried our luggage and provisions, each pulled by a team of bullocks.

We made slow progress, particularly over the rising ground in the southern portions of Tuscany where the road twisted and turned to negotiate the ridges through rocky pastures and ancient olive groves. Fences of piled rock lined the road and separated the fields. Limestone escarpments off in the distance reflected the hazy sunlight, chalk white streaks against the brassy, summer sky. Villages with stone watchtowers marked occasional promontories, with the houses and outbuildings clustered close by and spilling down the sides of the ridges helter-skelter, as if huddling in disorder under the protective shadow of the towers. Flocks of sheep and goats grazed about, casually tended in most cases by an elderly man or woman with a single dog.

A convent or a monastery generally stood on the highest ridges or promontories, with whitewashed walls gleaming in the sun and a church tower at one end. We saw several during the course of our first week on the road, each with its well-tended orchards and vineyards. We spent the night at two of them where we were welcomed and treated with much kindness, despite the austerity of the accommodations.

It was a peaceful journey. No prideful, warlike nobles contended for power over this part of the Pope's domains and those of his allies that we traversed. The country was free of bandits and highwaymen, full of bounty that its residents seemed willing to share without reticence. The cross and pennants of the Pope's Emissary, carried in advance of our party by the outrider, uniformly elicited a reverent and welcoming attitude. Despite these congenial circumstances, I found the journey difficult and burdensome, almost beyond bearing.

The heat and dust of that journey nearly undid me. We had come through similar country on our way to Rome the winter before along the coast road. But that was winter. The damp and chill that occasionally overtook coastal Italy in the cold season was nothing to an Anglo Saxon youth, raised in the north of England.

High summer in Tuscany was a different matter altogether. The heat beat on my head like a blacksmith's hammer. The turgid air seemed foul, devoid of oxygen, even in open country. The smell of grass and flowers had an edge of putrescence to it, a parasitic drag on the system. The horses hooves stirred the dust that overlay the dry chalky ground, filling the air with a flour-like cloud that turned to paste on the skin and in the mouth. Yet I dared make no complaint. For the others endured it without comment — and there was nothing anyone could do about it. I could choose to bear the burden or stay behind, no option at all in reality. Any remark on the rigor of the conditions would only lower me in Wilfred's eyes to no purpose.

Late one afternoon north of the Town of Siena, we topped a rise and began a descent into a long, wide valley shimmering in the heat. We could see the monastery where we planned to spend the night on a chalk ridge about four miles distant. Suddenly, the outrider leading us came to a halt and raised his hand. He turned and shouted something to the Cardinal and then pointed down the road. I shook myself to dispel the fatigue and heat torpor that dimmed my eyes in an effort to see what had caught his attention. It was not a simple matter. The heat waves created patchy mirage effects in the distance. The entire vista undulated with shifting lakes, rivers and ponds.

After a time, I could make out a dust cloud. Then a shift in the heat pattern seemed to convert a dark streak in the landscape into a large column of mounted men approaching on the same road that we were using. Even at this distance, we could see that they were moving smartly. Several outriders carried pennants on long lances in front of the column.

Our outrider glassed the approaching column with a small telescope and then rode back to confer with the Cardinal. Wilfred edged closer in an effort to overhear them. He did not succeed — but it was clear that the Cardinal did not like the news, whatever it was. Something about the approaching column caused him distaste and mild apprehension but not the fear he would have shown if he thought that such a large group of men posed a physical threat to us. We resumed our slow march toward the monastery in the afternoon's inferno, quickly closing the distance with the approaching column.

We could see them clearly now, men clad in black with gold trim on horses uniformly black. All of the men, in the first rank at least, wore chestplate armor, although none wore helmets perhaps in deference to the heat. Instead, they all wore soft velvet hats, black with a single black plume. All were heavily armed, swords, battleaxes and lances. They seemed unusually large and burly. All rode horses much taller and more heavily built than those common in Italy. Two of those in front carried standards bearing crests with elaborate coats of arms done in black, gold and dark red. Carved black eagles adorned the tops of the standards.

As the distance between our columns narrowed, two of the black riders spurred their horses toward us. They ordered us to clear the road with guttural shouts in French and a language I did not recognize. Cardinal Pellegrino signalled that we should comply. But then he gave us a surprising order. We were to concede the right of way to the approaching party but stand with our backs to them as they passed. We were not to acknowledge them or give them any form of greeting. As the road was closely confined by stone walls at that point, they would practically brush against us and tickle our backsides as they went by.

Although he said nothing, I could see that Wilfred liked neither the situation nor the instruction we had received. Nervous myself, I asked him to share his concerns. He leaned over and muttered so as not to be overheard.

31

"We have been ordered to show disrespect to someone who thinks himself important. Never a good idea unless you are stronger than he is, which we plainly are not. Worse, we'll be standing there with our backs to them, blocked by a rock wall so they can skewer us against that obstacle at leisure before we even know they have drawn their swords." He shook his head. "It's like spitting in the executioner's eye and insulting his mother just before you put your head on the block. Gives him encouragement to make a few preliminary rough cuts before he finishes with you." With a subtle movement, I saw him adjust his garment to improve access to the stiletto he carried strapped to his waist out of sight, whenever he was not on monastery grounds. Wilfred intended to go down fighting, a thought that did not reassure me.

The black column was on us now. Pressed against the uneven stone wall, my senses were rocked by the wind of their passage as well as the loud noise of the horses' heavy breathing, the hoofbeats, the smell of horse lather, the creaking saddlery, the metallic sounds of the armor, the all-encompassing cloud of fine white dust. Unable to restrain myself, I looked over my left shoulder toward the approaching horsemen of the column that had not yet passed. And there, just about to come abreast of us was the man who obviously commanded the proceeding.

He sat short and fat upon a magnificent horse of the most astonishing proportions. He wore a black tunic with gold trim, no armor. He carried no weapon but was closely surrounded by some of the largest and most heavily armed men I had ever seen in my short lifetime. His soft velvet hat differed from the others in that it had a small, tiara-type crown to the front, with a large red stone in the middle I took to be a ruby. All of his immediate retainers regarded us with frowns that bespoke the utmost scorn and contempt. A few of the soldiers had uttered vile insults as they passed us, although always in an undertone. I expected the same from their leader. Instead, he smiled slightly and nodded when he caught my eye. Taken totally by surprise, I nodded and smiled in return. I learned several hours later that I had exchanged personal greetings in that unexpected moment with Frederick II, Hohenstaufen, Emperor of the Holy Roman Empire and King of Sicily, en route to Viterbo in an effort to persuade Pope Gregory to withdraw his decree of excommunication.

In any case, the column passed us without incident and continued on down the road we had ascended. Even with our backs turned, only sneaking glances here and there, we noted the numerous palanquins that followed Frederick, transporting the women of his harem. Frederick, it seemed, was only at his best when he had several women available to quench his prodigious appetites as the fancy of the moment dictated. Word had it that he never travelled with fewer than a dozen, adding new and discarding old at regular intervals.

Our party reached the monastery roughly two hours later, amid the lengthening shadows of twilight. We entered the courtyard through a large wooden door with wrought iron and brass fittings. Tall whitewashed walls enclosed the space. It was shaded by several mature acacia and locust trees with rough cobblestones underfoot. Wooden planters and benches were scattered about against the walls and the trees to provide places for rest, prayer and meditation. Flowering shrubs and vines grew in abundance, contributing their riotous colors and scents. A simple fountain in the center of the space splashed water into a small pool lined with dark tile.

Benedictines had established this place perhaps five hundred years ago. Because the location commands the road — one of the ancient routes to Rome from the north — the monastery was built on the foundations of a fort that had stood there before. Both the fort and the monastery had been destroyed from time to time during the various barbarian invasions that had swept down the Peninsula over the centuries of the Roman Empire's decline. The fountain and some of the floor tiles were ancient remnants of the original construction.

The monks had expected our arrival. They had plainly not expected the Imperial visitation of Frederick's large party, and the place was still abuzz with that event when we arrived, road-weary and bedraggled, slightly winded from the long climb up that last steep rise. We got a full account of the Emperor's visit from one of the residents, a Brother Bernard of Swiss origins, at the dinner table that night. He was a gregarious fellow, self-important and effusive, who sat in the midst of our party both to satisfy his curiosity over our mission and to regale us with his tales. The flame from the candle on the dark dinner table wavered in the wind he created with his excited speech and extravagant gestures.

33

Brother Bernard spoke in French, a language commonly used in England and throughout Europe. If I concentrated, I could understand French, although I spoke it poorly myself. I strained to decipher Brother Bernard's rapid speech as I sat almost directly across from him, his jowls bobbling and sweat streaking his forehead. Wilfred sat next to me, much more relaxed than I as he listened and surveyed the room at the same time, taking in the other monks chatting over their meals. Cardinal Pellegrino sat next to the Abbot at the head table with Fra Dandolo attending him on the other side.

Brother Bernard had just described Frederick's entrance into the monastery compound on the heels of his burly Schwabian guards.

"Ah yes, let me assure you, that it is bad enough to get a visitation from an Emperor even when you are expecting him and have time to prepare. They have prodigious needs and expect you to provide for them. It is a disaster altogether to have one just drop in like that unannounced on a hot afternoon. At first, when I saw those accursed guards, I thought we were about to suffer pillage and martyrdom. I surely did." He cast his eyes upward and crossed himself perfunctorily, seeking the approbation of the others for his stalwart heroism at a time of such stress.

Brother Bernard took a deep draught from his flagon of wine, wiping his mouth with the back of his hand before continuing. "Perhaps pillage and martyrdom would have been better, all things considered." He nodded for effect and paused, obviously hoping to elicit a prompt to continue.

Wilfred showed interest.

"How so, Brother? It seems that they left without inflicting injury or causing damage. And they probably left behind a few gold coins to compensate for your provisionings and aid your relentless and unflagging pursuit of God's good work." He looked about the place innocently, as though seeking to verify his observation. If he intended sarcasm, Brother Bernard failed to infer it.

Instead, the good Brother shook his head emphatically, belched, leaned forward and waved a single admonitory finger in front of Wilfred's face. "You don't know the half of it, my good man. Not the half of it. You see, the Holy Father excommunicated Frederick II Hohenstaufen because he refused to take up the Cross and go on Crusade to the Holy Land after solemnly promising to do exactly that. God knows what heavy price we will have to pay in this life and in the next for playing host to such a scoundrel, even though we had no choice. And then, he profaned these sacred premises by his conduct and that of his companions, even more than by his own ungodly presence. No mere coins of gold could possibly compensate for what he did."

Brother Bernard paused, the better to nurture our curiosity. Then frowning, he leaned far over the table and whispered as though the information he wished to impart could not be spoken out loud. Even now, after all these years, I can visualize his fat, ruddy face, forehead streaming with perspiration under a fringe of straggly black hair, his shifty eyes betraying his zest for the tale as he attempted to project nothing but pious outrage.

"He brought his women into our courtyard."

The good Brother leaned back to let the full impact of that catastrophe sink in. His impressive belly pushed against his robe, almost as though he had a bag of flour perched on his lap. Brother Wilfred shrugged. "Why not? A hot afternoon, a long journey to complete, why withhold the hospitality of a house of God? Why withhold the bounties of your cool well waters and wine cellar from tired travellers just because they happen to be women?"

Brother Bernard snorted. "Because their presence within these walls is forbidden as you well know. But we would not put such a fine point on it if the issue had merely been a matter of tired female travellers, cool well waters and wine."

"Well what happened then, man? Enough of this rigmarole. Out with it." Wilfred smiled but he could not fully cloak his impatience with this fatuous, self-important monk. There was a point of prejudice in play here as well. Wilfred distrusted the piety and sincerity of all men of God — monks or priests — who were fat. For all his deviations from strict rules of piety, he was a loyal follower of our patron, Francis of Assisi. As such, he found corpulence inconsistent with an oath of poverty and a life of service. He equated portliness with corruption. I realized with a start that most of the residents of this monastery were far too well-nourished to meet with Wilfred's approval. His studied contempt for them all suddenly seemed as blatant as a slap in the face.

But Brother Bernard detected nothing but breathless anticipation in his listeners, so caught up was he in his juicy tale. He again leaned forward so that he could whisper and be heard above the noise in the room.

"After relieving himself and partaking of wine, Frederick climbed into one of the palanquins occupied by one of his women — perhaps more than one, we can't be sure — and committed the sin of fornication in the middle of our courtyard, in the middle of the afternoon."

Wilfred did not seem to share the shock felt by the rest of our little group. He in turn leaned far forward and whispered, mimicking Brother Bernard's breathless tone. "Tell me, good Brother. How do you know this to be true? Did you climb in with Frederick to get a better view or a whiff of the proceedings? Or did you just lift the curtain a little, the better to vent your curiosity as to the particulars of female parts?" He paused to take the full measure of Brother Bernard's sputtering before giving the barb one more twist. "Besides, as a devout celibate, how would you know the sin of fornication even if you did observe it in broad daylight in the middle of the monastery courtyard? What does it look like, pray tell? Please give us a detailed account of the appearance of a female bottom primed to receive carnal penetration, just to satisfy our unquenchable thirst for scientific knowledge." He leaned back and smiled expectantly.

I thought that Brother Bernard would fairly explode with indignation. "You Anglo Saxon swine. I waste my time talking to you about matters of proper conduct. It would be easier to train a wild dog. The great Roman Cicero was right when he said that it was a waste of money to buy an English slave because they could not be taught to do anything useful." He stood, lifted his robe, stepped over the bench and stomped away, sandals slapping on the stones of the floor.

Wilfred looked after him solemnly. I knew him well enough to know that he felt no remorse for the offense he had given. Brother Bernard was nothing to him. Less than nothing. A fat monk. Scum of the earth parasite.

The incident called to mind another incongruity between Brother Wilfred and his calling. He had little compassion for people he considered unworthy, for whatever reason, mostly having nothing to do with piety or Christian virtue and much to do with temporal virtues and practical skills. In his eyes, the worthy were few indeed. Although he and I had not discussed the matter, I sensed that he disdained most of the men in our party, along with Brother Bernard and the monks of this cloister.

His attitude unnerved me. The thought that we were embarking on a journey to the ends of the earth in an effort to find and win over formidable conquerors was daunting enough. My sense of dread grew by leaps and bounds as I realized that my more worldly companion saw none of the others as fit for the task. That being the case, and if he were right, how could we hope to survive?

After a few moments spent finishing our simple meals in silence, Wilfred spoke. "I am curious about this Emperor Frederick. I am curious about an excommunicant Emperor, on the road to Rome, who stops for refreshment at a monastery and openly fornicates with one or more of his women in the cloister courtyard. That is an unusual man, even for an Emperor. Particularly for a Catholic Emperor, excommunicated or not."

I was somewhat surprised. "So you think that Brother Bernard spoke the truth? Why then did you challenge him so?"

He responded without hesitation. "Because Brother Bernard is an ass. But yes, I believe he spoke the truth. There were at least twelve women in the palanquins in that party we saw on the road, all wearing court finery with jewelled crests and such like. Those palanquins were not large, particularly sturdy or soundproof. I'm sure anyone within thirty feet would know exactly what was going on in there after a man of Frederick's girth entered."

I persisted. "But as you say, how would Brother Bernard know what fornication sounds like or how it would cause a palanquin to move if he is a lifelong celibate?"

Wilfred laughed out loud. He looked me full in the face, smiling, eyes fairly spilling with friendly amusement. "You're a fine, innocent lad, Johnnie. I wager that before this trip is over, you'll know. And you'll know that that fat-arsed windbag Bernard knew as well because once you know, the whole thing is rather obvious. Brother Bernard knows because he probably fornicates with a woman or a boy or one of the brothers around here at least twice a week, corrupt as he is."

He paused, smiling, shaking his head slowly. "Oh, I believe him all right. Emperors have their way. A man like Frederick doesn't travel with

37

twelve women like that just to have them do his washing or rub his neck of an evening. He has them for the pleasures of the flesh, whenever the mood stiffens his member, you can be sure of it."

That seemed to end discussion of Frederick's libidinous ways. Dinner ended, followed by evening prayers. Later that night, I found Wilfred in quiet conversation with a spare, elderly monk whose name, I discovered later, was Brother Rodrigo. Tall, stooped, scholarly and soft-spoken, Brother Rodrigo was recounting for Wilfred the known history of Frederick II Hohenstaufen. Apparently Wilfred had circulated among the monks of the cloister until he found one willing and able to answer his questions.

The day had exhausted me and I had little interest in such matters. I left Wilfred to his inquiries and sought refuge in the cell that had been assigned to us.

CHAPTER FIVE

We were to travel from Venice to Constantinople on the Venetian galley Black Sea Queen. We first spied her moored at the dock next to the Palace of the Doge where the Grand Canal meets the Bay of Venice. We were housed in the monks' quarters at St. Mark's, adjacent to the Palace. It had the same dark stone walls, dank quarters and pervasive damp of Blackfriars, albeit without the chill.

The Black Sea Queen was a wooden ship of narrow beam with a single mast just forward of amidships, a high prow and a slightly raised rear deck where the captain and helmsman stood. The helmsman steered the ship by moving a large wooden tiller attached to a rudder that protruded beyond the ship's stern. A single square sail suspended from a boom that could be raised and lowered on the mast provided one source of motive power. She was also powered by long, sweep oars manned by convicts or slaves from a mezzanine deck just below the main deck.

The Black Sea Queen was a relatively large vessel with twenty-five oars each side. It had rudimentary crew quarters below forward, and finer quarters for the captain and special passengers to the stern. It could also carry cargo in a hold and in areas on deck.

The ship was equipped with a small catapult amidships for defense that could be rotated to sling its projectile in almost any direction. The catapult apparatus included a cauldron and fireplace so that pitch-soaked baskets and other incendiary materials could be used as weapons in battle with other vessels made of wood.

We would be travelling through the Adriatic, the Ionian Sea and the Aegean Sea. Although God troubled these waters from time to time with strong winds and violent storms, and they often witnessed the wars of mankind, we would be travelling at a time of calm insofar as man-made turbulence was concerned. No wars disrupted naval commerce. Even the pirates, so common at the eastern end of the Mediterranean, had been quiescent for many months. So we would not travel in convoy.

Nonetheless, our ship was to carry a unit of thirty Venetian marine soldiers armed with swords, daggers and crossbows. Arrangements for these men had delayed our departure. Cardinal Pellegrino had been aghast at the price demanded by the Doge for the services of fighting men in a time of peace. To his consternation, the captain refused to leave port without them, leading the good Cardinal to believe that he was the victim of a conspiracy to fleece the Holy See. Indeed, the Venetians had made no mention of the need to pay separately for extra fighting men when they had concluded the arrangements for our transport with the Papal emissary. But then, the Venetians had not become the richest trading nation by forswearing the opportunities for profit that the good and bountiful Lord presented to them.

Fra Dandolo sought in vain to gain relief from the burdensome imposition. Even his connections and exalted antecedents were unavailing in a case where the Venetians could exact any price that suited them. So the fighting men came along, despite the Cardinal's protests. He made that choice rather than waste a month seeking Papal intercession with no guarantee that the Doge or captain could be dissuaded, given the notorious independence and rapacity of the Venetians.

Wilfred had shown only mild interest in the crossbows the Venetians used. They were heavier and stronger than those he had tried in England. But they suffered from the same drawback, namely a lack of accuracy when compared to a longbow in skilled hands. The Venetian crossbows loosed a projectile with a blunt point primarily useful to penetrate armor and deliver a shocking type impact similar to that of a bludgeon. Crossbow projectiles were called bolts or quartels. In contrast, Wilfred's longbow loosed arrows with razor-sharp points that delivered a knife thrust like that of a rapier or dagger.

The crossbow was the weapon of choice throughout the Mediterranean. Men of England preferred the longbow and handled it with a skill possessed by no others. Command of the longbow requires more hours of practice. It was precisely because of this that Wilfred excelled. He used his longbow as part of his daily ritual, his practice an exercise in quieting and concentrating the mind.

Truly, I never saw him so much at peace as he appeared during his practice sessions, as though the art of the bow elevated him to a transcendent state.

*   *   *   *

We set sail one bright, windless morning, beating away from the dock at the height of the tide so that the ebb would assist us out to sea. Generally calm weather held for several days, allowing the use of sails only in the afternoon when a westerly breeze gained strength, dying down at dusk.

At night, the captain ordered the sail furled and our progress stayed until the following day. On the fifth night of our voyage, with a full moon to light the way, calm seas and a gentle following wind that continued after sundown, the captain decided to keep running rather than heave to for the night. He proceeded under sail alone, allowing the oarsmen to rest at their posts.

Wilfred and I had slept on the deck this night, as on many other nights, vastly preferring the balmy sea air and the endless sky to our cramped, foul-smelling quarters below. The gentle motion of the ship and the sound of the rigging had quickly seduced me into the oblivion of deep sleep. Awakening from time to time during the night, I revelled in the beauty of the night sky and the purity of the air. The luxuriant, lazy ecstasy of those calm Mediterranean nights on deck during our journey from Venice to Constantinople were among the finest nights I have spent in my entire life.

Shortly before dawn, we passed through the channel between the Island of Kithira and the Akra Malea Peninsula, the southeastern tip of the Peloponnesus and turned northeast into the Aegean Sea toward the cluster of small islands known as the Kikladhes, extending to the south off the Athenian Coast. The moon three quarters full stood low and large in the western sky, its light casting a broad path on the water to our stern, dancing on the uneven surface of the sea. The white cliffs of the islands and mainland caught the moonlight, providing muted beacons to guide our way. An occasional breaking wave would add a transitory streak of starker white at the base of the cliffs, showing bright and then fading with the pulses of the sea.

An orange streak along the eastern horizon with grey light extending upward into sky heralded the coming day. No clouds marred the perfection of the stars carpeting the sky from horizon to horizon, shining through in spite of the moon and the advance traces of coming sunlight.

Turkish pirates in three galleys attacked us just after dawn from the direction of the Island of Milos to the east. They waited until the sun had risen above the horizon and then rowed hard toward us with the blinding orb of the sun directly behind them. The lookouts heard the splashing oars and the shouts of their galley masters before they could make them out in the glare. The alarm spread quickly throughout our ship and sent men running everywhere. The ship's guard of Venetian marines quickly formed up and took their stations along the right side of the galley to face the enemy. Four men near the mast struggled to assemble the catapult and fire up the cauldron in which they would heat the projectiles. We could see similar fires on the three pirate vessels. The shouts of our own galley master grew louder and more frantic in tempo as the captain tried to outrun the smaller Turkish ships.

Through the haze of my own fears, I thought for an instant of the terror that must prevail on the rowing deck. Our rowers were all slaves or convicts, chained to their posts. If the Turks boarded and captured us, those of our rowers not killed in the battle would become galley slaves on Turkish vessels, never a happy prospect as, according to rumor, no man survived that service. If our ship was set alight either due to a mishap with our own catapult or from an enemy projectile, they would no doubt be burned alive, unable to escape. And if the ship went down, they would drown, trapped in their chains.

These sympathetic thoughts were fleeting indeed as I realized that, bad as things were for the rowers, my own circumstances were not much better. I would be killed or enslaved. If enslaved, I might be consigned to the rowing deck of a galley, I might be emasculated to perform the services of a eunuch in their society, if I survived the operation; or I might be sold to a sodomite for his pleasure. My mind churned as the Turks came steadily toward us, black and red pennants streaming from their mastheads. Their smaller vessels were clearly faster than ours. We could now make out their crews getting ready to board us as soon as they closed the remaining distance. Dark men, clad in loose pantaloons, bare chested and

42

marvelously well-formed, brandished vicious looking scimitars as they moved in. Their shouts made my blood run cold, even though I could not understand a word.

Realizing that we would be rammed by all three Turkmen if we kept to our course, the captain laid the helm hard over to show them our stern as we raced toward the Peloponnesus shore, perhaps three miles distant. Our turn cost us valuable yardage as the Turks continued to gain on us. But at least now, they would not be able to bring their rams into play. They would not be able to hit us hard enough to hole our hull while we all travelled in the same direction.

I gained a good look at them after our turn as they no longer had the sun directly behind them. Three graceful, small ships, built for speed with fierce gargoyle heads on their bowsprits and pointed metal rams plainly visible at the water line, they travelled with furled sails relying entirely on rowers. Their oars flashed rhythmically in the dawn sunlight, full of menace, like the legs of vicious waterborne carnivores.

All at once, I realized that I had been standing almost paralyzed, virtually holding my breath. I must have made quite a spectacle of wide-eyed fright to the sailors and marines rushing to prepare a defense. But although they were more functional than I, near panic prevailed among them on our ship's deck. Shouting and curses filled the air. Every man of them knew that we would all face horrible fates if we did not succeed in repelling the attack, an attack that would probably hit us from three sides at once.

The only reason we had not travelled in convoy through these waters was the Doge's belief that he had suppressed the pirates. Venetian ships had suffered no attack on voyage to Constantinople for more than a year now. It was our bad luck to encounter the first sign of a malevolent resurgence.

With a start, I realized that Wilfred was nowhere to be seen. I could not remember seeing him from the moment the alarm had been raised, although in my fright, I did not recall his departure. Just as the first crossbow bolts began flying back and forth between the ships, he reemerged on deck from below and came running toward me at the mast, heavy laden. In one hand, he held his longbow, extended over his shoulder. A basket of arrows hung by its handle suspended from the longbow down Wilfred's back, swaying crazily from side to side as he ran.

In his other hand, he carried a metal pot by the handle. He moved awkwardly but quickly under his load through the thin shower of lethal bolts hitting our deck from the Turkish ships.

By this point, the Turkish galley on our left had pulled roughly even with us at a distance of perhaps forty paces. It began to angle toward us clearly intending to get close enough for its soldiers to board. The pirates refrained from using their catapults, thus disclosing their intent to capture our ship rather than set it alight. We were all to be killed or enslaved with the ship taken as a prize. The Turkish boarding party huddled behind the parapet bulkhead of their vessel to shelter against bolts loosed by the Venetians as the distance between the ships closed.

Despite my panic, I became aware of Wilfred drawing his bow and loosing an arrow towards the helmsman on the Turkish galley. His shaft flew high and wide, landing harmlessly in the sea beyond. Wilfred leapt up and down in frustration.

"Goddamit man, stop these accursed shakes," he screamed at the top of his lungs. He put his bow down and stared in disbelief at his trembling hands. He shook his arms violently like a man possessed, dancing around in a circle. Then he picked up the bow, made a quick sign of the cross with a glance toward the heavens, drew an arrow from the basket and dipped its point into the metal pot.

Amazed as I was by his blasphemy, I did not fail to notice that he took a more relaxed and steady hold this time, the hold I had become accustomed to seeing during his long periods of practice. He missed his target again, the helmsman's torso. This time, the arrow struck the helm, driving through the helmsman's hand as it did so, pinning him like a bug to the wooden shaft beneath. The helmsman shrieked in pain, gyrating wildly as he tried to free himself.

Wilfred cursed shamefully again, albeit in a normal tone this time. "Christ shit on such a ragged release." But he had now registered the range and windage. His third arrow pierced the helmsman through, between the shoulderblades. His fourth struck the captain in the throat as he attempted to come to the helmsman's aid. The fifth struck deeply into the belly of another Turk who approached to help the captain, all in rapid succession as fast as he could pluck the arrows from his basket, dip them, draw and release.

With three of their number screaming hoarsely as they writhed their lives away, the other Turks hesitated before approaching the helm. Having lost its steering, the pirate galley veered directly toward us and passed just astern, requiring the vessel behind us to make a sudden turn in a vain effort to avoid a collision. The captain of the third vessel pulled away when he saw these unexpected maneuvers that left him alone in a position to engage us. Three-to-one odds had suddenly become one-to-one, with ours the larger vessel, our defenders more numerous than his possible attackers. Apparently he had no taste for that.

These events all transpired to the accompaniment of the most hellacious shouting, cursing and screaming imaginable. Crossbow bolts flew through the air like flocks of vicious sparrows, whirring and throbbing as they sought to pound their beaks into soft flesh. Oars splashed and cracked against each other. The Turks brandished their swords and shouted at us as though they could not wait to cleave us into quarters and feed our remains to the fishes. Our Venetians gave back similar invective, richly punctuated with the most arresting obscenities.

Our crew finally succeeded in lighting a fire projectile as the galley that Wilfred had incapacitated passed astern. The catapult had no difficulty lobbing the fiery mass among the Turks on deck at such short range. The burning pitch set the ship aflame from end to end in no time, the roar of fire punctuated by the screams of the doomed rowers. The water was soon dotted with swimmers who had jumped to save themselves. Somehow, the galley that had been directly astern also caught fire either by an accident or through collision with the vessel we had ignited. The third galley rowed rapidly away, leaving the swimmers and the roasting rowers behind.

Our captain did not hesitate. He brought our ship around to the northeast and resumed our course. Within a few minutes, we could no longer hear the shouts of the doomed men. Within a half hour, the flaming ruins seemed far away, almost an abstraction or a feature of the coastline, having nothing to do with murderous intent or tortured human remains. The sun was well up now and foretold a warm day. No breeze ruffled the mirror-smooth surface of the Aegean. A gentle swell raised and lowered the vessel in a pleasant soothing motion, in rhythm with the beat of the oars at cruising pace. The islands and mainland coast in the distance shimmered in a light sea haze that seemed to accentuate the chalk cliffs capped with dark vegetation. It would have been hard to imagine a more peaceful setting, well calculated to make the heart sing with boundless joy under different circumstances.

Our deck was littered with the enemy's crossbow bolts. Bolts had struck perhaps a half dozen of our Venetians. Two had died and a third did not have long to live. The others had but minor wounds. These were our only casualties, a modest toll under the circumstances, albeit devastating to those poor souls who comprised it.

It occurred to me later that many of the rowers in the burning boats were probably wretched Christian men enslaved by the Turks, some of them most likely men of Venice, like our captain and crew. I am sure that the captain knew the same far better than I. If he thought for even a second of attempting to save them, he showed no sign of it.

As we pulled steadily away from the scene of the encounter, word spread that we probably all owed our lives to Wilfred's longbow. Several of the crew had witnessed the chain of events he had wrought with the helmsman, the captain and the third man he had killed. In due course, the captain and then Cardinal Pellegrino himself came to congratulate and thank him. I understood the import of the message, although I could not hear most of the words so I cannot recount them for you. Suffice it to say that my protector had assumed a much enlarged stature in the eyes of the crew and passengers of that galley by virtue of his exploits. The Cardinal himself looked upon him as the right hand of God, the sword hand raised to strike down the infidels.

A familiar unpleasant odor slowly forced its way into my consciousness as I stood close in an effort to overhear these exchanges. In due course, I identified the metal pot as the source, a chamber pot at least half full of urine and excrement. As soon as the captain and Cardinal left him, Wilfred took the pot to the railing and emptied its noxious contents into the sea. As he turned back toward me, I asked: "Did I not see you dip your arrows into that pot before you loosed them at the Turkmen?"

"You did."

"Good God in Heaven, to what purpose?"

"To sour any wounds I might inflict." He paused in contemplation of my shock before continuing. "I would have preferred a faster acting poison, but I could lay my hands on none such in the short time I was allowed. There may be none on board this innocent vessel."

I was rendered nearly speechless. "Poison? Poisoned arrows?" To my shame, my voice broke with the word.

He replied with nonchalance. "Of course. Arrows freighted with human shit are not exactly the same as arrows anointed with a true poison, but they will do for a purpose. When the enemy sees that you are sending such stuff his way, it gives him pause. Even the bravest of men become more interested in dodging your missiles than in sending you his own. Even the bravest of men knows that a mere scratch from such a point can cause a stalwart warrior to sicken and die in good time. And all men understand the essence of the message when their enemy hurls his shit at them, as an adornment to a lethal shaft."

He turned to go below, motioning for me to follow. When he arrived at the hatch and I was not close behind, he realized that I still stood rooted to the spot. He regarded me for a moment and then returned to face me close on, his expression calm but voice stern and cold as the ice of the coldest winter. The first breath of a morning breeze somehow seemed to add power to his presence, as though he threatened to call forth the winds of hell to add emphasis to his convictions.

"If you cherish life, Johnnie, you fight for it with every means at hand. Only idiots and noblemen engage in mortal combat in accordance with rules that restrict the devices and tactics they may use in defense of their lives. Do you have any doubt that those Turks would have killed or enslaved us if they had taken this ship?"

I could not reply. He took me by both shoulders and shook me firmly. "Do you have any such doubts, Johnnie?"

I acknowledged that I did not.

He nodded. "Nor did I. Nor did I have faith that our good Venetian soldiers could overpower them, given that there were three of them and only one of us, more attackers than defenders and three sides of the ship to defend. It seemed that we would need a good bit of fortune to keep our heads attached to our necks. So I weighed in with all the force available to me as I have come to observe that fortune tends to favor those who try the hardest. I do not fear death, Johnnie, but I do not choose to die just yet. The thought depresses me when I consider the wonders we have yet to see and experience on this journey, let alone what lies beyond." He paused and looked back to the scene of the skirmish, the smoke of the burning galleys barely visible now at the horizon.

"Was it not the hand of God that saved us rather than just good fortune?" I asked.

He laughed for the first time since the encounter. Wilfred had a hearty laugh, a loud expression of uninhibited joy. His laugh always dissipated tension for me, never more than now. "The hand of God, my arse. If God had his hand in this journey, there would have been no Turkish pirates in the first place." He laughed again.

"As for good fortune, what do you call it when the helmsman I skewered falls in such a way so as to cause the galley he is steering to turn into the one directly astern of us, thus providing our catapult with a fat target for the hog roast? He could as easily veered off in the other direction leaving us still with two-to-one odds against.

"No, my lad. We were lucky back there, lucky to be alive this instant. I thank our Lord and Savior Jesus Christ for the luck, of course. But I do not see His hand in it. Life is full of such happenstance. Sometimes good, sometime not. I try never to waste the good because the bad will come, regardless of the purity of one's soul." He paused, looked skyward and crossed himself quickly, a familiar gesture.

"God did not bless us with life on this earth to have us waste it. To me, that means that one fights for one's life and tries not ever to squander the opportunities that fortune presents."

He smiled and beckoned. This time, I followed him in the direction of the hatch.

CHAPTER SIX

We docked briefly at the Greek port of Piraeus to take on water and to allow the Captain to report the pirate attack to the Venetian traders there. We stayed but half a day, slipping down the coast on the afternoon tide, to round the peninsula south of Lavrion. Passing between the mainland and the Island of Kea, we made for the open Aegean through the strait between Andros Island and Evvoia. No wind at all ruffled the surface of the sea, shining under a cloudless sky. We moved steadily to the rhythmic sweep of the oars. The Captain set the helm for the Island of Limnos across the heart of the Aegean rather than hug the shoreline, as was more customary in these treacherous waters. He judged the weather benign and sought to save the time we would lose on the more circuitous, albeit safer route.

The attack and fierce battle had left both crew and passengers in a sombre state despite the beauty of the surroundings. Only the sound of the oars and the shouts of the galley master broke the silence. The gentlest of swells from the southwest were all that disturbed the steady equilibrium of the Black Sea Queen.

The hours and days, and the passage of time, ceased to have meaning for me until the blue-grey outline of Limnos slowly rose up from the eastern horizon late one bright afternoon, then Gokceada off the Gallipoli Coast, and then the stark bluffs of the Anatolian Peninsula. Not until we moved close to that coastline could we clearly see the mouth of the Dardenelles, connecting the Aegean and the Sea of Marmara through a long, narrow defile between rocky shores that fronted sharply rising ground.

The weather changed as we entered the Strait. A stiff, southwest breeze filled our sail, allowing respite to our rowers. The escarpments on both sides of the Dardenelles seemed to funnel the wind to our advantage. We progressed at greater speed than we had attained during the entire voyage from Venice. Surely God must smile on our enterprise to favor us with such assistance.

The breeze cleared the air of all haze. Bright sunlight defined every angle and fold in the broken, rocky land, every crag, every outcrop. The sky filled with ranks of small, puffy clouds that cast shadows on the tawny hills of Anatolia, giving it the aspect of a spotted animal pelt, appearing to undulate with life as the cloudshadows moved across uneven ground on the hurrying air.

We cleared the Strait and ran before the wind close to the northerly coast of the Sea of Marmara. The walls of Constantinople appeared suddenly as we rounded a headland and moved along the south and then the eastern face of the City toward the Harbor of Phospharion at the mouth of the Golden Horn.

I have travelled far and wide, but never have I seen such a place as Constantinople. Never have I seen such high ramparts and strong towers, splendid palaces and soaring churches, so many that I would not have believed it but for the evidence of my own eyes. Never have I seen a City so large behind its walls, so long and so wide, appearing to be so wealthy, so rich in the diversity of its buildings. We passed close beneath the high gables and rich facades of great churches, St. John of Studium, St. Sergius and Bacchus, St. Mary Hodegetria and many others.

As we rounded the turn toward the Bosphorus and the Golden Horn, the dome of St. Sophia, the Church of the Holy Wisdom, came into view, an arresting sight beyond all description, all imagination, rising above the Palace Bucoleon on the commanding heights within the wall of ancient Byzantium. I felt as though I had travelled to the center of civilization, a place dedicated to Christ and nourished by a concentration of glorious structures for worship of Him unmatched anywhere in the known world.

No sooner had we landed than the impressions of grandeur gained from the galley deck, perhaps one hundred paces offshore, gave way to a sense of sinister decay. From within, the City proved filthy, crowded, unruly, the structures stained and decrepit, signs of ancient yet unrepaired conflagration on every side. Street vendors hawked their wares rudely, accosting passersby as though they would attack those who did not purchase their tawdry merchandise. Squatters lay about in the rubble of ruined structures, their clothes in tatters, their unwashed skin broken with sores, bare feet black with the dirt of months or even years unshod. Skeletal beggars implored alms at every streetcorner, some of them blind, others lacking a hand or a limb.

We were to stay in the City until Cardinal Pellegrino could conclude arrangements for the further progress of our party. The Venetians could see us through the Bosphorus and the Black Sea to Sebastopolis without difficulty. Venetian galleys made that trip regularly. We could not safely proceed further, however, except as part of an armed caravan under the guidance of a skilled leader who had arranged for peaceful passage. Although the route, the Silk Road, had been used for centuries in trade with the empires of the East, it was long and hard, traversing harsh desert lands, skirting several ranges of impassable mountains, beset by extremes of weather unknown to the European and Mediterranean world. These were the natural hazards, formidable enough. But a human hazard also fueled our anxieties, filling me with foreboding.

A sect of Moslem heretics known as the Assassins controlled the mountainous lands to the south of the Caspian Sea under the leadership of a bloodthirsty sheik known as the Old Man of the Mountain. These men, it was said, were noted for their stealth, capable of entering a camp on the darkest of nights and cutting the throats of all who slept there without waking a soul. Armed guards proved equally defenseless against them, collapsing without murmur from a thrust delivered by an unseen black-clad assailant. No caravan could hope to traverse the lands under sway of the Assassins without their consent — a consent on offer only at ruinous price. Even so, one ran the risk that the Old Man would recant his word if the prize of plunder appeared richer than the price he had exacted.

I had listened to these tales told among the soldiers and sailors of the ship during the long hours at sea. My mind grasped them in paralyzed horror, the way a small animal freezes in the presence of a serpent. The prospect of having my throat slit during peaceful slumber, of dying without ever awakening to appeal for God's mercy in my last moments in this life, filled me with peculiar revulsion. As the prospect of entering the realm of the murderous infidels drew ever more imminent, anxiety grew within me.

Given the demands of our journey, we understood that it might take Cardinal Pellegrino several days to make the appropriate arrangements. We might then wait several days more to accompany the ships traveling east to provision our caravan. For even though the men of the caravans rarely traveled west of Sebastopolis, the goods that they carried to barter for the treasures of the east generally came through Constantinople, a trade controlled by the Venetians.

Wilfred, Fra Dandolo, the other members of the Papal mission and I were to await departure at the Monastery of Magnana, close against the eastern Wall, but a short distance below the Churches of St. Irene and St. Sophia, immediately below the old Greek Acropolis known as the Hippodrome in the time of the Emperor Justinian, seven centuries earlier.

I stayed close to Wilfred as we walked the short distance from the ship to the Monastery, through the seething chaos of the City, trying to ignore the baleful stares of hostile men, swarthy of complexion with curly black hair. Wilfred noted my fight.

"Uneasy are you, Johnnie? These lads have you on edge, do they?"

"Aye."

He smiled tightly. "Me as well. There is something amiss here, I know not what, nor have I heard what it might be." The sweep of his gaze stopped suddenly to study the upper reaches of St. Sophia, more visible now above the rooftops. He pointed.

"See there, Johnnie. The windows of that great church are gone."

"Perhaps they are under repair."

He shook his head. "Where then is the scaffolding?" There was none to be seen. A better vista opened up as we passed a cross street leading up the hill. Wilfred stopped to point again.

"Look there. See the columns with nothing atop them. See the places on the walls where icons or decorations have been removed, and none too gently at that." He shook his head again. "That church has been the object of sack, and not recently by the look of it."

He turned to me, eyes wide with astonishment. "How can it be that the grandest church in all of Christendom stands pillaged in a Christian City?"

As if to punctuate the sullen atmosphere, four armed horsemen cantered down the stone street scattering the foot traffic, driving us into doorways and against the walls of buildings to avoid being trampled. The style of their clothing, their armaments, their saddlery and horse livery identified them as Frankish knights. One of them brushed against Wilfred nearly knocking him off his feet, causing him to drop his longbow and the small bag in which he carried his belongings into a gutter that ran with the discharges from neighboring buildings. I saw my friend's eyes surge with the cold anger that seized him at such moments.

"Go your way, Frank bastards. May Christ cause the pox on your balls to blind you and your brains to spill out of your arse." He shouted after them, a booming voice that reverberated in that noisy street like the sound of a trumpet. No challenge, no call to war could have been more clear. If the knights heard or understood him, they did not show it. Several passersby laughed at him, somehow a derisive gesture in the circumstances. I tugged at the sleeve of his robe to hurry him toward the monastery. None of our party seemed even to note his blasphemous profanity or his rage.

*   *   *   *

We stayed in the monastery for two days before venturing up the hill to see St. Sophia. The monastery itself was in a poor state, occupied by Latin-speaking monks who appeared to be followers of St. Benedict. We had almost no discourse with them. They did not make us feel unwelcome. At the same time, they clearly wanted as little to do with us as possible and would not lament our departure.

Something about that monastery felt out of place, slightly askew. I could not discern a specific cause for the dissonance I felt, yet I felt it clearly, as though the place and the occupants did not suit each other. Wilfred being withdrawn and pensive, I did not discuss the matter with him. Indeed, we said very little as we went about our devotions. When we had had no news of a departure for the East by the third day, Wilfred proposed that we visit the great church.

A brisk wind cleansed the air, driving away the stench of the City, as we climbed the steep hill to the square in front of St. Sophia. The bright sky overhead enhanced the dome of the structure, surrounded by its jumble of elegant subsidiary towers.

The great size and rich complexity of the church must be seen to be comprehended. The main portion is built on a rectangular base, roughly 70 yards wide, 75 yards long. But the sense of enormity one gains from the exterior is nothing to the vastness of the interior vaulted spaces. Upon entering, one feels rendered small, both physically by the pure height and depth, and spiritually by the rich grandeur of the aisles and galleries, the arched balustrades, the detailed artistry of columns and column capitals, the intricate inlaid work on every surface. We wandered toward the nave almost in a trance, heads thrown back to admire the ceiling of the dome, mouths agape in awe. Had I not seen it, I would not have believed that the hand of man could erect and embellish such a great and beautiful edifice in tribute to Christ — or any other god, for that matter.

We encountered the first officer of our ship as we made our way through the transept. He accosted us as we progressed, our eyes cast aloft in wonder. It was a friendly greeting, virtually the first we had heard since our arrival in this surly City. Wilfred was a hero in the eyes of the ship's company, even more so to those of the company who had witnessed at first hand his pivotal role in the fight with the Turkish pirates. The first officer, Pietro Santangelo, had stood stalwart on the bridge through the entire battle and had seen it all.

"So, Brothers," he said, "this must be your first visit to St, Sophia." He smiled, an expression of cheer on a face cheerful by nature. We nodded.

"Too bad then that it remains in disrepair a full 23 years after the sacking."

"What sacking?" Wilfred asked.

Pietro laughed. "Ah, you are ignorant of the history of this City, then." We admitted that deficiency.

"Well, in the Spring of 1205, the Frankish knights of the Fourth Crusade, led by the great Doge of Venice, Enrico Dandolo, sacked this City, stripping it of all its treasures, including the treasures housed in this great place of worship built by the Emperor Justinian fully seven hundred years past. Do you recall the great bronze horses above the door of St. Marks Cathedral in Venice?" We did.

"Taken from this place. Do you recall the sculptures and reliefs on the north and south faces of St. Marks? They, too, were stripped from this place, as were the decorated glazings." He laughed again.

"And inside, in the north transept of St. Marks, hangs the miraculous icon of the Virgin Nicopoeia — the Bringer of Victory — which the Byzantine Emperors took into battle for centuries. The Treasury of St. Marks brims with the art of this place, so much that it cannot all be displayed, all taken during three days of wanton plunder and transported back to Venice."

My mind could not grasp these things. Wilfred, too, seemed perplexed. "How could this be? Was not the Fourth Crusade summoned by the Pope to smite the infidels?"

"It was."

Wilfred shook his head. "Was this not a Christian city and the seat of a Christian Empire in 1205?"

"It was."

Wilfred shrugged, his face disclosing pure bewilderment. "How then could such a thing take place?"

Pietro Santangelo smiled at him broadly, his handsome face alight with mirth, dark eyes twinkling. I could not tell if his amusement was sincere or tinged with irony.

"I will tell you. The reason is quite simple, quite straightforward.

"The knights of the Fourth Crusade contracted with the Republic of Venice to provision and transport them in their enterprise. When the time came to embark, they could not pay the agreed price. So the Doge consented to take them anyway if they would first regain for him the City of Zara on the Dalmatian Coast, recently wrested from the Venetian Republic by the King of Hungary. They did so. The fleet then came here where Venetians have always maintained a trading enclave.

"The Empire was then in weak hands. Alexius III sat athwart the throne, a feckless youth with little appetite for the rigors of governance. After a time, Enrico Dandolo saw the opportunity to displace him and establish a Venetian fiefdom on the throne of Byzantium. He persuaded the Frankish knights to support the enterprise by offering them the traditional three days of rape and pillage of the City accorded to conquering armies."

Wilfred shook his head again in disgust and wonderment. "So the treasures of this holy place and this Christian City were sacrificed to slake the greed of those who had taken up the Cross to smite the infidels."

Pietro Santangelo nodded, smiling still. "And the City put to the torch, the Byzantines put to flight, remaining in exile to this day. The governance of the City is now divided between my countrymen and the boorish Franks who can agree on nothing, with little effort to repair the damage or arrest the decay or control the sullen chaos that pervades this City in all its neighborhoods and alleyways."

For the first time, I thought that I detected a note of dismay in Pietro's account, a note of shame. I could not be sure. But his tale prompted a closer examination of the interior of Hagia Sophia, an examination that revealed many evidences of the desecration that had taken place here. Several moments passed in silence as we looked at our surroundings with fresh perspective. Then, I heard the rustling of parchment. Pietro Santangelo unrolled a scroll and spread it upon a bench.

"I copied this from a letter to the Pope from a man who saw the sack of this place, Nicetas Choniates. I found the letter in the library at the Palace of the Pope and it moved me. Allow me to read a portion of it." He paused, squinting at the parchment.

"'They smashed the holy images and hurled the sacred relics of the Martyrs into places I am ashamed to mention, scattering everywhere the body and blood of the Savior. They destroyed the high altar, a work of art admitted by the entire world, and shared out the pieces amongst themselves. They tore the jewels from the holy chalices. They brought horses and mules into the Church, to use as a stable and the better to carry off the treasures they had stolen from the pulpit, the throne, the doors and other places. When some of these beasts slipped and fell, they ran them through with their swords, fouling the Church with their blood and ordure. Everywhere could be heard the cries and lamentations of the matrons, innocent maids, even virgins consecrated to God, to whom they showed no mercy.'"

My mind raced back to Fra Cipriani. I thought of he who had sacked the city and stabled his horses in the Grand Mosque at Bukhara to proclaim himself God's punishment. I thought of the deeds of that great Conqueror who was the very object of our embassy. It was one thing to

56

talk of such events, another thing altogether to stand in a place where a catastrophe, eerily similar, had in fact taken place. And in Christ's name. I wondered if Wilfred had the same thoughts. His face showed nothing but gravity and opaque absorption.

Pietro Santangelo was not done with us. He beckoned that we follow him to a gallery off the main transept. There in a sombre alcove stood an enormous, dark tombstone. Despite the bright sunlight outside and the rows of lofty windows without glazing, open to the sky, very little of the light streaming in to illuminate the great vaulted spaces of this hallowed structure, reached the alcove's recesses. It took several moments for our eyes to adjust to the gloom, for the inscription to emerge from the shadows and reveal the identity of the hero buried here, in a place reserved for saints and martyrs of the Church. Enrico Dandolo, Doge of Venice, leader of the Fourth Crusade, he who had stripped the Church of its treasures in a profane ceremony of pillage to enhance the grandeur of St. Marks, had chosen this place for his own consecrated burial, to await the Day of Judgement. I crossed myself quickly. May Christ have mercy upon his soul.

When we returned to the monastery, we discovered that the Black Sea Queen would depart for Sebastopolis at dawn the next morning. Cardinal Pellegrino had finally arranged for the caravan we needed and paid the Venetians' price in full with the Holy Father's gold.

Wilfred rebuffed my meagre efforts to discuss what we had seen at Hagia Sophia and what we had learned from Pietro Santangelo. His dark mood and withdrawal persisted for many days. I had seen him like this before and was not greatly troubled by it. I transcended such periods in our relationship with prayer, awaiting the bright emergence that always followed his bouts of introspection.

The voyage to Sebastopolis proved uneventful. And we traversed the jumbled land of the Assassins without so much as seeing a member of that fearsome sect. When we emerged from the mountains of the Caspian unto the vast plain beyond, we entered the domains of the distant power with which the Cardinal sought contact. We saw no sign of it as our camels swayed eastward, at their own, maddening pace.

CHAPTER SEVEN

The desert wind billowed the walls of the yurt. The poles holding the structure creaked and groaned against the wind's assault. Torch flames flickered and danced on the shifting air currents that penetrated the seams in the hide walls and the hole at the top left to allow smoke to escape.

The wind had blown steadily for the last three days, ever since we left the forlorn settlement at Ashgabat on the road to Bukhara. It was a hot dry wind from the northwest and each gust raised a swirling dust cloud. At night, the wind seemed to increase in intensity, the gusts carrying a freight of sand and dust particles that could sting the eye and skin of anyone foolish enough to face the blow head on. Even at daytime velocity, the wind quickly became irksome, without mention of the heat, the featureless country, the swaying discomfort of the camel's back to one unused to the motion.

Exhausted, uncomfortable and sore, I lay near the wall of the yurt on one of the rugs used by the nomads for flooring. The Mongol herdsmen mostly used animal skins for their tent floors. The caravans and higher Mongol officials more typically used the rugs woven by Persians and Turkmen from sheep wool, colored with vegetable dyes, decorated with bright, intricate and roughly symmetrical patterns. Our yurt this night had flooring of the latter type, richly colored rugs of reds, blues and browns. As an official embassy from an important power to the court of the Great Khan, we had apparently qualified for such treatment.

For we now knew that we were on a journey to the Court of Ugedei, son of Ghenghis Khan, ruler of the Mongol Empire. In Constantinople, in Sebastopolis, no one had heard of Prester John. We were told that it was Ghenghis Khan who had declared himself the punishment of God from the holy altar of the Grand Mosque at Bukhara. His armies had sacked the cities and massacred the inhabitants throughout the former domain of the Khwarazm Shah. Mongol hordes slaughtered the infidels on their eastern frontiers whenever the spirit moved them. Our embassy could have been directed by God to no other power, given its purpose. Ghenghis having died in 1227, we sought contact with Ugedei, his successor as Great Khan.

On this night, I was indifferent to the privilege conferred by the finery on which I reclined. I was fatigued enough to have slept on a bed of nails, and sufficiently uncomfortable to despair of sleep altogether.

We had been on the trail that day for almost sixteen hours, pushing hard to traverse some particularly inhospitable country. The road skirted the southern fringe of the Kyzyl Kum Desert, a vast dry area of alkali flat, wind sculpted sand dunes and meager grass with no reliable waterholes. The Kara Kum Desert lay just to the south of our route. The road followed a relatively narrow band of sparse country between the two deserts. But at least here, on the margins of the desert lands, we could find grass for the animals and a bit of rank water that could serve to keep a man or beast from dying of thirst.

I found the journey very difficult. For one thing, we seemed to be travelling through a featureless wasteland that stretched on to an endless eternity. The mountains that stood on the horizon never seemed to change, never closer, never further away, always there as though some great force kept moving them at exactly the pace of our camels. The heat was oppressive, the wind a great burden. Sometimes I felt as though I was standing at the vent of a blacksmith's furnace so searing was the air.

Then there were the camels, an abomination. I found it difficult to get used to their irregular gait, swaying and jolting along for hours on end. They stank. They were infested with fleas that quickly infested their riders. Flies swarmed around them. They were unruly and complaining, hard to control, recalcitrant beasts.

This night, I seemed to feel the misery of our circumstances more acutely than usual. I was travel sore and covered with insect bites. Dinner had consisted of a fiendishly distasteful concoction that I could barely swallow despite robust hunger. I had dared not ask what it was for fear of the answer. I felt filthy and irritable in my skin, desperate to plunge fully clad into a cold river or lake of which there were none in sight or in prospect for many days to come — not until we reached the Syr Darya

River within a day or two of Bukhara. So I lay in discomfort on my robe against the seething wall of our shelter, facing the wall and trying to suppress the urge to scratch my fleabites, hoping without much hope for the gentle oblivion of sleep to overtake me.

Toward the center of the yurt, Wilfred reclined in quiet discussion with Rashid ad-Khabar, a Mongol Court official of Persian extraction who had been sent out to accompany us when word of our embassy had reached Karakorum. Rashid seemed a remarkable fellow. Roughly thirty years old, he had the dark skin, jet black hair and dark eyes typical of most of the peoples we had encountered since reaching the lands beyond the eastern shore of the Caspian Sea. Unlike the Mongols, his face was sharp and thin with a nose like a hawk's beak. His mustache and beard were closely cropped, neatly trimmed and full, unlike the straggly style of the Mongols and other peoples of the steppe. He wore fine robes and an Arab headdress on the trail, held in place with a rope made of fibers that appeared to contain gold.

We never obtained an accurate account of Rashid's history. We assumed that the Mongols spared him when they conquered and destroyed one of the Persian cities. They had a habit of sparing craftsmen and scholars upon condition that they take up service to their Empire.

Rashid had apparently been sent out to meet us because he had command of rudimentary Latin and might better be able to ascertain the details of our embassy. When it became clear that neither Cardinal Pellegrino nor Fra Dandolo had any interest in attempting to broaden the scope of communication, either by attempting to expand his Latin or learn another language in which he was fluent, he had lapsed into a smiling silence, conversing from time to time with the caravan leader.

I cannot recall when Wilfred first approached Rashid. But at some point, I became aware that they were spending a lot of time together, riding and in camp, Rashid teaching Wilfred the Mongol and Farsi words for various objects and Wilfred teaching Rashid the Latin and French. Each day, one could see them pointing at various objects and exchanging the words for them, correcting each other's pronunciation. In the evenings, they sat together over parchment learning the writing for the words of the day. I had no way to judge the progress of these efforts because I was not included in them, nor did I wish to be. Before long, however, I noted

61

Wilfred exchanging small bits of conversation with the caravan leader, some of the camel tenders, some of the herdsmen and travellers we met along the way. Their responses showed that they understood him.

This evening seemed no different than the others, except that Rashid had unrolled a few parchment scrolls that he had been carrying. I found out later that one was written in Arabic and the other in the language of the Uighur people, the script that Ghenghis Khan had adopted as the official written language for use in the Mongol Empire. The Uighur were a people of the high plateau west and south of Mongolia that the Mongols had subjugated and who had become an important mainstay of their Empire.

So this night inaugurated Wilfred's efforts to become a scholar of written Arabic and Uighur in addition to the other languages that he sought to master on our long journey east. As he would often say, the effort kept his mind busy during the hours of travel through the emptiness of the Central Asian steppe. As a scholar and high court official, Rashid was a godsend for him.

In due course, Rashid and Wilfred put out the torches and repaired to their sleeping robes. Wilfred preferred to sleep outside, but the howling wind of this godforsaken place precluded his doing so that night. So he came and lay down near me. As I could not sleep for all of my discomforts, I asked him what he and Rashid had been trying to discuss through their limited, albeit expanding, channel of communication. Wilfred did not reply for a moment. At first, I thought that perhaps he had fallen asleep and had not heard my question. It quickly became clear that he was wide awake, and I had ventured into a sensitive area of deep inner turmoil.

"Rashid's an infidel, a Moslem. I assume you knew that."

I had not thought about it. Thinking on it now, I could not recall Rashid praying or performing any other act that might disclose religious leanings.

"If that's the case, why do you spend so much time with him?"

"Because he can teach me what I yearn to know." He paused. "Besides, although I have not had occasion to test him truly, he seems very wise. If he were not, the Mongols would have killed him with all the others of his city when they took it."

"What is it that you yearn to know, Wilfred?" This question was far more important to me than trying to assess why Rashid would consent to work for a power that had slaughtered thousands of his co-religionists, defiled their shrines and destroyed their seats of learning.

Another pause. It was absolutely dark, a total absence of light. Clouds blocked out any moonlight that might have shown through the chinks in the yurt. Only the sound of the wind and the groaning of the hides and poles created any fodder for the senses to feed upon.

Eventually he spoke, his voice subdued. "I am not sure, Johnnie. My mind is all confusion, trying to figure out the right and wrong of who we are and what we believe."

"I don't understand why you are so confused." True enough.

"Nor do I. But if the Lord God created the earth and all the people in it, then he created this place along with the infidels and the unbelievers that inhabit it, correct?"

"But what if this is the devil's work, Wilfred?" It would have been easy for me to believe in a purgatory not unlike this place.

"Where in the Scriptures does it report that portions of the earth and portions of humanity were created by the devil, Johnnie?" I heard him move in his robes. I could visualize him in my minds eye, head in palm propped up on an elbow. "The devil attempts to take over the hearts and souls of men, but he did not create them. God created them. Including those that have never had the opportunity to know Him. Is that not correct?"

I could not argue. I was too fatigued, even if I had had an argument. Yet I could sense the excitement that Wilfred felt whenever he stood on the threshold of a new revelation. He was an absolute slave to a restless and questing spirit, a willing rider on a runaway horse.

"Tonight, Rashid showed me Arabic and Uighur script. The Arabic is a book of Persian poems, the Uighur some sort of government directive, neither very important. But the writing itself is a thing of great beauty, rounded and flowing with exquisite intricacies, more beautiful than the finest Latin calligraphy that we spend years illuminating. I cannot help but see the hand of God in such beauty, even though created by men and not Christian men at that."

63

At times I trembled for the soul of my protector. He seemed almost regularly blasphemous to my more regimented mind. I admit now, as I did then, that I lacked Wilfred's imagination, his genius, his energy. It occurred to me more than once during our years together that all these things might have had a demonic origin.

"Do you understand this writing, Wilfred?" I asked.

"Not yet. Rashid instructs me and I hope to know it some day. In the meantime, we teach each other words that we can practice during the long hours of the day. Our ability to speak and understand each other grows. I have even come to understand from him some of the similarities between the religions of these regions and Christianity. My language is not yet good enough to understand the details of dogma and doctrine. But the organizations are similar in many of their essential qualities, which is a disturbing and important revelation to me."

My flea bites tormented me and I knew that I could not fall asleep while such urgent itching persisted. So despite my fatigue and lack of real interest, I hoped to divert my mind by further exploring Wilfred's ideas.

"What are these similarities?"

"Well first, a great schism divides the infidels. A schism of which we Christians know nothing. Apparently cousins and other direct descendants of the Prophet Mohammed fought amongst themselves over who should control their holy places. Many murders were committed in these struggles, violent quarrels over who was the proper interpreter on earth of the true word of God — Allah, as they call him. The murders and contention occurred more than five hundred years ago and crystallized into rival branches of Moslem belief, with the followers of each branch hating each other. From what I am able to understand, the doctrinal differences between the contending sides seem quite insignificant, although it is possible that I miss the point because I am still a neophyte in the language."

"You learned this from Rashid?"

"Yes."

"How so?"

"I wished to know why he would consent to work for the Mongols when they appeared to be the enemy of his people and destroyers of the sacred places of his religion."

"What did he say?"

"I didn't understand all he said, but I think that he is of one sect and the cities the Mongols have most recently destroyed were largely populated by members of the other. In any case, he believes in the power of the Mongols. He wishes to remain part of their governing structure. He considers them invincible. Rashid believes in the value of this life. So he prefers to work for the winning side in this life as a way to prolong it and fill it with comforts. He prays to his God in his own way for the benefit of his soul in the next."

My fatigue and discomfort impaired my ability to follow the thread of Wilfred's thinking. Where were the similarities? My question provoked laughter.

"You are a good Roman Catholic, Johnnie, one who asks few questions. You will undoubtedly go to Heaven. Perhaps I should keep my mouth shut and refrain from challenging your mind with impure thoughts."

"Jesus will protect me from any such impurities, Wilfred. Please share your thinking with me. I will keep it in confidence, regardless of its blasphemous nature."

He paused again, as though unsure where to begin. He trusted me, of that I was sure. "You are aware, are you not, of the schism between Rome and the Eastern Orthodox in matters of Christian doctrine?"

"I have heard of it. I know not what it is about."

His answer came instantly. "It is about power, of course. Power here on earth, just as with the Moslems. But the apologists for the east church and the west church — the clerics hired by the contenders for power to justify their claims in religious terms — have cooked up a doctrinal dispute over the true nature of Christ, disputes that no earthly evidence can ever resolve. And then there are the followers of Nestorius, the heretic prelate of the fifth century, excommunicated by the eastern church, whose followers are apparently numerous in these regions and well accepted by the Mongols. Have you heard of the debate over whether Christ is more God than man; or more man than God?"

I had not.

"I will describe it. Although the subject is more complex, it has provoked intense learned debate and been the stated cause of several wars that were really about power — whether Constantinople would be subordinate to Rome or the other way round, whether Nestorius or a rival prelate would prevail in debate before the Byzantine Emperor."

He shifted position before continuing. A violent gust rocked the yurt. He waited to let it subside, speaking in a low voice.

"If Christ were more God than man, then he didn't truly suffer on the cross and he knew at the time that he would be restored to his Godly place, a fact that could reflect upon the sacrificial purity of his faith. As a God, he would need no faith because he would know the answer. On the other hand, if he were a man — born the son of God but a man nonetheless — then he suffered as we have been taught to believe that he suffered; and he must have had the purest of faith to believe in his example to mankind and in his own resurrection." He paused before continuing.

I had not heard any of this before. I found it perplexing, the more so because each thesis seemed plausible to me, impaired as I was at the moment. "Which do you believe to be correct, Wilfred? Was Christ purely a God or did he have a dual nature?" He responded with fervor.

"Why does it matter what I believe or which is correct, or if there be a correct answer? Do we not follow the man or God or man/God because of his teachings? Is such a contrived argument worth serious debate, let alone wars in which people actually burn cities and kill each other? Nestorius believed that Christ must have been more God than man because one cannot imagine the true Christ as a small child, petulant, self-absorbed, incontinent. He staked all on his point of view, and a conclave of bishops cast him out. His followers fled east, to these lands, to escape persecution. To what end?"

He spoke now with intensity. I could tell that anger and frustration filled him. It startled me to think that he could become so agitated in this place over such abstractions when it seemed far more important to me just to survive the coming days of arduous progress through these accursed lands. When I did not reply, he continued.

"You know, of course, of the Pope's Crusades against the Cathars and Waldensians in Toulouse and Provence. You recall that we were required to make a detour to avoid cities and towns under siege in those provinces on our way to Rome."

I remembered all too well. We had been forced to spend at least two extra weeks on the road, navigating around those travails. He continued.

"The Frankish knights who conduct those Crusades have taken up the Cross in the name of the one true faith, of course. But the Pope, with the approval of the King of France, has given his sanction that they may keep the properties of all the heretics they dispossess, as well as the lands of the dukes and counts who have suffered the heretics to live within their domains. Now I ask you, Johnnie. Do you think that these good and God-fearing knights would have taken up the Cross in the absence of such earthly inducements?"

Wilfred's question bore a rich freight of sarcasm. I felt almost as though I were being accused of some sin, so intense did he sound. The total darkness of the tent and the howling of the infernal wind added to the atmosphere of threat. I could not keep the fear and concern out of my voice. "Please Wilfred. I know not."

He answered in a calmer tone. "Nor do I, Johnnie. But I doubt it. Oh I don't mean to suggest that Simon de Montfort who leads that Crusade by the Pope's appointment is not a devout and God-fearing man and a mortal terror to all heretics condemned by the Holy Father. Somehow, I don't see him turning over the vast estates he has taken from the Count of Toulouse by conquest in the Crusades to some charity or other. He has shown no sign of any such intentions. Indeed, he lives on the fat of those rich lands."

I felt lost. These thoughts had churned my friend and protector's mind into a state of great agitation. To what purpose? I could not even begin to guess.

"What does all this mean, Wilfred? Why do you concern yourself over such matters?"

I heard him stir, as though shifting in his sleeping robes. I sensed his agitation and deep concern. Profound silence added weight to the oppressive darkness before he answered.

"I am beginning to doubt earthly religions, Johnnie. All of them. Whatever their origins in miracles, acts of pure faith, martyrdom and revelation, they quickly become mere codpieces for the exercise of temporal power by men. When these men become rivals for power within the framework of a religious structure, they create nuances of doctrinal difference, claim sole ownership of godly truth for their particular nuance and seek to destroy all those who disagree."

He paused, perhaps to let the weight of his words sink in before continuing. I heard him take several deep breaths, as though his thoughts constricted his lungs. For a moment, I thought that perhaps a vengeful God had stricken him. He continued with agitated conviction.

"I believe that I have been sent to this place, untouched by Roman Christendom, with peoples foreign to our way of life, to discover the truth. I believe that if they all act similarly to Christians in matters of faith, regardless of the faith they profess, then perhaps we will have profound evidence that God does not exist at all except as a creation of the human mind, questing for immortality and grasping at fragments of vagrant mystery as giving false promise that man can indeed transcend death. Only the scraps of mystery and the interpretations vary from people to people and place to place. The underlying motive force remains the same, everywhere, to all peoples. Mortality." He stopped for a moment, audibly struggling for breath as though in a wrestling match with his thoughts. His voice was lower and more calm when he continued.

"While in the meantime, the institutions created in the name of the various beliefs simply serve as vehicles for the exercise of power by certain men over others, as well as forums within which potent men can contend with each other for power."

I could not be sure, but it seemed to me that a particularly powerful gust shook our yurt at the conclusion of Wilfred's statement. I trembled at the depth and breadth of his heresy. It did not help to realize yet again that I was inextricably bound up with him. I had no alternatives in all of this limitless, abominable land.

We continued to talk in a desultory fashion for several hours more. His mind wandered away from the deep discord at the core of his soul, focusing on more mundane things. He wondered how the camels fared on a night such as this, or the small herd of sheep that travelled with us to contribute to the dinner pot. We discussed the likelihood of reaching a body of water that would serve to purge us of our coating of dust. We speculated on possible unguents to assuage the sting of flea bites or to prevent new onslaughts of affliction.

None of these subjects settled the unrest that he had raised in my mind when he revealed the questions that troubled his soul. For Wilfred was my family, all that I had in all the world. And it was no small thing to me to have him share what he had shared — reasoned doubts over the very existence of God.

The bleak dawn found me still awake. A profound melancholy settled over me and did not begin to dissipate until we reached the Syr Darya and plunged into its chill waters.

CHAPTER EIGHT

We stopped at the City of Samarkand on our way eastward toward Karakorum. Six roads connected the gates of Samarkand with a square in the middle of the City. Elms, poplars and maples lined the roads to provide welcome shade against the fierce summer sun. Trees also lined the large square paved with river flagstones. A fountain stood in the square, slightly off-center. The fountain itself served also as a water supply for the center of the City with an underground aqueduct leading to it from the River Zeravshan. The water gushed from an upturned bronze spout shaped like a horn of plenty, then splashed down a tiled pyramid to a pool below whence it could be drawn with pottery or metal vessels. Excess water overflowed into a drain that returned to the River with some of the waste of the City. The blue and white tiles of the multi-tiered fountain formed an intricate pattern with many of the tiles inscribed in a flowing, Arabic or Persian script.

Quite beautiful in their simplicity, the fountain and aqueduct performed a strategic function as well, conveying water to the City center, even when hostile forces controlled the space beyond the walls. The builders had disguised the take-out point at the River with great care and ingenuity. The underground aqueduct was hidden in like manner. Despite the turbulent history of the region and the numerous attacks the City had suffered, no besieger had ever found either the take-out point or the aqueduct. Although the City had been taken and sacked on several occasions, no siege of Samarkand had ever succeeded due to a lack of water for the defenders.

A large, ornate building stood on the west side of the square, built of clay and stone with a tile roof. Its light tan color derived from the natural clay of the region and shone almost white in the afternoon sun. It had sixteen, ribbed domes on tall drums of varying height in two groupings at each end of the building. Ceramic mosaic facings and bold use of patterned brickwork gave variety to its aspect. A trellised entryway made of fine hardwood, richly overgrown with flowering vines of a species unfamiliar to me led to a large wooden door with black iron fittings. The remains of minaret towers at the four corners of the building betrayed its origins as a grand mosque. Tiles with Arabic inscriptions embedded in the clay of the structure also identified the building as a former house of Moslem worship.

The Mongol hordes had inflicted serious damage to the mosque when they captured the City in 1221, deliberately defiling both interior and exterior. As in Bukhara, however, their destruction had had a strategic rather than religious purpose. The Mongols did not hate or despise Moslems or Islam. To carry out their conquests, they attacked those who resisted them. If the resisters happened to be Moslems, the Mongols attacked their houses of worship as they did the houses of worship of all their enemies — to demoralize by demonstrating that they were impervious to the wrath of their victims' God, whomever or whatever that God might be. Once the Mongols established hegemony, they tolerated almost all religions. Indeed, they seemed to encourage such diversity, so long as no sect sought to become too grand and hence a potential source of unrest or rebellion. According to legend, the Great Khan Ghenghis once said: "We Mongols believe there is but one God, by Whom we live and by Whom we die, and towards Him we have an upright heart. But just as God gave different fingers to the hand, so has He given different ways to men."

Despite these views and the presence at court of Buddhists, Nestorians, Moslems and Taoists to all of whom he gave rapt attention, he and his successor Ugedei remained primarily shamanists, dependent upon fortune-tellers who foretold the future from the char patterns in burnt shoulder bones of sheep. Thus it was that Moslems still used the old mosque on the town square in Samarkand as a house of prayer, although the authorities prohibited repair of the exterior damage or enlargement of the facility. Here again, their reasons were practical. They did not wish the building to become a potential fortification and hence a focal point of unrest.

We were housed at an inn on a narrow cobbled side street, just off the square. The street itself was just wide enough to accommodate two camels or two horses passing in opposite directions. Even so, the riders' outer legs would brush against the adjacent building front. Any person on foot at such a time and place had to run or dodge into a doorway to avoid being jostled or pushed underfoot. The residents seemed to accept these circumstances with an equanimity I could never muster during our sojourn in the City.

A depressed drain in the middle of the street carried away waste water as well as the discharges of the animals horses, mules and camels used for transport. Despite a few low hills within its walls, Samarkand is relatively flat. As a consequence, the drains functioned sluggishly, fostering swarms of flies as well as unpleasant odors, particularly on warm, windless days and nights. Hordes of drain-breeding mosquitoes made the still nights particularly tedious. But in this regard, Samarkand was no worse than Rome, Constantinople or other cities where our travels had taken us. In some respects, indeed, Samarkand was better for being lightly populated by urban standards of the times.

The population had never fully recovered from the great slaughter of the 1221 conquest. We saw many large structures with only a single inhabitant or family, some with none at all. Many of the guild and craft establishments seemed understaffed. Only a half dozen men toiled in a metal-working facility near the main square that would easily have accommodated fifty. The camels and horses of our caravan were housed in a stable with more stalls empty than full. Much of the damage done during that awful event had not been repaired — and much of what had been repaired had been done badly.

Yet the City teemed with a life befitting a crossroads of commerce. Torches flared in the square most nights. Camels groaned and bellowed morosely as they navigated the narrow streets. Traders and peddlers pitched and struck their stalls near the fountain as the spirit and tides of trade moved them, stridently hawking their wares and bargaining in a lively fashion with their customers. Fresh produce, live poultry, lambs, goats, fine rugs and tapestries, precious jewels, rare spices, all could be purchased in the raucous bedlam that was the bazaar at the center of Samarkand, all day and all night, every day and every night as the women of the town came and went with vessels for the waters of the fountain.

Just off the main square, prostitutes of all ages, shapes, sizes and races of humanity loudly offered themselves to the camel drivers and other caravan people, often trading the favor of their bodies for opium or hashish or other non-monetary goods as well as the usual talents of silver.

As if in mortal combat with the rampant and overt sin lurking at the edges of the square and beyond, the muezzin at the mosque called the faithful at the ritual five times per day, the bells at the Nestorian Church sounded at regular intervals, Eastern Rite Orthodox priests wandered through the streets in their black robes holding high the ornate form of cross they favored, the followers of various oriental religions sounded their cymbals and chimes as they walked or danced through the streets and shamans of various stripe practiced their magic and performed their ritual sacrifices indiscriminately.

We saw the same rich mix of humanity in Samarkand that we had seen in Venice, and more so in Constantinople. But here, Mongols and other Asiatics were very much in evidence. The Mongols were particularly striking — short of stature, powerfully built, with large, flat faces and slit eyes, heavily hooded. They had dark complexions and leathery skin. Their hair was coarse and black, beards and mustaches thin and uneven. They were uniformly bowlegged, reflecting their years on horseback beginning at the most tender of age. Those who I observed unclad had virtually no body hair. According to legend, Ghenghis had been a remarkably tall and rangy man for a Mongol, endowed with uncommon strength and ability to endure pain, cold and other hardships. In my travels, I saw no tall Mongols, but all that I encountered were strong and stoic to a degree that seemed inhuman.

All through the day and night, Mongol couriers clattered through the streets of the City carrying the post, transporting important papers and valuables. Small patrols, usually ten in number, moved through on their way to tributary lands to collect revenue or escort shipments of tribute back to Karakorum. The Mongols travelled on short, shaggy horses, a breed they domesticated in a land far away to the northeast beyond a river known as the Yenisei at a time long before Christ, at a time when the world was covered with great glaciers. Those horses had already become a major part of the Mongols' legend due to their speed, their endurance and their toughness under extreme conditions.

All of the Mongols carried short, compound bows as their primary weapon, with scimitars in scabbards. Those bows fashioned of bamboo and yak horn were also a major part of the Mongol's invincible legend.

Between the mosquitoes, the cacophony from the square and the exuberant sexual proclivities of guests in neighboring rooms, we got little rest. So spent much time mingling with the throng. We became familiar with several of the vendors who greeted us warmly enough each time they spied us. Wilfred had advanced sufficiently in his language lessons that he could exchange a few words with some of them. When Rashid accompanied us, we learned much concerning the commerce of the area, what products came from Persia, which from Armenia, which particular items of tapestry had true value and which did not, and so forth. But Rashid had official duties to perform in the City that kept him occupied. So Wilfred and I mostly wandered on our own, trying to make sense of this incredible new world.

One warm afternoon, we sat at the edge of the square watching a Mongol official attempt to bargain with a Persian trader for a magnificent blue, red and gold rug woven of rich wools in a delicate pattern. It seemed to us that the rug merchant was toying with the official, deliberately insulting him with no intent ever to make a sale. Their exchanges climbed the scale of intensity, sounding to our untrained ears like two dogs trying to outdo each other in a contest of staccato yelping.

Just as we thought that they might resort to violence, we were distracted by the sight of a tall, white-haired man crossing the square in the direction of the mosque. He wore the white robe of a priest with a huge, ornate cross on a gold chain around his neck. We took him for a Nestorian. To our surprise, he entered the courtyard of the mosque. We could see, however, that he did not go through the large wooden doors into the place of worship reserved for the faithful. Instead, he ducked down and went through a low door on the left into a wing off of the main mosque building.

Without a word, Wilfred arose and followed him with me close behind. Although I would not have had sufficient interest to follow the priest-like figure on my own, I had less interest in remaining in the square alone with what seemed like a bloody fight about to break out between two angry men armed with daggers, scimitars and God only knew what else.

The priest had left the door slightly ajar. We slipped through it to find ourselves in a long, narrow room with whitewashed clay walls. Wooden beams supported a vaulted wooden ceiling, the beams carved with a repetitive, stylized rendition of the signs of the Zodiac. A dark wooden table ran down the middle of the room with low benches on each side. The walls were lined with low shelves filled with scrolls and books, many of great antiquity by the look of them.

At the end of the room to the right as we entered stood a partition made of rough unfinished planking that extended from the floor to the wooden beams but not all the way to the ceiling. A door in the partition led to another room beyond. We could see the flickering light of a candle or small torch reflected on the ceiling beyond that rough hewn wall. Small windows covered with oiled parchment were placed high on the walls of the room, admitting little light despite the afternoon sun. We could see that the eaves shaded those windows even at the brightest hour of the brightest day, giving the room a gloomy cast that the candles on the table did not dispel.

The stark contrast between the joyous sunlight without and the dinginess within seemed to magnify an overpowering sense of melancholia. The room smelled of mildew even in this dry season. The animal fat in the burning candles and black residue left by candles consumed long ago added their malodorous freight to the fetid air. Thousands of dust motes moved slowly through the small columns of light admitted by those windows facing the direction of the sun. The air itself seemed to lack all sense of life.

The priestly figure in white robe sat at the end of the table near the partition poring over a parchment scroll that he had just unrolled. He had an ornate silver pointer in his hand that he used to follow the script. He barely acknowledged our presence as we entered, although it seemed quite clear to me that we were not welcome. The candle in front of him shone on his face so I could see him well, even in the gloom. He had thin features and blue eyes, closely cropped beard and hair, both stark white. His hairline receded at the temples and forehead, giving emphasis to the height of his imposing head. I guessed his age at fifty years, perhaps a little older. He must have been a handsome and arresting figure in years past. Now, his expression, the lines of his face, the cast of his eye bespoke profound detachment from life and a crushing sorrow, ominous in its portents. I confess that his aspect made me uneasy, as though he might be a ghost or an incarnation of the angel of death.

If Wilfred felt any of this, he did not show it. He spoke to the man deferentially, with a nod of his head and gestures of respect.

"Please, forgive our intrusion, sir. But we could see as you crossed the square that you are a man of Christ, as are we. As men of Christ are rare in these precincts, we sought to make your acquaintance and perhaps share a brotherly word."

He bowed again and extended both hands palms up. The figure did not so much as look up. His silver pointer moved slowly over the page in front of him from right to left, his lips moving silently with the progress of it, his brow knit in concentration.

Suspecting that the man might be hard of hearing, Wilfred repeated his greeting in a louder tone. No response. He tried French, again with no luck; then rudimentary Persian with the same result. Despite his undoubted humility before God, Wilfred was a proud man among men who gave due respect to others and expected no less in return. I could sense the anger rising in him in lock-step with my apprehensions. He advanced and leaned both hands on the table palms down, staring hard at the white clad figure at the end of the table. He muttered in our native English tongue, loud enough for anyone in the room to hear. "God's blood. I will not be treated as an apparition by a bookworm with a scepter up his arse."

This oath got the priest's attention. Although I doubt that he understood the words, he no doubt heard a threat. He engaged Wilfred with his sad, unblinking blue eyes and spoke to him in Latin, with an accent I had never before heard.

"Man of Christ, you say? Thou art man of Rome. Not man of Christ. We have nothing brotherly to exchange, you and I. I know not and care not what brings you and your Roman overlords here to die, as die you shall. For your sake I hope quickly and not in accord with some of the local customs. As a man of Christ, I offer up that prayer for you and no other — except that you leave me in peace to pursue my work."

The man spoke in a cold, detached tone; bloodcurdling as though from beyond the grave, all the while holding Wilfred's eye with a fixed stare. I expected a lightning bolt to dart forth from those eyes on the instant to strike Wilfred into dust.

The man's speech had reduced Wilfred to cold fury. But before he could advance and place his hands on the priest's throat in accord with his intent and desire, the door in the partition at the end of the room opened and Rashid ad-Khabar stepped into the room, smiling broadly with white teeth flashing in his dark face framed by the fresh white burnoose in which he was clad. He extended his arms as though symbolically embracing all men on earth and not just those in the room. He spoke haltingly but clearly in Latin, his skills with the language having greatly improved under Wilfred's tutelage.

"Ah, gentlemen. So good to see that you have become acquainted with each other. I had intended to introduce you and it is only through my deplorable manners that I have not yet done so. Let me correct that failure immediately."

With a flourish, he turned to the priestly figure. "Alexis. May I present to you Friar Wilfred Wilcoxen and Friar John Wheelwright who are Franciscan brothers from the land of the Anglo Saxons far far to the west of here, an island in the winter's sea at the edge of the earth where I have never been and of which I have heard very little." The priest sat back regarding Rashid thoughtfully before turning to look at us. For the first time, I detected a slight glimmer of warmth emanating from him. Rashid then turned to us with a similar flourish.

"Friar Wilfred, Friar John. May I present to you Patriarch Alexis Petrachos, former secretary to the Metropolitan of Merv and currently the man appointed by the Court of the Great Khan to preside over the collection of religious texts in this region, to catalogue those texts, translate into Uighur script those not written in that script and see to their preservation for the greater glory of the Khan, his heirs and his most illustrious and all-powerful Empire." Whereupon Rashid made an elaborate and deep bow to the Patriarch and then to us. That exaggerated gesture finished the task of dispelling the hostility remaining in the room.

We all held our places for a moment. Then Rashid turned back to Alexis in a more serious tone. "You see before you a most unusual man of the Roman Church, indeed of any follower of Christ or of Islam for that matter." Indicating Wilfred with a gesture. "A man with an open and inquiring mind. He seeks to learn languages for which he has a remarkable gift. He seeks to learn of the beliefs of others and not just bludgeon them into accepting those he holds himself. In short, he is like yourself, Alexis. Who better than you to address his questions while we sojourn in this vibrant crossroads of incivility and barbarism?" He waved his hand toward the general bedlam in the square where the dispute between the vendor and the Mongol official had degenerated into some sort of brawl.

"And the other?" Alexis nodded in my direction.

"Ah. The young Friar John. He says nothing. Gives no offense. I suspect that he hears and retains all. If I am wrong, it matters not. You need pay him no attention." Thus was I included in the exchange.

As the Patriarch had another engagement that afternoon, he agreed to meet us at dawn the next morning to give us a tour of the scrolls and books under his care.

*   *   *   *

The warm night seemed fragrant with the smells of grasses and flowers, reminiscent of a night in verdant country. Like the conductor of a musical ensemble, the atmosphere had signalled suppression of the sour odors that normally prevailed and fortissimo for the scents from the land beyond the walls, freshened by a short but fierce afternoon shower.

We sat on the low tiled wall that enclosed the fountain, bathed in the light of the full moon. Only a few stars were bright enough to make themselves seen in the eastern sky where the power of the moon's light prevailed. Moonlight defined the City, etching a sharp line between the irregular dark of the buildings and the softer light of the sky. Here and there, the dim glow of a torch broke the darkness unevenly. But mostly, the City rested in the moonlight as though the great bulk of the remaining inhabitants had closed their shutters or hung robes over their windows to turn inward, away from the outside world.

A few women clad in sandals and robes came to the fountain to fill their vessels for the evening's water as we sat in conversation. They paid us no attention as we talked. Despite the absence of the torches that usually burned in the square in the early evening, I could make out

79

Rashid's features as he spoke in his makeshift Latin, so powerful was the moonlight.

"Yes, Wilfred. You see, Alexis is deeply troubled by recent events as are many of us. Many personal issues and bereavements beset him. He toiled long and hard for the Metropolitan of Merv, a beautiful walled city that once stood in rolling country at the foot of mountains several days ride to the southwest from here. The City was then part of an area controlled by Seljuk Turks, although located within what used to be ancient Persia, the Empire of Darius the First, land conquered by Alexander the Great when he defeated Darius' grandson. An area rich in tradition, learning, civilization, a civilization nourished by rich soil, bountiful lands enhanced by irrigation works built centuries ago."

"The Seljuks tolerated Christians in their midst?" Wilfred asked. We had always been told otherwise. Indeed, we had always been taught that the Seljuks slaughtered Christians whenever and wherever the opportunity to do so arose.

"Oh yes. The Seljuks did not insist on religious uniformity. They were tolerant, in the tradition of the great Saladin. Indeed, Christians and followers of Islam have generally lived in peace throughout the vast tracts that stretch from the eastern shore of the Mediterranean to these regions here, except from time to time when outsiders — such as the so-called Crusaders — have broken the peace with intolerant zealotry, a thirst for mortal combat and a penchant for atrocity. The wars of these regions, of which there have been many, have been tribal wars or racial wars, wars in which religion sometimes has been implicated but mostly in aid of a different goal. Conquest for its own sake or the sake of a tribe or clan."

I could see Wilfred nod slowly. Rashid's portrayal of the Seljuks was a revelation to him, and to me as well. Rashid continued.

"So Alexis travelled far and wide in these regions, carrying the word of Christ to the nomads. He lived among them, rode their horses, ate their disgusting food, endured their hardships and learned their languages and barbaric customs. And in the end, he succeeded in his efforts beyond all expectation."

"How so?"

"In the Spring of 1218, I believe it was that year, 200,000 men of the

80

Kira Khitai tribe presented themselves at the gates of Merv for baptism and blessing by him. Can you imagine such a scene? Two hundred thousand pagan savages to be accepted into Christianity in a single chaotic ceremony. A horde fourfold the size of the entire population of Merv at that time. Now it should be obvious to even a committed believer such as yourself that not all of the members of a multitude of that size were truly moved in their hearts and souls to receive Christ as their Savior at that exact moment. In fact, Alexis had won over their so-called king; and he, in turn, ordered the others to convert on pain of death.

"But whatever the cause, that baptism took place. It was his doing. Those men accepted Alexis as their priest, their Apostle, their confessor, their conduit to salvation in a great outpouring of brotherly love and religious passion. The festival of baptism lasted a full joyous month, I am told. The encampment of the Kira Khitai sprawled for several miles in all directions outside the main gate of the City."

Rashid paused as we all pondered the scene in our minds' eye. Someone lit a torch at the far corner of the square. A few sparks ascended the column of heat straight up into the windless night. The flickering orange light of the torch added a nuance to the unwavering white of the moonlight, bringing the shadows of the square to life. After a moment, Rashid continued with his tale, tone unchanged.

"Now, the Kira Khitai are native to the lands one thousand miles or more northeast of this place, between the mountains of the Altai and a Lake known as Baikal. I have been to Karakorum and have seen the Altai range but I have never seen the Lake, reputed to be a true jewel of harsh beauty. That country is also the homeland of the Mongols to whom the Kira Khitai are related and with whom they are allied through arrangements forged by the Great Khan Ghenghis.

"A few years after the mass conversion and while they still professed adherence to the teachings of Christ, the Kira Khitai returned to Merv as part of the Mongol army. That army took Merv by storm, destroying it utterly. Nothing but ruin remains of it today. The Mongols slew all the men of Merv as well as all the elderly women and infants. They enslaved the young women and youths of the population. They nailed the Metropolitan of Merv upside down to the main gates of the city. The soldiers urinated in his face as he gasped his last breath."

81

Rashid turned to contemplate the flickering torch as though to seek profound meaning in the flame. His face reflected the orange light as he continued.

"To Alexis Petrachos, they offered a choice that he had earned due to his role as the confessor and spiritual father of the Kira Khitai, his willingness to live among them and his interest in their language. He could share the fate of his Metropolitan — or he could become an official of the Mongol Court, in charge of collecting, organizing and translating religious writings as part of the cultural heritage of the Empire. He chose life over martyrdom. And in that choice, he sees himself as a traitor to his friends, his protectors and his faith. He sees himself a coward who could not face either an excruciating death or the stark truth that his great accomplishment — the conversion of the Kira Khitai — had proved to be nothing but a chimera. A mirage in the desert of a wasted life."

Rashid stood up, stretched and stepped away, turning to face us. He pushed his burnoose back off his head, showing his rich dark hair and handsome features. I could see the moon reflected as a gleaming white dot in his dark eyes.

"So, my friends." He spoke again in a calm tone. "You must understand and respect that my dear friend Alexis bears a great burden of personal anguish. He is afflicted with doubt, self-hatred and loss of faith. He retains a grip on sanity only through his work. I hope that you can treat him with understanding as you seek to gain enlightenment from him."

He bowed slightly and strode away.

Wilfred muttered softly, barely audible. "He describes himself as well, I think."

"What?"

"Rashid's people were also destroyed by the Mongols and he too was spared in exchange for a commitment to do their work. Yet he seems to do it well and without a grudge. He blames only himself. He too has chosen life, despite his adherence to a faith that exalts martyrdom." His voice trailed off.

We sat for several minutes in silence watching the torchlight dance against the night sky. The moon stood much higher now. More stars shone through. A large shooting star flashed from north to south, burning brightly and provoking startled exclamations from the water carriers and soldiers lounging in the square. Judging by their agitation, some of them must have taken it for an omen, whether of good or evil I could not say. I heard Wilfred mutter again, more to himself than to me. "So Fra Cipriani was an idiot."

"Who?"

"Fra Cipriani. Remember? He of the upraised arm and the injunction that we go forth to convert these heathens. How much did the good Alexis Petrachos and the burghers of Merv profit from his act of conversion? And on top of that, the man — Cipriani — was too prejudiced to take note of his surroundings.

"He dragged his bones around these regions for how long? Two years? Three? No Christians here, he says. No sign of Christian men.' God's blood, the very nomads who saved his unworthy, tremulous arse were probably God-fearing Christian men."

I cannot explain the reason why I felt sympathy at this moment for the devastated apparition who had suffered so profoundly in his trek. In any case, I argued with Wilfred. "Perhaps he only considers adherents to the Roman faith Christians in the true sense. As I understand it, all of these out here are adherents to the Nestorian heresy."

Wilfred thought for a moment. Then he shook his head. "Perhaps, but not likely. He would have mentioned heretics by that reference. He said, 'no Christians.'" Wilfred spat with contempt. "It makes little difference. We are here in large part because of that idiot. It appears that we are on a fool's errand to convert men who will cut our throats with joy in their hearts whether they share our religion or not. And this Cardinal Pellegrino does not impress me either."

"Why not? He is certainly an important official, the Holy Father's personal emissary."

Wilfred spat again. "Right. And he lacks the charisma to convert a servant girl, let alone proud and willful freemen and conquerors, even if he could speak their language which he makes no effort whatever to learn." He paused. This was more than a manifestation of Wilfred's prejudice against corpulent prelates, although the good Cardinal certainly did fit the description. His aloof, disapproving demeanor and overall passivity rendered him particularly unfit for the task at hand. Wilfred shook his head.

"There is no turning back now. We have no choice but to play out this journey, wherever and however it ends."

He paused again. His voice took on a tone of quiet determination. "By God, I have no intention of just sitting back and letting things happen, Johnnie, indeed I don't. Our salvation lies in getting as close to these people as possible in every way possible — through customs, language, everything."

Salvation through human action other than prayer, avoidance of sin, loyalty to the teachings of Christ. Open expression of such ideas with such fervor and conviction filled me with the customary discomfort. How many times I prayed to God to become reconciled to the ways of my companion I could not count, all to no avail.

He stood up, stretched and we started back toward our hostel. Alexis had told us that he would see us at dawn to start our instruction. We would need to work fast as the caravan was scheduled to leave Samarkand for Tashkent in three days time. Every daylight hour would be precious to Wilfred's undertaking.

As we rounded the corner into the dark street on which our quarters fronted, a figure emerged from the shadows directly into our path, speaking quietly in a language I did not understand. A woman. She stepped forward into the moonlight pushing the hood back off her head and opening her robe. She had glorious black hair that seemed to cascade all the way to her waist, almond shaped eyes, regular and beautiful facial features. She wore nothing under her robe. I could see her full breasts with their prominent nipples, the dark hair of her genital area and full thighs. She had apparently anointed herself with a oil as her body glistened in the moonlight. The oil must have been scented as the aroma of lilac filled the air. She held out her arms as if to embrace us both.

Wilfred grabbed my arm and steered me around her, saying something to her in the Persian language I had heard him practice with Rashid. She dropped her arms and did not follow us as we entered the hostel. I thought that I would faint. The effort to climb the stairs almost undid me. I concentrated as hard as I could on the Compline Hymn we recited at Blackfriars every evening:

From all ill dreams defend our eyes,

84

From nightly fears and fantasies;
Tread under foot our ghostly foe,
That no pollution may we know.

Her image tormented me that night and on many others with disturbing dreams, yearnings formless yet insistent, strange stirrings in my loins and profound agitation. I had not believed that the human form could attain such beauty and provoke such profound unrest. I have formally confessed on several occasions that I lusted mightily after that woman and would have thrown over my vows in an instant to lie with her, even without knowing what to do if the occasion had ever arisen. For the first time, I understood the irony of the so-called St. Paul's canon to which Italian priests so often referred: "Si non caste tamen caute." If you cannot be good, be careful.

Just a Persian harlot, according to Wilfred. He seemed to take little notice of her. But her sudden appearance on that night, as though she expected us, made me wonder where Wilfred went when he vanished for an hour or so in the middle of the night, as he often did. "Just seeking solace from the prayers of matins and lauds," he would say. The time for those prayers took place during the dark hours certainly, but Wilfred's observances seemed sporadic now that we were no longer in the Abbey where the prayers were offered every day. The faint scent about him when he returned from his prayer sessions in Samarkand seemed evocative of hers, albeit ambiguous and less strong.

I lay in bed grappling with my fears, Wilfred's injunction that our survival depended upon knowledge we had yet to acquire, and disturbances emanating from the vision of female nakedness glistening in the moonlight. The night seemed to last an eternity. Dawn's light found me still greatly agitated.

*　　　　*　　　　*　　　　*

Alexis Petrachos was already there when we arrived at the library. The day had dawned clear. It would be warm. For our purposes, strong light was most important as it was difficult to read in the library by candlelight. Alexis was busy collecting certain texts with which he intended to work that day. Wilfred had stated that he did not want Alexis to depart from his regular routine. Instead, he wished to be included in that routine with the freedom to ask questions. Somehow we quickly departed from that plan. Within no more than ten minutes, Alexis was giving us a general summary of religious beliefs, attitudes and mythology within the Mongol Empire.

"The Mongols, you see, show much religious tolerance. Within the Empire you will find Moslems, Christians, Hebrews, Mannicheans, followers of the Buddha, of Taoism and of various forms of sorcery as practiced by shamans, witch doctors. It is said that the Great Khan Ghenghis became a follower of Buddha a few years before he died. Whether he did or not, he did not adopt Buddhism as an official religion of the Empire. But it comes down to this. Government in this region is not based upon religious persuasion as it is in Byzantium, areas that acknowledge the Apostolic See, or even among the Moslem Turks."

Wilfred interrupted. "Forgive my ignorance, but I have never heard of Buddhism, Taoism or Mannicheans. I am interested in the Empire's approach to religious belief in general. But I would learn more of these specific things if you can enlighten me."

Alexis laughed and shook his head ruefully. "I can only read to you from some of the relevant texts, Friar Wilfred. I find these beliefs impossible to understand and totally foreign to the structure of my mind. It is as though I had a blockage of some sort. Perhaps you will suffer from no such disability. Perhaps I can learn from you and not the other way round."

He stood and walked to a section of shelves in the corner of the room from which he extracted two scrolls and an ancient, leather bound book. Returning to the table, he carefully spread one of the scrolls in the shaft of sunlight admitted into the room through one of the eastern windows. We could see that it contained ornate symbols arranged in columns. Alexis took up his silver pointer and laboriously worked through the text, reading out loud as he progressed.

"The Tao that can be discussed is not the enduring eternal Tao; the name that can be named is not the enduring eternal name. From the unnamed sprang heaven and earth; the named is the Mother of the ten thousand things. Verily: Only he that is desireless can discern the secret essences. Unrelieved of desire, we see only shells."

86

Observing Wilfred's confusion, he read it again. Then, without comment, he turned to the second scroll. He opened it on top of the first and read, again with his silver pointer moving slowly over complex self-contained characters in column.

"Great, it passes on. Passing on, it becomes remote. Having become remote, it returns. Therefore, the Tao is great; Heaven is great; Earth is great; and the sagely King is also great. Man's law is from the Earth; the Earth's from Heaven; Heaven's from the Tao. And the law of the Tao is its being what it is."

He looked up, regarding our confusion with calm amusement. "I do not profess understanding of this, you see. But I believe that Tao and Buddha share a common belief in a larger force that is of God but has nothing to do with any individual man or soul. Followers of those faiths do not pray to an all powerful god to seek salvation or protection for themselves or their souls, nor do they seek to avoid punishment for the commission of sins. They seek some sort of harmony or unity with a larger current that encompasses all life of which they are but small and insignificant parts."

He stood and secured the scrolls with tender care. Then, he pulled the ancient book toward him. "This commentary may help. It helps me a little." He picked up his silver pointer and again worked carefully down columns of characters.

"The True Men of old knew nothing either of the love of life or of the hatred of death." He looked up. "I take the term `True Men' to mean those true believers who have attained the exalted state of enlightenment." He resumed his reading. "Entrance into life occasioned them no joy; the exit from it awakened no resistance. Composedly they went and came. They did not forget what their beginning had been and they did not inquire into what their end would be. They accepted their life and rejoiced in it; they forgot all fear of death and returned to their state before life. Thus there was in them what is called the want of any mind to resist the Tao, and of all attempts by means of the Human to assist the Heavenly. Such were they who are called True Men. Being such, their minds were free from all thought; their demeanor was still and unmoved; their foreheads beamed simplicity. Whatever coldness came from them was like that of autumn; whatever warmth came from them was like that of spring.

Their joy and anger assimilated to what we see in the four seasons. They did in regard to all things what was suitable."

Alexis sat back, looking at us solemnly, without expression. "Obviously, the antithesis of Christianity in any form. Right?"

Wilfred nodded. "No quest for salvation, no attempt of the Human to assist the Heavenly. Hence no credence to the belief that Christ or any of the Saints cannot thrive but upon our prayers. No attempt to invoke the personal help of an all-powerful God through prayer, good works, even a dutiful life." He paused, thoughtfully stroking the light beard that he had allowed to grow over the last several days. "If those passages truly reflect belief in the Tao, then a dutiful life can lead to nothing but benign resignation."

Alexis spread his hands wide in a gesture of agreement and bowed slightly. "And no credence to the pagan beliefs that their gods depend upon sacrifice, whether of man, beast or worldly goods. And hence, presumably no credence for the significance of the Eucharist or the wine of the Mass." I thought briefly of the vial of the blood of St. Thomas á Beckett that we had taken from the Archbishop of Canterbury to the Pope as an offering. I thought of the other relics that played such a portentous role in our faith, the battles fought to possess fragments of the true cross.

These thoughts did not suppress a growing discomfort. As unschooled as I was, I could recognize the profoundly heretical nature of these teachings. I could not contain my alarm. I half expected some form of God's punishment to invade the room to wreak vengeance upon us.

"How can we even discuss such ideas, Wilfred? They can only be born of the devil."

Alexis smiled at me. "You must make that choice for yourself, young John. Leave if they give you discomfort. I discuss and study these ideas because it is my role within the Empire, a role I must play to remain useful and create value for my life in the eyes of those with the arbitrary power of life and death over all who sojourn within these borders, including yourself and Brother Wilfred. Unlike the True Men of old in the tradition of Tao, I prefer life and resist any premature exit from it. The fates have tested that premise for me and it now stands beyond argument." He paused with his eyes elevated, as though he sought to see beyond the oiled parchment windows to the blue sky beyond before continuing, his voice low, almost a whisper.

"Besides. I find that I am fascinated by the ideas behind these texts. Who is to say where the truth lies, or even if there be but one truth, or any at all?" He lowered his gaze to look directly at us, his voice shedding all wistfulness. "But suit yourself. Don't violate your faith on my account. My work will continue whether you are here or not, long after you depart. I estimate at least ten year's work merely to translate what is here, let alone catalogue and organize it in any meaningful way."

The discussion continued. I found that I could not leave, nor could I stay. The discussion repelled me, but I had no wish to return to the inn or walk about the City alone without Wilfred. None of the others of our party would suffer my meager companionship. I knew not where to find them in any case. In the end, I stood in the doorway watching the comings and goings of the square, catching only snatches of the conversation within. I heard more of the Tao. And then a new subject piqued my interest, a question Wilfred put to Alexis.

"Of what region are you native, Patriarch?"

"Antioch, the City of Antiochus on the Mediterranean Coast. On the road from Constantinople to the Holy Land."

"If you don't mind my asking, of what extraction, what nationality?"

Alexis smiled. "My forebears are all of Greek and Macedonian extraction. My father and his father before him were born in Sebastopolis at a time when that was an important City of Byzantium on the eastern shore of the Black Sea. They were both successful traders who travelled far and wide from that City."

Wilfred nodded. "I know that City for it is where we took leave of our ship and first learned of the horrors of camels."

A moment or two of silence passed before Wilfred revealed the issue that agitated his curiosity.

"You do not have the complexion or features of any man of Greece or Macedonia that I have seen. In the land of the Anglo Saxons, many people have fair skin and blue eyes as you do. Not so here."

Alexis nodded. "I assume it was Norsemen who cast that seed in the land of the Anglo Saxons. Correct?"

"So it is said."

"And so it is said here as well. Over five hundred years ago, Norsemen brought their longboats down the Volga River to the Caspian Sea and spread their seed all over these regions with much violence and drunken exuberance. I am nothing but residuum of that orgy along some distant, violated branch of my family tree."

Another long moment passed in silence. Perhaps Wilfred shared the wonder I felt that more than five hundred years past, the same Norsemen who consistently shattered the peace of our home islands had done the same in these farflung regions. Here again, I confronted the specter of men so foreign to my nature that they might as well have been of a different species, men so restless that they would wither and die if forced to stay put. Depriving such men of the risks and rigors of thousand mile violent forays into the vast unknown in pursuit of rape and plunder would be the same as cutting off their breath.

A reference to the Great Khan interrupted my musings. Wilfred had asked if Ghenghis had worshipped Christ, a query that elicited a full-throated laugh from Patriarch Alexis. The question did not seem so outlandish to me. If the King of the Kira Khitai would order his entire nation baptized, why not the Great Khan? And was he not said to be Prester John by none other than the Pope himself? When his laughter subsided so that he could speak, Alexis gave definitive answer.

"The Great Conqueror knew not Christ and revered only as servants the Christians he elected not to dispatch, the way a huntsman reveres a useful dog selected from a litter, all the rest of which are put to death. As a youth, he made obeisance to pagan gods through the office of shamans he employed to conjure up storms and other calamities to confound his enemies. It is said that he defeated the Naiman tribe of the northern steppe among others in this fashion. His shaman called forth upon them a great hailstorm that ravaged their camp on the eve of his surprise attack.

"In his later years, he became a professed follower of Buddha." Patriarch Alexis laughed again, another expression of sincere amusement before he continued. "For that reason, I am instructed by none other than his son and successor, the Great Khan Ugedei, to concentrate the larger portion of my efforts on Buddhist texts." He paused, chuckling this time, shaking his head in quiet amusement before continuing.

"Ugedei himself worships intoxicants, lavish foods and slave girls who massage his parts with exotic oils, feathers and similar tactile stimulants, when he is not out leading his hordes in battle. He has little time for Buddha. So I study for us both; and, of course, to honor the hallowed memory of his father." Words laden with scorn, delivered in a tone of utmost disrespect, although his countenance seemed bland and noncommittal.

I felt the hackles rise on the back of my neck. First heresy and now sedition. Sedition against a ruler who routinely killed thousands of innocents. Less than twenty-four hours ago, Alexis had predicted that this same ruler would kill us. I felt as though I stood at the lip of a great chasm, with no ability to move to safety as the ground crumbled away under my feet. With profound constriction in my gut, I walked out into the sunlight of the square and sat at the edge of the fountain. I waited many hours there for Wilfred to emerge.

*   *   *   *

I discovered that evening that Buddha and Buddhism had aroused Wilfred's curiosity. He and Alexis had discussed the subject the whole day long. Alexis himself was a student but not an expert, only just now becoming immersed in the sacred texts. He had read many passages during the course of the day that the two of them had then attempted to understand.

In his description over our evening meal, Wilfred told me why the subject had aroused the fire of his most intense curiosity.

"From what Alexis told me and from some of the things that he read, it seems that the Gautama Buddha — the fellow who originated the line of thought that serves as the base teaching of the religion, if you can call it that — was the son of a wealthy man. He spent his early life in pampered luxury, full of privilege and indulgence. When he reached maturity, he renounced all of that life and all earthly possessions to become a mendicant wanderer seeking after truth."

He regarded me without expression. "Of what does that tale remind you, Johnnie?"

I drew a blank. Wilfred did not prolong my embarrassment.

"Francis of Assisi had a similar upbringing and selected a similar renunciation, did he not?"

91

True enough, as far as that part of the tale went. I nodded. "So was the Gautama Buddha a Christian? Did he attempt to exemplify the word of Christ as Francis does?"

Wilfred smiled, shaking his head. "Alexis can find no such references in the texts he is studying. Nor does the teaching run in that direction. Indeed, it seems almost to be the opposite in many respects, as though the two systems of belief could not exist in harmony in the same soul." He sat back and let his gaze drift away, out through the door into the dim light of the narrow, congested street. "But as interested as I am in these teachings of the Buddha, my mind simply cannot contain the notion that the Great Khan was a believer in those ideas."

"Why not?"

"Because they are rooted in renunciation of all earthly wealth, power, desires, acquisitiveness. The Great Khan Ghenghis sought to appropriate to himself and his people the wealth and possessions of all those he encountered. He sought to extend his power over the entire earth. Far from renunciation of desire, he sought to fulfill his through enslavement of female captives by the hundreds. According to what is written, he became a follower of Buddha at roughly the same time as he destroyed the empire of the Khwaryzm Shah, the fellow of whom Fra Cipriani spoke, at roughly the same time as he, Ghenghis, proclaimed himself God's punishment. According to what is written, his caravan back to Karakorum from those conquests extended for ten miles with camels carrying his plunder. The plunder included forty women he had selected for his own amusement from among the captives." He rubbed his beard thoughtfully. "How could such a man be a Buddhist?"

An answer, perhaps not the answer that Wilfred sought, came to mind immediately. "Perhaps in the same fashion that Henry the Second, or Philip Augustus or Frederick II Hohenstaufen can be rich and powerful Kings and, at the same time, followers of Christ."

He nodded. "Yes. But this is different, I think. I sense something more mysterious and slippery here. I also feel in my gut that it is something we should explore if we are to hope to understand." What? He had stopped as though the question had tripped him up. Then he leaned forward and caught my eye with an intense gaze.

"You're a sharp lad, Johnnie," he said. "Please come with me

92

tomorrow. I want you to hear these teachings first hand for yourself. I need to have someone with whom to ponder them. Rashid has no interest in the subject other than the bigotry and contempt of a devout Moslem for beliefs not based on the Old Testament or the Koran. If he were the Great Khan himself, he would hold an inquisition and burn all Buddhists within the Empire. You're the only one to whom I can turn. I ask this of you as a favor. I feel that all this is important, although I cannot explain why."

And so another die was cast.

*   *   *   *

The dawn seemed an exact copy of the day before. The air smelled fresh, with a crisp edge to it, carrying the scent of dried grass and wild blossoms from beyond the walls. The hills of the City cast elongated shadows. The oblique light of the new day etched and enhanced the diverse pattern of City forms — elaborate structures composed of tawny clays and bright blue tiled domes gleaming in the sunlight, drab and subdued in shadow, with new light sharpening the contrast.

Alexis was already at his table with several texts spread out before him when we arrived. The dingy light and overused air within had not changed, nor had my sense of foreboding. I felt that I had entered a musty den from which no good could possibly emerge. Once again, as had often occurred on our journey, I felt trapped in a place of great potential for misfortune, with no feasible means of escape.

Alexis acknowledged us without smiling as we entered. I felt distance, not disrespect. On this day and to the extent we sought to be enlightened on matters of Buddhist belief, we facilitated his own studies. He welcomed us as foils. In all other respects, I sensed that we were nothing to him. He did not wish us ill or well. He sought neither connection nor enmity. Whether we stayed or departed was of no concern, so long as we did not bother him or seek his help beyond what he proposed to do, whether we were present or not.

Without a greeting beyond the barest of nods, he turned to one of the scrolls laid out on the table and looked up at Wilfred. "I have found the

Fire Sermon of which I made mention yesterday." Whereupon, he took up his silver pointer and began to read laboriously.

"'O priests, the learned and noble disciple conceives an aversion for the eye, conceives an aversion for forms, conceives an aversion for eye-consciousness, conceives an aversion for the impressions received by the eye; and whatever sensation, pleasant, unpleasant or indifferent, originates in dependence on impressions received by the eye, for that also he conceives an aversion. He conceives an aversion for the ear, conceives an aversion for sounds, conceives an aversion for the nose, conceives an aversion for odors, conceives an aversion for the tongue, for tastes, for the body, conceives an aversion for things tangible.'"

He trailed off in his reading, searching for an endpoint, and then continued.

"'Conceives an aversion for the mind, for ideas, for mind-consciousness, for the impressions received by the mind, for this also he conceives an aversion. And in conceiving this aversion, he becomes divested of passion, and by the absence of passion he becomes free, and when he is free, he becomes aware that he is free and he knows that rebirth is exhausted, that he has lived the holy life, and he has done what it behooved him to do, and that he is no more for this world.'"

He looked up, his face expressionless. Then he spoke in a neutral voice, without judgment.

"So we have here teachings based upon total and absolute denial of human thought, feeling, emotion, desire, of temporal possession, in an effort to become one with an all-encompassing current from which all life originates, to which it all must inevitably return; that life, that moment, in which such a union occurs, at which point the soul reaches a permanent state of mindless bliss." Regarding us thoughtfully, as though assessing the impact of his reading, he observed. "And these supposedly became the beliefs of the Great Khan."

He moved several scrolls in an effort to find something, as though he had seen it before and had misplaced it in the pile before him. In due course, he found that for which he was seeking and began again to read.

"'The radiant life-monad,' the one who has transcended life and reached the state called `nirvana' which appears literally to mean without

94

wind'" lifting his eyes quickly to see our expression before starting over. "'The radiant life-monad rose from the earth, greater and more brilliant than the sun, yet without color, crystalline, immortal, omniscient and omnipotent, boundless and without weight, passing upward through all the heavens. The released weightless monad is not to be reached by any prayer. It is all aware but indifferent, unthinking; alone yet everywhere. It is without individual character, personality, quality, or definition. It is simply perfect.'"

Wilfred shook his head in wonderment. "What could be the appeal of such beliefs?"

Alexis shrugged. "The urge to find peace from want, from unfulfilled expectations, from the ills of this world perhaps. Who knows?" He paused, smiling. "Rashid has a theory."

"And what is that?"

"The Buddhists and also the Taoists acknowledge torture by cold. The notion of hell as a cold place is consistent with much of their teaching. As the winter season in these regions is long and incredibly cold, perhaps these people quickly embrace a system of beliefs that teaches rejection of life in cold climes as an escape from hell and an ascent to heaven. Who is to say? With Rashid, one can never be sure if he is joking. Besides, he is a Moslem, devoted to his faith. I doubt that he gives serious thought to any other."

For the next several hours, Alexis read from various texts. He and Wilfred exchanged desultory observations. I discerned no profound insights from either party; but then my attention span was short and my continuing anxiety distracted me. Indeed, I barely heard Alexis' description of the strange practice of something called yoga that the Buddhists had adopted as a device to aid in their meditative reveries. I barely noticed when he showed Wilfred pages with diagrams of various yoga postures. The session droned on. I quickly lost the thread of it, preoccupied as I was with the road ahead.

*   *   *   *

We took our leave of Samarkand two days later, climbing aboard camels at dawn to depart by the northeastern gate. The caravan consisted of our party and twenty camel loads of cargo with the cargomasters and camel drivers.

Rashid accompanied us with two assistants who had joined him in Samarkand. He rode at first with Cardinal Pellegrino and Fra Dandolo in a further attempt to ascertain the details of His Holiness' embassy to report to his masters. Apparently, the Cardinal was as taciturn and aloof as before. Rashid was soon riding with Wilfred and me and they resumed their drilling in the linguistic skills each sought to aquire from the other. I soothed my boredom and abhorrence of camels by concentrating on the features of the land we traversed, the sky overhead and the far horizons. I sought to steep myself in these things rather than the meaning of ugly sounds invented by various branches of humankind to serve as inadequate vessels for banal thought, deception and obfuscation.

Before we left Samarkand, the lovely Persian girl appeared before us twice more, once in twilight and once in full dark. She did not reveal herself as she had done at first but she left no doubt of her purpose. I could only assume that Wilfred had had liaison with her, for why else would she pursue us as she did? I wondered what price she placed on the favors of her body. I wondered how Wilfred had paid the price. I would have given her all that I had or could obtain by any device, even though I would not have known what to do with what I had purchased. In any case, the vision of her beautiful eyes, flowing dark hair and fulsome body had troubled my sleep on restless nights after she first exposed herself to us. Disturbing and fascinating, her image often floated before me as I balanced on the edge of unconsciousness during the long, swaying hours of travel.

The season was now well-advanced. In a month's time, we could expect to experience hard frost on the occasional night. A month thereafter, we should expect snow, perhaps fierce winter storms. We had rising ground to negotiate through lands more thinly populated than those we had already traversed. All these factors created a sense of urgency that we had not felt before. Our caravan leader made it clear that he intended to travel hard and that those who could not keep up would be left behind. I found no joy in our situation as we pushed ever eastward over these vast and empty lands.

CHAPTER NINE

At some point on our progress to the East after we crossed the Amr Darya River, the Mongol authorities decided to add their own note of urgency to our mission. Rashid received instructions that our party should separate from the caravan with which we were travelling and proceed on horseback.

The rider who brought the message was himself one of the high speed couriers of the so-called *yam* system — relay stations with fresh mounts established to facilitate communications within the vastnesses of the empire. Couriers of the *yam* had been known to travel three thousand miles from the Volga River to Karakorum in little more than thirty days. Many of these riders switched mounts at full gallop.

It should go without saying that none of our party were sufficiently skilled on horseback or hardened by practice to proceed comfortably in this fashion. Unfortunately for us, our hosts either did not understand or concern themselves with our limitations. They gave us mounts and expected us to proceed as they were accustomed to do. Thus began a period of hardship in our travels of which I had not seen the like in all my years. As difficult as it was for me, a young lad of sound body and good health, one can only imagine the hell on earth endured by Cardinal Pellegrino and Fra Dandolo, both elderly and soft men whose slack physiques reflected their long lives of privileged contemplation.

The Mongol horses compounded our discomfiture. Compared to European horses, they were small, spirited and jerky in motion, stocky, without grace. The Mongol horse possesses a powerful neck, thick legs and a dense coat. It is noted for a fiery spirit, vigor, endurance, steadiness, sureness of foot and ability to survive on thin rations over long periods.

The ensuing days and nights merged into an endless, pounding hell as we raced eastward, driven remorselessly by our Mongol guides. I recall mountains of incredible height and severity topped with brooding glaciers, vast reaches of desert, endless swamplands with few towns or populated areas. I could not possibly have imagined such emptiness, nor could I have imagined that the human body could endure such a pounding as we took during our progress. Most nights, we made camp exhausted, desperate for a sleep that the pain of the day's journey kept from us. Most mornings, we arose before first light to face another day of dread, shivering in the pre-dawn chill.

When the moon stood full or nearly so, whether waxing or waning, our guides required that we travel through the night without stopping, in the Mongol fashion. I vividly recall one night in particular when we pushed through the last high pass before descending to the plain of the Mongolian heartland. Gorges, black as night flanked our narrow path, bounded by piles of rock akin to the fortifications of some vast city, a place of fantastic imagination. We passed through yawning gateways flanked by bastions of vaulting height, gleaming dully in the moonlight. Rock formations resembling towers, pyramids, crescents and domes, dizzy pinnacles and crenellated heights of surpassing majesty, capped in snow and ice surrounded us, pressing in upon the road we travelled, all invested with unearthly grandeur by the magic beams of moonlight - but exhibiting in their wide breaches and indescribable ruin, that they had been battered by ferocious and incessant winds, thunder, hail, the onslaught of countless winters, all the mighty artillery of time.

In this fashion and through such portals, we made our way to Karakorum.

CHAPTER TEN

Karakorum was little more than a sprawling city of tents, spread in haphazard fashion in the midst of rolling grassland. Located not in territory originally controlled by the Mongols but rather in the land of the Naimans, a conquered and now subject people, it stands in the valley of the Orkhon River at a traditional crossroads of the steppe nomads. Forest dwellers had passed this way for generations on their annual migrations to and from the south. Moslem traders with the Sung and Chin peoples had crossed this Valley from east to west and back for centuries. Steppe nomads had moved their herds and fought their battles over these lands since before time began.

The architecture of the few permanent structures was more functional than artistic, particularly when compared with the sights that had greeted our eyes in Venice, Constantinople, Samarkand and other places through which we had travelled. But then the Mongols were practical people, dedicated to the nomadic life even at the very apex of their Imperial power, not much interested in the trappings of sedentary civilizations. Even so, they had decorated the City with stone carvings of massive tortoises and other animals that perhaps served some sort of spiritual purpose in their heathen observances. And small but graceful stone towers adorned the City walls at regular intervals, topped by forms that resembled the helmets worn by their horsemen in battle.

Only a nomad of the region could have appreciated the location of Karakorum. We had travelled for days before through country that seemed exactly like the Orkhon Valley in almost every respect, with absolutely nothing to commend any part of it to my eye. Low, treeless hills stretched endlessly in every direction. Forbidding mountains brooded on the eastern, southern and northern horizons, far away, sometimes obscured by intervening hills. We travelled for days without sighting a tree of any kind other than perhaps a lone willow or poplar clinging to life along a meager watercourse. A dry wind blew almost continuously, day and night. The lack of firewood meant that we cooked and warmed ourselves over fires of dried dung, evil smelling and temperamental, producing little heat.

The nomads prized this land for its grasses. Even these seemed sparse except in a few places scattered about where the arid lands grudgingly yielded precious moisture. Having tended the garden at Blackfriars, I was familiar with plant life. So I could see that these were annual grasses. Their bounty would fluctuate radically from year to year in response to modest changes in rainfall. It would have been obvious to the most introspective traveller that rainfall was a capricious commodity in these regions. For on our entire progress east of the Caspian, it seemed that we never stood far from a forbidding desert considered impassable or nearly so by the local inhabitants. Karakorum is no exception as it lies not far from the Great Gobi, a wasteland that I learned is so vast, harsh and desolate as to defy description.

I kept these observations to myself. Rashid had warned us that we should not reveal any agrarian knowledge or interests in dealing with the Mongols.

"They consider all persons who till the soil lower than the lowest of beasts. They would not deign to work the soil in any fashion as it falls beneath the dignity of the nomadic horseman. So it is thus that they kill peasants without remorse, casually, whenever and wherever they encounter them. So it is thus that they have destroyed the agrarian cultures in the path of their conquests and that lands once rich and bountiful are now fit only for meager pasturage during short periods of the year."

I could not help but think of the long, pleasant hours that we had spent at Blackfriars tending the orchard and garden. I could not help but think of the reverie that possessed Wilfred when he engaged in these activities, his special communion with the plantlife of our compound. Rashid had not completed his harrowing tale.

"After the Mongols captured and sacked the city of Kai Feng and conquered the Chin, their great general Subedei proposed that the Mongols kill all of the peasants of the entire country to preempt their employment as footsoldiers in future uprisings. To understand the enormity of this proposal, understand that there are more peasants in the land of the Chin than there are stars in the skies. It is a vast, vast land with more populace than any other place on earth. Why, more peasants struggle to sustain life in the valley of the Yellow River alone than exist on this plain from here to Persia and beyond. And yet, the Mongols intended to carry out Subedei's plan and kill them all."

Wilfred raised up on a elbow, his interest piqued. "And did they in fact conduct such an impressive massacre?"

Rashid shook his head. "No. They were dissuaded at the last moment by a Chin counselor whose life they had spared at Kai Feng so that he could work for them." Another case like that of Petrachos, like that of Rashid himself. "This man, Yeh Lu Chu Tsai, who is in Karakorum now and who you might meet, explained to the Mongols that they would collect no tribute if they killed all the peasants as the land would be laid waste and would produce no bounty. It took the Mongols a while to grasp the notion that a land could be bountiful and yield tribute in some form other than that of grazing animals. In the end, they accepted the wise counsel of Yeh Lu. As they have done in many other particulars since." He paused, in a form of sad wonderment. "But not in all, unfortunately."

The eternal wind rocked our ger, setting it to creaking and groaning, as if to underscore Rashid's observations with an affirmation from the dark heavens. Not for the first time or the last, I faced the jarring contrast between the personalities of the Mongols I had come to know and the history of their dark deeds. On each such occasion, I felt more isolated, as though lost on a hostile sea in a small boat. I had no one but Wilfred. And as I knew him and loved him, I could not but see how he was drifting away from all that was familiar to our world, he by choice, pulling me behind because I had no other.

*   *   *   *

The ger in which we took up residence at Karakorum was located adjacent to the palace wall. Cardinal Pellegrino, Fra Dandolo and their immediate entourage were conducted to a more luxurious ger inside the walls, closer to the site of Imperial administration. Persian carpeting covered the earthen floor in their ger, whereas ours was covered with the animal skins typical of all but the highest officials.

With time on our hands, we explored the City on foot, working our way slowly to avoid getting lost, as there were no street markers and no one with whom we shared a common language apart from Wilfred's few words of Uighur. Karakorum seemed more of an encampment than a city, with no paved streets. Gers and tents of all descriptions stood at random along poorly defined thoroughfares, twisting and turning to no discernible pattern. Horsemen travelled in all directions among the pedestrians with no attempt at separation or precaution. Traders leading laden camels or donkeys were as likely to be run down as the casual pedestrian. No one even attempted to moderate the chaos of the busy intersections, where "every man for himself" was the controlling rule. Dust and noise filled the air. The sounds of hoofbeats, the shouts of riders and pedestrians, the bleating of goats and sheep, the bellowing of camels all added their burden to the atmosphere of the City, continuously agitated by swirling wind. Despite all this, the tension and energy seemed lighthearted to me, full of good will and empty of threat.

The City was not as chaotic in its organization as it first appeared. It was divided into various quarters, one for clerics, another for builders and engineers and so on. It contained the beginnings of European colony, consisting mostly of artisans who had found their way to various cities of Persia and Mesopotamia and who had been spared when the Mongols sacked those places. It contained no less than twelve Buddhist temples, two mosques and a church. Along the many highways that linked the City to the empire flowed an unlikely traffic of priests, ambassadors, mystics and charlatans, come to beg indulgences or attempt to capitalize on the superstitious nature of the people.

I recall coming upon a market square one afternoon, accompanied by Wilfred and Rashid. A bare chested shaman stood in the square chanting, eyes raised to the heavens. Twenty or so people stood in a circle listening to him. We joined them and Rashid translated for us.

The shaman recounted the tale of the Great Khan's death during the campaign against the Tangut in the land of the Chin in August of 1227. Ghenghis did not die in battle. Despite advanced age, he had insisted on accompanying his army to rally and lead his soldiers during this last campaign. The burden of years finally took him after a last audience with his sons during which he instructed them on the succession.

In his final hours, Ghenghis chose to be buried on a mountain known as Burkhan Kaldun in a range that rises near the sources of the Onon, Tuula and Kerulen Rivers in the northeast of the Mongolian heartland. The original forebears of the Mongol nation, the Blue Wolf and the Fallow Deer, mated at this location, consecrating the ground as the birthplace of the Mongol people.

"There was a Blue Wolf which was born, having his destiny from heaven above. His spouse was a fallow doe. They came, passing over the Great Sea. Batacaciqan was born when they camped at the head of the Onon River at Mount Burkhan Kaldun. And Batacaciqan begat Tamaca whose line became the Chosen People."

Chanting in singsong fashion, the shaman recited a long string of begatings, in a fashion that reminded me of the Old Testament, until he came to Temuchin, the man who declared himself Ghenghis Khan in 1206.

Ghenghis' body lay in state for three months while princes and ambassadors travelled to pay their respects, although no record exists of any from the Roman Church, from Byzantium or from any European King or Prince. At his burial, forty bejewelled slave girls and forty of the finest horses were sacrificed and buried alongside him. Then a thousand horsemen rode over the ground to disguise the site, of which no sign or exact memory remains.

Within two years, the steppe devoured the final resting place of Ghenghis Khan, wiping it from the face of the earth and the memory of man, even as his Empire flourished.

*   *   *   *

We had little to do after our arrival but await word of Cardinal Pellegrino's embassy. We knew that he sought audience with Chancellor Yeh Lu Chu Tsai and perhaps even with Khan Ugedei himself. We would not be part of that audience. So once again we spent our time wandering in the City, exploring its recesses and attempting to learn its rhythms. The Mongols saw to it that we received provisions. Otherwise they left us alone. We saw Rashid sporadically. He had his duties to perform in this place. Those duties did not include entertaining the lowly retainers of distinguished ambassadors.

We had been in Karakorum for four weeks when Rashid brought us arresting news. He appeared one morning, his face grave. He spoke slowly in Latin, obviously seeking to achieve clarity in a tongue that came awkwardly to him, now that he did not practice with Wilfred on a daily basis.

"Pellegrino and Dandolo both died during night."

We looked at him. Incredulous. Wilfred spoke first. "Surely, you jest. We have heard nothing of ill health."

Rashid shrugged. He had cared for neither of the deceased. They had both treated him with disdain. He brought us news, no more. His message carried no hint of emotion. "It is true nonetheless." He shrugged again. "It appears that they ate something adverse to their systems. They were both of advanced age. Perhaps their time came. Who knows?"

Could they have been poisoned? The thought struck Wilfred as it did me. We could not ask such a question of Rashid, of course. Wilfred had another to ask, however.

"What do you know of the progress of the talks between the Cardinal and the Khan, Rashid?"

"What talks? There have been none — and might never have been any. The Cardinal brought only meager gifts and refused to acknowledge the Khan as ruler of the world. He refused to declare himself or the Pope servants of the Khan. I doubt that Ugedei Khan would have held an audience for him. In any case, none had taken place before the men died. Nor had they met with the Chancellor, Yeh Lu."

We observed each other in silence for a moment. To my mind, there could be no doubt that the emissaries had been done in, the Empire having no use for them, no desire to support them in luxury at Karakorum, no interest in conducting them home at Imperial expense. They had been brought to Karakorum in the erroneous belief that they had important concessions to offer from the Apostolic See. Instead, they sought only vague talks about possible future cooperation in which the armies of the Empire would shed blood for the benefit of the Roman Church. Wilfred had the same thoughts. In contrast to my paralysis, he acted on them.

"Let one thing be clear, Rashid. Johnnie and I make obeisance to the Empire. We acknowledge the authority of the Khan over all the earth. As you know, we have nothing. But we offer our services to do the type of work that Alexis performs in Samarkand."

Rashid nodded, bowing slightly. "I will report your words to the Chancellory." He turned and departed, leaving us in a swirl of doubt and confusion.

With Rashid gone, we could share our suspicions over the demise of both emissaries, on the same night. In the end, whether they died through coincidence or at the hand of the Mongols made little difference.

*   *   *   *

Our mission died with Pellegrino and Dandolo. We had no reason to be in Karakorum, indeed anywhere within the Mongol Empire. And yet, there we were. Six thousand miles from Rome, further still from Blackfriars. We had no money and no means of returning without the assistance of our hosts. We lacked purpose or importance, flotsam cast up on a foreign shore.

Bad as the situation seemed, it was far worse in fact. Two days after informing us of the deaths, Rashid woke us in the dead of night to warn us of our peril, based on information newly come to him. He spoke in a whisper, without light, as though he wished to attract no attention, wished not to be seen with us.

"Wilfred. Johnnie. I must warn you that the Mongols may kill you now that the ambassadors have died. You are persons of low station. You are no one's envoy. You are of no potential use to them. They will assume from your station that nothing you say will carry any weight with those who sent you."

I felt a chill grip my belly. He was right. The Papal See would give us no credence. That being the case, what reason did the Mongols have to feed us, with winter approaching? What reason did they have to supply us with transport so that we could return home? We could not purchase favors for lack of funds, even if any had been on offer. I could tell from his tone that the baleful news had also taken Wilfred by surprise.

"Come, come, Rashid. Are they so quick to kill those who come to them in peace, on a mission of peace?"

Rashid snorted quietly. "The Mongols kill for far less reason than you provide to them, now that your envoys are no longer alive. Your lives are nothing to them." He paused, his voice becoming more calm and measured.

"You must understand two critical things about these people. First, they believe that life does not end. It simply returns to an eternal stream of life, when the temporal being is destroyed. It then reemerges from that stream in another corporeal form. Therefore, they don't destroy your ethereal being when they kill you in the traditional sense. They simply rid themselves of a tangible inconvenience. They themselves view their own lives in this fashion, a state of mind that makes them fearless warriors as death holds no terror for them."

He paused for a moment again, choosing his words carefully, groping for the correct Latin phrases. When he resumed, he spoke even more quietly than before, his tone and the total dark of the ger adding ominous portent to his message.

"Second, these people believe that all beings on earth and all material possessions are placed here for their exclusive use and enjoyment. They take what they wish, use what they wish, destroy what they wish in any manner they choose without scruple or restraint of any kind. They derive exquisite pleasure from torturing other human beings. Sadly, they are not alone in this. But in my experience, they are alone in their total conviction as a matter of tribal and now Imperial belief that they have the right to do it to whomsoever they wish — to whatever poor wretch falls under their sway. Thus, they do not just kill. They kill cruelly, after inflicting great agony. It is a matter of both policy and practice with them. I have seen it with my own eyes. Done to my own people before my own eyes, as also in the case of Petrachos and Allah knows how many others who work in their service as an alternative to a protracted death." I could hear his voice break slightly at this, even as he whispered.

Silence reigned in the tent for several minutes. I could hear the pounding of my heart resonate in my head like a great drum. Terror constricted my belly and chest. Wilfred spoke at last. His voice sounded calm to me, especially compared to the croaking sound that I would have made.

"Is it possible that you could obtain audience for us with Chancellor Yeh Lu, Rashid? I would speak to him."

"Possible. What would you say?"

Wilfred sounded more confident now, as though the plan he was about to reveal had gathered strength, a shrub of hope taking root in a bleak desert of threat.

"We can be useful. We are worth far more alive than dead, particularly to Chancellor Yeh Lu."

Rashid could not hide his skepticism. "How so? The Mongols do not need an archer or an interpreter in training. And what can Johnnie do, as he does not qualify for either of those two pursuits?"

Wilfred did not hesitate. "We are trained illustrators of sacred texts." A slight exaggeration in my case although certainly not in Wilfred's. "I have observed with interest the Uighur and Persian writings that the Empire seeks to preserve. Chancellor Yeh Lu's personal project, I understand. Our art would serve as well to enhance such work as it does the Christian texts for which we have been trained." He paused for a moment. I could imagine him shaking silently with controlled mirth in the darkness. "We will be required to make some small stylistic adjustments, of course. But we will have motivation enough for such a minor accomplishment. Indeed, I have already practiced the rounding so much favored in these regions and found it no great trick."

Rashid did not attempt to hide his relief. Whatever he felt for me, he appeared to have grown fond of Wilfred. This device, he could see, might keep us out of deadly peril at least for a time. He and Wilfred agreed that he would seek an audience with the Chancellor on our behalf.

When he had been gone awhile, I asked Wilfred if he thought we could do it. He replied in a manner that had become all too typical on this journey. "What choice do we have, Johnnie? I do not choose to end my life buried alive or impaled on a stake just yet. Nor do I recommend anything like that for you."

"But what will we use for tools?"

"I brought mine," he said. "We will have to use local materials for dyes. We know they have such stuffs here. We need only find out what they are and how to get them. Surely the all-powerful Mongol chieftains can command that material for us."

"What will we do with the tools and dyes? How can we illustrate texts we cannot read with figures and representations that are foreign to our teachings?"

He laughed out loud this time. "What choice do we have, Johnnie?" Again, the maddening question. He paused and spoke in a more serious vein. "I will seek Rashid's help with the texts until I learn them myself. As for the illustrations, we must quickly learn to copy what we see." He reached out and put a hand on my shoulder. "You have a sharp eye, lad, and a good memory. At first light tomorrow, make drawings of everything that you can recall from the mosaics we saw in Bukhara, Samarkand, Tashkent and the other places we have passed through. Keep a keen lookout from now on for everything that we can use to refine our work and I shall do the same. It is too bad that this City is too young and too raw to possess any art of note. So we must start with imagination built on but few shreds of memory. Had we known how important it would become, we might have remembered better. But so be it."

I could more sense than see him lay back. I pictured him staring up at the blackness in the ger with no moon or stars this cloudy night to cast even a glimmer for the eye to fasten upon. He spoke, barely above a whisper. "It is too bad that we are not more gifted as illuminators. I never thought that my life would depend upon that particular skill. But, by Christ, we shall become gifted enough to fool these heathens and survive into the bargain."

Wilfred quickly fell asleep. Lacking his conviction and being more fearful than he, I lay awake until dawn's light roused the City to its day's work in a welter of raucous commotion.

*   *   *   *

Chancellor Yeh Lu projected a strange, tranquil power for a man of such small statute. He stood no more than five feet tall. Of indeterminate age — but not young, surely — he had a complexion like tanned leather, wisps of white hair and a thin white beard and mustache. He stood straight, wiry and strong, but somehow slightly out of proper shape like steel bent just past the point of total resilience. His deeply lined face had a grave aspect to which his slanted eyes lent an exotic cast. His face had the classic features of an elder from beyond the Wall with the skin of a nomad.

He gave us audience at Rashid's request in a room of the inner palace that served as his office. It had walls of brown, rough stone, two openings high up to admit meager light under a roof composed of wood that the Mongols had imported from the forests to the north. The room contained no furniture at all save for a low table with rough cushions for seating. I assumed that the cushions were filled with wool, although I could not be sure. Skins rather than woven carpets lay about on the floor.

Two torches burned in metal holders that had been affixed to the stone walls to add light in the dingy setting. Their flames danced in the ceaseless wind that tormented this place at all seasons, finding its sneakthief way through cracks in the stone walls to agitate the air in the room. The guttering torchflames created shifting patterns of light and shadow, adding a restless quality to the setting.

Chancellor Yeh Lu conversed with Rashid in the tongue of the Uighur of which I understood nothing but a few scant words. Wilfred knew more, but not enough to follow the conversation in all its twistings and turnings. So my account was shaped by Rashid's translation into his version of the Latin tongue that I had come to understand.

After a few pleasantries, Yeh Lu got right to the point.

"So you have come to plead for the lives of these two, whose value in the eyes of the Khan is less than that of a lame horse. What can you say for them?" Yeh Lu smiled. It was well known that he did not believe in the gratuitous shedding of blood. But it was also well known that he served the Great Khan faithfully and did not resist Imperial practices for small cause.

Rashid bowed, arms outstretched before raising his eyes to engage those of the Chancellor. "It is true that these are mere handmen and retainers of the envoys who have unfortunately died. It is also true that they adhere to the Christian faith. Not the tolerant and unobtrusive version practiced by the followers of Nestorius who have long lived among us, but indeed, the Western version that demands adherence by all men and condemns those who resist." He waved his hand almost dismissively in our direction before continuing.

"But these two can nonetheless be of use to you, so long as they promise not to preach their dogma and work diligently."

"How so?" Yeh Lu continued to smile, seated in a relaxed posture on his cushion, cross-legged and yet erect of back, head held high.

"The Christians practice a high art of illustrating sacred texts in a manner that makes them more pleasing and better understood by those who study them. Both these men are skilled in those techniques, the older one," indicating Wilfred, "having become learned in the skill over many years, and the younger," pointing to me this time, "having served as his apprentice.

"As you know, Chancellor, Persian and Uighur works of the type that you seek to create and preserve as part of the legacy of the Empire are often illuminated in a similar fashion. I believe that with practice, these men could learn to perform their function in a manner more versatile than just the style adapted to the Christian writings in which you have little interest. I bid you give them an opportunity to demonstrate their ability in that field. It will cost little as they live simply."

Rashid had the good grace not to mention the most important, albeit awkward, argument in support of his position. At the moment, Yeh Lu had no alternatives to carry out a project in which he himself had a personal interest. Nor did he have other prospects. Worse, he had no alternatives because the three men he had chosen for the job, from among the captives brought to Karakorum after the sack of Kai Feng, had been butchered by Subedei in a careless moment. A careless moment brought on, so it was said, by excessive drink that had obliterated memory of Yeh Lu's express instruction. Subedei, the great general, having a stature and importance that transcended Yeh Lu's authority, the offense had gone unpunished. Yeh Lu's need for skilled illuminators for his compendium of the Empire's conquests had gone wanting.

It quickly became clear that we would have our period of probation. If we succeeded, we would acquire a station high within the entourage of the Chancellor himself. We would succeed, as failure was unthinkable.

But Yeh Lu did not dismiss us. To the contrary, he waved us back into our seats as we rose to leave. He spoke directly to us, using Rashid as an interpreter.

"I will question you concerning your mission in more detail in the future. I also wish to learn as much as possible about the people whence you come. Now, however, we have a more urgent matter to consider. What should be done with the Venetians?" The Venetian marine soldiers who accompanied us - I had forgotten about them.

"You see, the people of the Great Khan accord great respect to official envoys from other chiefs and princes who acknowledge the Khan. In contrast, they grant no respect whatever to soldiers who do not fight from the back of a horse and who perform no other valuable function within society as you yourselves propose to do. With the unfortunate death of the envoys, the Venetians have fallen to a low station here. If one of the Khan's more boisterous subordinates decided to use them for target practice or as the objects of a group manhunt, no convention of this society could prevent it."

My blood chilled at these words, spoken and then translated casually, as though the discussion concerned nothing more momentous than the price of a head of sheep. Wilfred held the Chancellor's eye as he replied.

"You are right, Your Excellence. Besides, the Venetians can perform no function here. They are good fighters, surely. But they are men of the sea who fight best from ships. Send them back under a safe conduct pass. It will assist relations between your Empire and the Republic of Venice when they return and tell of your kindnesses and solicitude for them."

The Chancellor continued to smile as though bemused. "Why should we care about that? We have no relations with the Republic of Venice, whatever that may be."

Wilfred nodded. "Some day you may. They are a great trading nation of the sea, a potential source of fruitful commerce. As they care for trade and little else, they will not send you envoys seeking to persuade you of the merits of any particular religious belief or seeking to engage you as an ally in wars not of your choosing."

Wilfred delivered this statement without expression and it took a moment for Rashid's translation to sink in. After a moment, Yeh Lu's eyebrows arched suddenly in surprise. A great smile fractured his face into thousands of creases as he took in the full sweep of Wilfred's little joke at the expense of the dead Pellegrino and Dandolo. He laughed quietly.

"Just so. In deference to their unique qualities among westerners and on the basis of your good offices, we will give them transport and a safe conduct. If they leave at once and move with speed, they may escape the full wrath of winter on the steppe." He laughed again. "As you so aptly say, we should encourage contact with westerners interested solely in trade and who do not seek to convert our wretched barbarian selves to their strange creed." He paused, eyes twinkling. "Pray tell me, good sir. If your last statements reflect your true beliefs, how is it that you were on this mission?"

Wilfred shrugged and smiled in turn. "To escape boredom, Your Excellence. And perhaps to learn from those who know far more than I." He turned toward me, indicating. "Young John here accompanies me as I am his protector and he has no other choice. I pray that you will grant indulgence to one so poorly situated that he must rely on such a one as myself for that purpose." At this, the Chancellor laughed out loud.

The audience quickly concluded thereafter. But Wilfred had struck a responsive chord with the Chancellor. Our lives were spared. The Chancellor brought us into the chancellory to work on his project of creating a literature of quality to validate the empire of the barbarians.

The Venetian soldiers left within a week. They elected, fatefully, to travel by camel despite urgings that they proceed by fast horse, using the benefit of relays to speed their progress ahead of the gathering winter. They declined as they were not acclimatized to horses, being men of the sea. They had suffered mightily on the trip east and did not wish to repeat the experience. The portion of our journey to Karakorum on the backs of horses had been hateful to them, the swaying of camels more familiar to seafaring men. They disappeared on the road west, murdered by man or the elements, no one knows which.

112

CHAPTER ELEVEN

Vice Chancellor Tsai Chou tugged thoughtfully at the thin white wisps of his beard as he shifted through the scrolls and sheets in front of him. He spoke the Uighur dialect with a heavy accent that made him difficult to understand. And as he spoke softly, I had to strain both to hear and to understand him. He had summoned us to attend him and receive instructions.

We had now worked diligently for the Chancellory for a full three years. With his gift for languages, Wilfred had quickly learned to carry on simple conversations in both Uighur script and Mongol dialects, with the sporadic aid of Rashid and others of the Chancellory who Yeh Lu had assigned to assist us in our endeavors. I had only recently begun to feel comfortable with the rudiments of Uighur, a guttural language of monosyllables with a structure totally unlike English, Latin or French. Despite it's nature, foreign to anything in my experience, the script came more readily to me - and I had become fascinated with the beauty and intricacies of the figures.

Tsai Chou cleared his throat, and with other gestures, made plain his intent to impart something of importance to us. He spoke the Uighur dialect with a heavy Han accent that made him difficult to understand. As he spoke softly, I had to strain to hear him.

"Our task, in which you are engaged as workers, is nothing less than to keep and preserve the wisdom of the ages. Only this Empire among all the peoples of the world has the power and self-confidence to pursue such an undertaking." He paused, leaning far back on his silken cushions to gaze reflectively at the fluted wood dome of the room, whitewashed and brilliant in the afternoon light. "In this, we pay homage to the wisdom and humanity of Ghenghis, the Great Khan, who commanded tolerance for all thought and belief within the realm even as he himself came to embrace Buddhism."

Indeed. Only the Empire had plundered the sacred archives of so many peoples that it could even contemplate such a task. Only the tolerant, wise, humane and ultimately devout Great Khan, of all the conquerors in human history, had ordained such a massive plundering. So now, we would aid the Empire in becoming the keeper of all humanity's birthright. For whether he was a Buddhist or not, the God Tengri, the Great Blue Sky of the Steppe that had ordained the supremacy of Temuchin over all the peoples who dwelt in felt tents, had expanded Genghis' mandate until it extended over all humanity, the temporal and spiritual possessions of the entire world.

Wilfred and I both shifted restlessly on our cushions. We said nothing. Ever since Yeh Lu had turned us over to his deputy, we had sensed a distance, a rising tension between us and our hosts.

Tsai Chou pushed forward from his reclining position and reached for an irregular stack of paper and parchment arrayed on the carpet before him.

"I wish to begin with a brief summary of the religions. I wish to organize it by reference to various writings that exemplify and explain the beliefs. I wish the summary to be succinct. Later, we will create libraries of source materials and essays for those interested in more profound research, exploration of the subtleties and complexities with which all are infused. I have collected these papers for you to copy and illuminate to begin your work."

He searched through the stack carefully and withdrew a sheet.

"In honor of the Great Khan's faith, we shall begin with Buddhism and the Buddha's Sermon." He read slowly, in a singsong style, without apparent emphasis on any word, without rhythm.

"'All life is suffering; The cause of suffering is ignorant craving; The suppression of suffering, nirvana, can be achieved. The Way is the Noble Eightfold Path: Right Views, Aspiration, Speech and Conduct; Right Vocation, Effort, Mindfulness, and Rapture.'"

He regarded us as though seeking a reaction. I had none. I felt only tension. I was too preoccupied with my own anxieties to search Wilfred's face for any expression. Tsai Chou smiled an opaque smile before continuing.

114

"This is a perfect point of beginning for its contrast with the essence of Islam, Christianity and Persian faith based on the teachings of Zoroaster. The laws of nature or of the universe hold no interest for the Buddhist, who seeks a way out, a way to be free of such laws. There is no moral law derived from God for there is no God; and the gods espoused by men are the traps that the yogi must evade. The Eightfold Path seeks to kill all fear and desire against the order of the universe; and with victory comes rapture and compassion for all those yet to break the bonds."

He replaced the sheet from which he had been reading and withdrew another from the stack, regarding us out of the tops of his narrow eyes as he prepared again to read.

"You followers of Christianity will recognize the truth of these words: `The revealed Christian truth consists of one God in Three Persons, with his pantheon of angels arrayed against various devils, communion of saints, forgiveness of sins, and resurrection of the body. It includes the presence in every consecrated drop of wine and bread of the Mass of the dead and resurrected Son of God, both God and man, born miraculously of a virgin mother.' Thus, it is a faith based upon belief in miracles, free will and worth of the individual, seeking the attainment of reward and avoidance of punishment in an afterlife based upon adherence to dogma. The very antithesis of Buddhism. And yet, the Eightfold Path does not stand as the opposite of Christian belief. Quite the contrary."

Again, Tsai Chou smiled his enigmatic smile. Complacent. Self-satisfied. Superior.

"I tell you these things not to engage you in discourse. For in truth, your views mean nothing to me or to the Chancellor or the Empire. I simply seek to explain the task. This Chancellory wishes to create a body of written wisdom to serve as a resource for scholars and sages. It will take many years to complete the work. Indeed, it may never be truly completed. But we are the architects. You are but the lowly craftsmen who will execute the design. You will do what we say, without comment or argument. Do you understand?"

We understood. For the last six weeks, the allotment of food vouchsafed to us by the Chancellory had become quite sparing and of poor quality. We had no money with which to make up the deficiencies. In subtle ways, we had been given to understand that we were being punished for inadequate submissiveness. Wilfred had questioned the methods we had been directed to use in one case and we had both requested improvement in certain aspects of our circumstances. These questions had obviously been taken as impertinences of a type that would not be tolerated.

The lives of subject peoples had little value in Mongol eyes. We were totally at their mercy, a cold and fleeting commodity under the best of circumstances. We would do whatever Tsai Chou commanded. And we would closely emulate him in the art of the enigmatic smile.

*   *   *   *

"But what of the oral traditions of the peoples of these regions, Honorable Sir? Why is it that we work only with writings?" Wilfred propounded his question sincerely, in a tone of total innocence, abject deference.

We had been employed on Tsai Chou's new project for a full six months, receiving his quiet and somewhat grudging approbation. We knew that he approved of our work even more than he allowed. I could see that my own work approached the quality of Wilfred's even as his seemed to improve, to become more infused with life now that he stood clear of the restraints of monkish tradition. We had been obedient to the point of servility. Whether through work or adherence to the discipline of subjugation, we had reversed Tsai Chou's stern attitude towards us. He now saw us as useful — perhaps irreplaceable — and devoid of intolerable insolence. Our food ration had become more bountiful. Servants of the Palace brought us warm cloaks and jerkins, felt boots and fur hats. We returned from the market one day to discover men repairing the rents in the felt panels of our ger.

Tsai Chou raised his eyebrows at Wilfred's question. "Of what do you speak, Fra Wilfred?"

Wilfred bowed his head slightly as though speaking to a superior, a mode that we had both learned to adopt with him. "Forgive me Your Honor for raising a question. I have kept in mind your orders that we do as bidden and that you have no interest in our views or innovations. So I hesitate to offer an opinion of such little worth." He stopped for an instant, head bowed. When the Vice Chancellor said nothing, he continued, maintaining his pose of deference.

"This Empire is the most vast and powerful of any Empire in human experience. It has its genesis in the energy and insight of peoples who have not maintained a written history. Yet, they are a people with a rich tradition of epic events and legendary heroes, a tradition passed down through the generations by story tellers and various renowned shaman." He looked up and engaged Tsai Chou directly. "Why is it that we copy and preserve only the traditions of the tribes and nations whose vitality has proved no match for the people of this Empire?" He stopped with that. A challenge. Unmistakable, albeit uttered quietly.

Tsai Chou smiled, although it seemed to me that his eyes did not participate in the expression. "What is it that you propose, Fra Wilfred?"

"With the utmost respect, Your Honor, I request that you send us a venerated shaman of the Mongol people. Let us hear from him the legends and teachings that have been passed down through the generations. And let us write them down in the script of the Uighur to preserve the true traditions of the people who have created this triumphant Empire, all subject to your approval, of course."

A slight shiver flowed from my lower abdomen and ran down my legs. For me, Tsai Chou's presence was always unpleasant, full of tension and vague threat. In my eyes, he had the aspect of a poisonous serpent. At any moment, his hooded eyes could open wide with hatred as a prelude to a deadly strike. I sensed that he held us in contempt, considered us no better than slaves, dishonored by our origins as well as by the fact that we were totally at his mercy. He used us to carry out his project. He fed us well to improve our ability to do his work, not our own. Now Wilfred was proposing a different project, perhaps one in which the Vice Chancellor would have no interest whatsoever.

And besides, our Uighur script was not yet of the highest quality. We could copy in it. But I feared that we might lack the versatility and understanding to capture the nuance and subtlety of speech, particularly the mystical and ethereal speech of a traditional shaman. Once again, I feared that Wilfred had jumped off a cliff into a dangerous and unexplored void, dragging me after him.

Tsai Chou did not respond to Wilfred's request, nor did his expression betray any reaction to it. Instead, he handed us several scraps of literary material that agents of the Chancellor's office had rescued from various conflagrations and sent us off to create complete copies of the fragmented works. I felt that he had rejected Wilfred's proposal as beneath contempt, unworthy of response.

So it came as a surprise when we received a visit from Lo-Poqti less than one week later. He simply appeared one mid-day as we worked, entering our ger unannounced and without seeking our leave. His appearance compounded the shock of his unheralded arrival.

Lo-Poqti was tall for a Mongol. Equal to Wilfred in height, but thin — skeletally thin. His dark and wrinkled skin hung on his bones like a leather garment several sizes too large. In contrast, his face seemed full, with high cheekbones and eyes that were little more than slits. All hair on his head, eyebrows, straggly beard, thin mustache, was dead white, like snow. The deep creases in the skin of his face gave him the aspect of great age. Yet he stood erect, moving lightly and with grace in the manner of a younger man. All this was remarkable enough, but much less than the total arresting picture.

Lo-Poqti wore nothing but a leather loinpiece, amulets, sandals and a shaman's headpiece. Although it was late April, winter had not fully loosed its grip. I recall that day as being quite chilly, with dark sky, north wind and snow flurries alternating with freezing rain. Yet Lo-Poqti showed no sign of discomfort. He announced the purpose of his visit without formality.

"The honorable Tsai Chou sends me to recount the truths of the Chosen for you to record." He stood, regarding us as though from a great distance, a great height. His eyes, though bright, seemed vague and unfocused. His headdress and overall appearance announced that he was a shaman.

Wilfred was far better than I at adjusting seamlessly to the unexpected. Saying nothing, he bowed, took sheets of clean parchment and sat to face Lo-Poqti with quill in hand. He beckoned to me, indicating that I should emulate him, stating in English: "Write down what he says so we can compare notes. We must get all this correctly as they will know if we do not. It is their story, after all."

Over the next two days, Lo-Poqti recited the spiritual Genesis of the

Empire in the person of he who became Ghenghis Khan. He spoke in a sing-song voice with no particular emphasis or emotion, in the manner of Tsai Chou. Omitting the extraneous detail and digressions with which Lo-Poqti enriched it, the tale proceeds thus:

In the beginning, the peoples born of the Blue Wolf and the Fallow Deer fought each against the other. None of the tribes or clans were strong enough to claim leadership or to resist oppression by the Hsiung-nu — Huns — to the west or the Chin to the east. In this time of chaos, a clan known as the Bjorjin of the Qiyat tribe was taken by surprise and all of its members slain save for a young boy, one Chuqti.

Lost and orphaned, he lay in despair among the corpses of his family members. While in that condition, the spirit of Tengri, of the Great Blue Sky, came to Chuqti and commanded that he proceed westward to the Mountain of the White Leopard — the highest peak in the Kunlan Shan Range that lies on the boundary of the land known as Xinjiang, or the land of the Uighur, and the high mountain land known as Xizang or Tibet — there to receive the wisdom and commands to be imparted to him by the spirit god of that place, a giant snow leopard. Somehow, with great hardship, Chuqti made his way through the Tarim Basin, the Takla Makan Desert, finally reaching the base of the high escarpment of the Kunlan Shan at the place where the River Qurqan rushes down in a cascade of raging foam, laden with glacial silt.

Wilfred and I had travelled to Karakorum through the Tarim Basin, skirting the northern edge of the Takla Makan desert. I have seen the gleaming white escarpment of the Kunlan Shan to the south, rising to the heavens, dwarfing the Alps to my eye, its waves of violently upthrust rock capped with glaciers to the limits of the horizon. Thus it was that Lo-Poqti's recitation of Chuqti's ordeal struck a true chord with me.

The raging water, the sheer escarpment, the snow and ice daunted Chuqti, already exhausted from his trek. All hope of finding White Leopard Mountain abandoned him. He sensed the proximity of death and resigned himself to entry into the spirit world. He took shelter in a small scour cave by the riverbank to await his fate. Shortly thereafter, he fell into a deep sleep in which he dreamed that he was drifting weightless through the blue void on the breath of Tengri. He saw White Leopard Mountain high above him, rising to a dark stony peak above a glacier field, the remains of an ancient tree leaning crazily at the pinnacle with the great snow leopard himself reclining on the topmost rock, gazing upward.

He awakened to discover that he had been transformed into a raven, the most intelligent of birds, slow but powerful and without enemies. Rejuvenated by his rest, he took to the air, using friendly wind currents to assist him upwards. Attaining the crest, he quickly found the mountain of his dreams and flew to a perch on the ancient dead tree. The snow leopard regarded him gravely before calling him by name.

"Greetings, Chuqti. Although the vessel of your body has been transformed, you remain as before and as you will forever."

"But why have I been commanded to come here, Oh Great One? And who are you?"

The leopard regarded him with his large yellow eyes. The raven noted the beauty of the animal with his white pelt, grey markings and regal bearing. The leopard replied in a quiet voice. "I am the voice of the river of life. The spirits speak through me because a leopard is solitary, strong, quick and deadly. And I am all those things and more. I symbolize the fiercest beauty by my form, a joy to behold but fearsome both to my enemies and all those creatures placed on earth to sustain my life in these austere climes. As for you, your spirit will shortly depart from the raven's body to rejoin the eternal stream from which all life emerges and to which all life returns. You are here because the spirits ordain that you be instructed as to your destiny as the leader of the Chosen." The leopard stood, stretched and lifted his head to fix the raven with his baleful eyes.

"Your spirit when next summoned from the eternal stream shall infuse the body of a man with the energy, insight and stubbornness to unite the Chosen, all of the peoples who live under felt tents, and thus celebrate the true glory of Tengri. With great hardship and suffering, you shall prevail over your enemies and spread the rule of the Chosen over all the world. And you shall say unto them: 'My people shall wear gold, they shall eat the choicest meats, they shall ride the finest horses, the men shall hold in their arms the most beautiful women and they shall take for their own the best of all that exists in the world for it exists for them and them alone.' And you shall deliver all that you have promised and more."

Excitement quickened in the chest of the raven as it spoke in Chuqti's voice. "And who is the man in whose form I shall do all these things?"

"Temuchin. Of the Bjorjin clan of the Qiyat tribe. The great ladle of the spirit world will dip the spark of your soul intact from the eternal stream of life to invest his body with the force required to carry out his mission. And I, the Great Snow Leopard, shall inhabit his body with you so that he shall have the best of us both."

As the raven watched, the leopard began to lick one of its upturned forepaws with its large, grey tongue. With its paw held thus, the raven could see on the main pad the clearly defined symbol of the drawn bow, the symbol that now appears on all the battle pennants of the Empire.

Lo-Poqti recounted many other fables of a similar sort that Wilfred and I dutifully wrote down. None struck me as new. I am not widely read, but it seemed the fables of the Mongols departed only slightly from those of other peoples.

Fables and legends did not satisfy Wilfred for long. When it appeared that Lo-Poqti would continue indefinitely with tales of that sort, Wilfred interrupted him.

"Honorable Lo-Poqti. I would know the facts of Temuchin's rise to the position of Great Khan. I wish to record those facts for future generations. Although those facts are not as profound or meaningful as what you have told us, since they deal with the affairs of men and not of the universe, can you honor us with a recitation of them?"

Lo-Poqti smiled, his face seeming to break up as thousands of creases appeared at the corners of his eyes and mouth. The expression revealed that his teeth were black, either from disease or a dye of some kind. I had not noticed that remarkable feature before.

He paused for a moment, looking upward to the ceiling of the ger and then began in his singsong voice, as though reciting the tale to himself.

"When Temuchin was born, the Chosen did not obey one another. The Ong-Khan, leader of the Keriyat and Saqiyat was the most powerful but he could not command the respect of all the Chosen. Thus, the tribes and clans vexed each other, fighting continuously. And because they were weak in their disunity, they were sore beset by their neighbors."

"When Temuchin rose from the grade of childhood to the degree of manhood, he became in the onslaught like a roaring lion and in the melee like a trenchant sword. In the subjugation of his foes, his rigor and severity had the taste of poison, and in the humbling of the pride of each lord of fortune, his harshness and ferocity did the work of fate. The Ong-Khan befriended him and they became allies. The Ong-Khan enjoyed the fruits of Temuchin's loyal support.

"But within a short time, the sons and brothers of the Ong-Khan and his courtiers and favorites became envious of the rank and favor Temuchin enjoyed. They accordingly cast the nets of guile across the passage provided by opportunity and set the traps of treachery to blacken his name. They planted the seed in the Ong-Khan's ear that Temuchin secretly planned to cast him out and take over his realm."

"The Ong-Khan became suspicious of Temuchin and then fearful of him as his power and fame grew. So it was decided that at dawn, while the eyes of mankind are hooded with sleep and rendered negligent by repose, the Ong-Khan and his men would attack Temuchin and his followers to snuff out the threat that he posed. But the attack was betrayed by two youths, Kishlik and Bada, who went to Temuchin to warn him, allowing him and all those in his camp to steal away."

Lo-Poqti ladled a cup of water from the urn that we kept by the door of the ger and drank deeply. He then went on to describe the protracted battles between Temuchin and the Ong-Khan in which Temuchin ultimately prevailed. Then he recounted the consolidation of power.

"And when Temuchin's cause prospered and the Ong-Khan lay dead, his wives and daughters in Temuchin's service and his family as slaves, the stars of Temuchin's fortune were in the ascendant. He dispatched envoys to the other tribes also. And all that came to render submission he admitted to the number of his commanders and followers and regarded them with favor and indulgence. As for the refractory and rebellious, he struck the breath from their bodies with the whip of calamity and the sword of annihilation until all of the tribes were of one color and obedient to his command. Thus, he established new laws and laid the foundations of justice."

"Whereupon the venerable shaman Teb-Tengri came to him and said: 'God has spoken to me and these are his words — I have given all the face of the earth to Temuchin and his children. Bid him administer justice in his fashion.'" So the Mongol Empire was God's justice translated to the Conqueror by the interpreter Teb-Tengri, who stayed at Temuchin's side and told him of God's will for many years thereafter, in matters great and small. Temuchin never acted without Teb-Tengri's counsel and never transgressed against the counsel thus given.

When Lo-Poqti left at the end of the second day, we did not know if he would return. His departure was as enigmatic as his arrival. Wilfred and I did not find much in his teaching worth extended discussion, with one exception.

"I see now why these men are such fearless fighters," he said.

"Why is that?"

"It is as Alexis said. They don't fear death, as death merely liberates their spirit to remerge with the eternal stream, whence it will be reborn." He laughed. "The virtuous Christian knight fights without fear because he expects to go to Paradise. The cowardly ones usually have weight on their conscience, although they otherwise might be the best fighters just because they are less restrained by virtue, so-called. These people dispense with such complications. So the nastiest ones can fight without fear as well." He chuckled, shaking his head.

I regarded him carefully, pondering the wisdom of my next question and whether it would be better left unasked. "What do you think of the beliefs that Lo-Poqti described in his recitation of fables and legends, Wilfred?" He shrugged.

"No Christian can credit them. But what difference does it make? They may believe what they wish as long as they allow me to do the same." That closed the subject for him.

I have remembered all that Lo-Poqti said in great detail, as I had to write it down. I wrote first in English and then helped Wilfred translate it laboriously into Uighur script in a bound parchment volume that we delivered to Tsai Chou one day. He acknowledged the work but never commented upon it.

*   *   *   *

Wilfred turned to a stack of fragments that we had recently received from Tsai Chou. "We had best get to work on this stuff, Johnnie. This is the

Vice Chancellor's project and he has made plain his indifferent regard for ours."

He withdrew a sheet and beckoned me to come view it with him. We worked out the words together. "Keep walking though there's no place to go. Don't try to see through the distances. That's not for human beings. Move within. But don't move the way fear makes you move." And then another. "I have lived on the lip of insanity. Wanting to know reasons. Knocking on a door. It opens. I have been knocking from the inside."

More of Salaludin Rumi, Tsai Chou's favorite. A passionless man devoted to the work of a most passionate poet. A man obsessed with control devoted to writings that advocate abandonment of all constraint on the human spirit. Contradictions churned my mind into a quagmire that bogged down all coherent thought. I did not do well in the face of competing certainties or mutually exclusive beliefs. From all that I had heard, read and written over the past several years, I could only clutch this much as valid, shining still and bright through the turmoil. "Don't try to see through the distances. That's not for human beings. Move within."

And banish fear. I would have found that impossible even in far better circumstances than we enjoyed.

CHAPTER TWELVE

I know not how Wilfred befriended Tolui. I found them one day in conversation, sitting cross-legged on the ground outside the ger where we worked. It seemed that they had known each other for some time, as they both exhibited an easy familiarity that belied the human gulf between them. I could tell that they bantered with each other even as I found it difficult to follow the twists and turns of the Mongol tongue. And although he always denied it with wide-eyed indignation, I am convinced that Wilfred swore like a trooper when he spoke in Mongol or Uighur dialects, freely employing profanities that he would never use in English except under extreme duress.

In any case, Tolui seemed to spend a lot of time with us, hanging around, watching us work, chatting idly with Wilfred about various matters, answering his incessant questions about the nomad life and affairs of the Empire. During periods of our work when the required degree of concentration did not preclude conversation, Wilfred would share with me what he learned.

"This man, Tolui, is a third cousin of the Great Khan Ugedei through one of the several wives of one of Ghenghis' brothers. Or something like that. I can't be sure. Anyhow, he is an aristocrat but not of high station. He leads a squad of ten light horse in the Mongol army."

We had learned by that point that the Mongol army was divided into units of ten, one hundred, one thousand and ten thousand men, each of the units being led by an officer who reported to the leader of the next larger component. The leaders of the ten thousands, or *tumen*, reported to the commanding general.

"Why is he so interested in our work, Wilfred?"

He shrugged. "Can't say. But he's a fighting man and the fighting men of this army live for plunder. He may think that as we are artisans of sufficient skill to receive support for our work from the Imperial treasury, perhaps we will be able to teach him the value of objects he might steal when next the Mongols sack a city." He shrugged again. I searched his face in vain for sign of an expression that might betray feelings behind what he had just said.

"Has he fought in many battles?"

"So he says, yes. The Tangut, the Naiman, one of the sieges of Kai Feng. He claims to have participated as a leader of ten in the campaigns against the Khwarazm Shah. He claims to have been at the sack of Merv."

So he may have been one of those who slaughtered all of Alexis Petrachos' people. It was one thing to hear of such atrocities, another thing entirely to stand in knowing and close proximity to one of the perpetrators. I felt my stomach constrict.

"What do you find of interest in him?"

Wilfred shrugged again. "He sought me out, not the other way 'round. But he's a cheerful enough fellow. Answers my questions about the local customs. Told me how they make their bows. Told me how they ferment mare's milk to make that foul stuff they drink." He smiled. "The man's generous as well. Offered me one of his wives for an evening's diversion. When I refused, as politely as possible, of course, he offered me one of his daughters. When I cited Christian vows of abstinence, he reminded me that the Christians of these parts fornicate freely and at every opportunity."

Ah yes. Even Nestorian clergy were not celibate. And the followers of Christ throughout the Empire — including highly placed members of the royal family — were adherents of the Nestorian heresy. Like most of the other men of the region, they had as many wives and consorts as they could afford.

"How did you get out of that without giving offense?" It did not occur to me at the time that Wilfred might have accepted Tolui's offer. His face betrayed nothing as he replied.

"I told him that I had taken a vow of abstinence, a solemn promise to God as binding upon me as any vow he might make to Tengri, the spirit god in whom he places his faith. My reasons were mine. And I asked that he

126

respect them as I would respect his, were our roles reversed. He accepted that. We clasped hands on it. And although we have spent much time together since, and I have even seen some of the comely maidens who he took as slaves after some of his more recent battles, he has not renewed his offer."

Comely maidens. I could only imagine. In all of Karakorum, in all of the time that we had spent there and in the immediate environs, I had yet to lay eyes on a single female I would describe as comely. The local women looked much like their men. And those who had been taken as slaves quickly lost whatever lustre they might once have had under the duress of their captivity.

After a time, I realized that Wilfred had not yet answered my question. So I renewed it.

"Comely maidens aside, why do you spend so much time with him?"

Wilfred stepped away from his work and moved close, as though fearing to be overheard. It seemed strange, as there was no one there and none in the City who spoke English in any case.

"Think ye, Johnnie. We are helpless here. We live at sufferance. We totally depend on these people for food and shelter. We could not strike out for home and hope to survive more than a few weeks. We need friends. We need to become valuable to well-placed people. We need to learn all we can about these people and their Empire so that we can use the knowledge to survive and make the most of our situation."

He stopped and looked carefully around the ger, as though attempting to detect anyone who might be eavesdropping through the walls or at the junctions where the felt sections were sewn.

"And besides," he continued. "We have been plunked down by God's good grace in the very heart of the most powerful Empire in the history of mankind. How could we not take note of our surroundings and attempt to learn as much as possible about them? Is that not a superior choice to awaiting a horrible fate with fear and trembling, expecting each night to feel a dagger between our ribs or a garrote around our necks?"

He laughed at my expression.

"Yes, Johnnie. I seek constant learning as a way to avoid wallowing in the utter hopelessness of our situation, if one aspires ever again to see England. You may wallow in whatever you wish. But before I go that way, I might first become more Mongol than the Khan himself just to explore what that might feel like. Have you no such curiosity?"

I admitted that I did not. No more curiosity than to know what it might feel like to be a snake, or a rat, or some other low form of detestable life. I found nothing about these people attractive or interesting. To the contrary, they seemed fearsome, repulsive and in many ways subhuman to me. Among other things, much of their food disgusted me. Their ability to inflict pain with enthusiasm and without shadow of restraint appalled me. Their casual cruelties to each other seemed more of beast than of man.

No. I did not care to know what it might feel like to be Mongol, but I could see Wilfred's point. And I could see that it would behoove me to support and assist him in his efforts — because of the two of us, he alone could keep us safe here and perhaps lead us home some day. I had no chance without him.

So we cultivated Tolui as Wilfred thought best. We answered his questions. We treated him with exaggerated respect and deference. Shamelessly. Over time, it became clear in small ways that we had come under a sort of protection that he provided — no small thing. For despite being the leader of the smallest common unit in the Mongol army, the group of ten, Tolui and his unit were members of the Imperial Guard, ten thousand strong. In addition to protecting the person of the Emperor himself, the Great Khan Ugedei while we resided at Karakorum, the Imperial Guard constituted the elite unit of the Mongol army. For these reasons, the officers of the Imperial Guard commanded respect and privilege. They received a disproportionate share of the spoils of war. The Emperor provided them with assistants to tend their flocks for them. In exchange, the Guard trained continuously in the arts of warfare.

*   *   *   *

The black horse galloped at top speed across the rolling plain, its rider bent low over the horse's neck. A sack made of hides and stuffed with straw bounced wildly over the uneven ground, tethered by a woven rope to the horse's saddle. The rider jerked the rope irregularly, further agitating the gyrations of the hide sack.

A large contingent of mounted Imperial Guardsmen pranced restlessly as the rider approached. At a signal from their commander, the Guardsmen broke into a gallop in rough single file, paralleling the course of the single rider, thirty to forty yards distant from him. As each Guardsman came abreast of the single rider, he loosed an arrow at the sack and then veered abruptly away to stop in line with those who had gone before. They had not long to wait before a second single rider followed the track of the first, also trailing a hide sack that the Guardsmen pursued in a disciplined file, each loosing an arrow and then veering away to repeat the operation again and again.

This exercise that we witnessed on regular occasions would often take a contingent of two hundred riders a distance of four or five miles during which progress they might make as many as a dozen attacks on hide sack targets. The riders who dragged the targets were exhorted to make them as difficult as possible to hit. The Guardsmen were equally exhorted to score hits and could expect to receive a cuffing from their officers should they fail to do so. Requiring the Guardsmen to loose their arrows to the left on one day, the exercise would be repeated in reverse on the next so that the soldiers developed facility to hit moving targets on either side of their mount while at full gallop.

But developing skill at horseback archery was hardly the sole purpose of these exercises. Teaching coordinated and intricate maneuvering of the horsemen was at least as important. One could immediately see how the Mongols in battle capitalized on any movement of the enemy army through the quick and deadly forays of their mounted archers.

We had come out this fine, autumn day to watch Tolui lead his unit as part of the exercise. A stiff wind added to the challenge. The hide sack targets were often engulfed in clouds of dust. Yet the targets quickly picked up a hedgehogs' array of brightly colored shafts as the deadly attacks hit home. We sat on a small knoll watching the show, in awe of the skill displayed, enjoying the sights and sounds of it, the taunts of the target draggers and the shouts of the mounted archers.

When the last single rider had raced past, Tolui and the rest of his unit rode over to where we sat watching. We stood as they approached, hard-eyed, fierce men with broad faces, skin of seasoned leather. Several of them wore only a sleeveless vestment despite a chill in the air, their massive

129

arms sinewy with fearsome musculature. We could smell both men and horses as they moved close, an unsettling presence.

Tolui raised his hand to bring the horsemen to a halt as he addressed Wilfred.

"It is said that you are a bowman. Is that a true tale or a fairytale?"

When the Mongols had sent out the contingent of thirty to take us away from the slow-moving caravan and bring us to Karakorum at speed, they had confiscated Wilfred's longbow. They did not allow foreigners to move through their territory bearing arms. It had now been five years since Wilfred had last drawn. He nodded, as much a slight bow as a nod.

"I once drew a longbow, Captain Tolui. But as you know, I am not allowed that right here, as a foreigner. Nor have I ever drawn a Mongol bow. We English use a type of bow that would not serve well from the back of a horse as yours do."

Tolui nodded. He then turned abruptly to one of his men and barked an order in a dialect we did not understand. The man dismounted and approached Wilfred with a compound Mongol bow and quiver in hand.

"Show us, Brother Wilfred, if you have the power of arm and back to draw the bow of the Mongol horseman. Be forewarned. We know of no foreigner who can do so."

Wilfred smiled and shrugged as he took the weapon in hand. He chose a shaft and put it on the string, looking about for a suitable target. One of the hide sacks lay where the last rider had left it, perhaps fifty yards distant across a swale, directly against the stiff and swirling wind. He flexed the bow gently a time or two, extended his left arm, arched his back and drew in the English fashion with the bow vertical, drawpoint at the right corner of his mouth directly under his right eye. Despite Tolui's warning, the effort did not appear to tax him.

His technique startled the Mongol soldiers. We had observed that the mounted archers of the steppe drew to their chests with the bow held either horizontally or at an angle. Although they achieved good accuracy through long practice with this technique, it imposed handicaps. A shaft drawn to the chest instead of directly under the eye is harder to align with the target. A bow held at an angle casts the arrow at a similar angle, thus adding another variable for which the archer must allow, a variable that a perpendicular bow tends to eliminate if properly drawn and released.

In any case, the Mongols had barely begun to murmur their disapproval of Wilfred's methods when his first shaft flew crisply to within a few feet of the sack. Having registered the range and gauged the power of the bow, he placed the next six shafts squarely in the middle of the sack, drawing quickly and without apparent effort. The speed and stability of the shafts in flight showed the he was getting the most out of the weapon, as anyone skilled in archery could easily appreciate. After the last shaft hit the target, Wilfred nodded to Tolui, thanked him for the opportunity to test an excellent Mongol bow and handed the bow and quiver back to the soldier who had delivered them.

All of the Mongols maintained impassive visages, but it was clear that they had not expected to witness such an exhibition from a foreigner, particularly a foreigner not of the steppe. It occurred to me that they might now consider Wilfred dangerous and decide to rid themselves of him. One never knew with these people, although one knew only too well that they placed a low value on the lives of those not of their tribe.

Tolui's face was set in a frown.

"You could not shoot arrows thus from the back of a horse."

Wilfred neither argued nor agreed. "Why not? It is merely a matter of practice. I admit that you cannot hold a vertical bow in a position where the horse obstructs the lower limb, but you can shoot to either side quite well. Is that not where you shoot most of the time in battle?"

Tolui regarded him solemnly. "True enough. But why should our soldiers concern themselves with such a technique?"

Wilfred bowed in deference. "I would not be so insolent as to suggest that the conquerors of the entire world need alter anything that they do." He paused, regarding Tolui with a solemnity to match his own, unmarred by the slightest note of sarcasm. "But why not consider an alteration that could increase the accuracy of aim and effectiveness? In the tactics you pursue on the battlefield, you occasionally shoot from dismounted ranks, do you not?"

All knew that they had done so on many occasions, from ambush or in setpiece situations. Wilfred continued.

"You will find the English method more sure in its aim and less tiring,

131

more accurate with greater rapidity over a series of several volleys when the volleys are loosed by men on foot. As a result, your massed volleys will become more deadly. You need only try to prove the truth of it."

Tolui shook his head. "We have our traditions."

I trembled at Wilfred's rejoinder. "Do you prefer your traditions or do you prefer victory? Even I, a foreigner new to your country, have learned that the Mongols were a divided and impotent people, a little people, subjugated and reviled by most of the tribes from whom you exact tribute today, until Temuchin departed from the traditions of futility and adopted practices that brought you victory. Until he taught you new ways, the Naiman, the Keriyat, the Polovtsy, the Tanguts, many others, drove you off the best pasture lands and took your women for their amusement whenever they wished. Would you eschew his example or would you follow it? What say you? What would Temuchin himself have answered to such a query?"

"He would have struck off the head of any foreigner who propounded it."

Wilfred nodded, smiling. "Perhaps. But he would have tested the practice, as you well know, Captain Tolui of the Imperial Guard. And no stiff-necked prejudice would have prevented him from adopting it if he found it effective." Through all the tension of this exchange, there could be no doubt that Wilfred had struck a chord.

Tolui did not respond to Wilfred's last sally, delivered in a tone of complacent insolence that nearly set me trembling with fright. Instead, he sat his horse frowning, right hand slowly stroking his thin beard. After a moment, he ordered his men to dismount with their bows and quivers to begin the task of learning the English method of archery, as taught by Brother Wilfred Wilcoxen of Blackfriars' Abbey, Yorkshire.

As Tolui's unit proved the value of the technique, others sought Wilfred's guidance. So he became an instructor to the entire Imperial Guard and a teacher of other instructors who spread the method throughout the army. Our value to the Court thus rested on two foundations, rather than one. Judging solely from the increased comfort of our accommodations, the improved quality of the food vouchsafed to us and the slaves offered to assist us in the pleasures and chores of daily life, it seemed clear that the Mongol Court valued military skills more highly than the literary work in which we had been solely engaged previously.

So in this regard as well as others on which I have remarked, the Mongols seemed not so different from other nations, so-called civilized nations, that profess interest in affairs of the mind but give primary emphasis to the profession of arms.

*   *   *   *

Late one autumn afternoon — so late in fact that we had lighted torches to continue our work — Rashid ad-Khabar appeared at the door of our ger. He was alone and had come unannounced, despite his high station at Court. Normally, a Mongol functionary of the Court would travel with retainers and visit only those given time to prepare appropriately.

We had seen Rashid only from afar for many months. He had not answered the two messages that Wilfred had sent to him during our sojourn in Karakorum, when we felt the need of informed friendship. So his visit came as a surprise. He did not help himself under the circumstances by entering our ger like a long-lost brother, smiling broadly and greeting us with elaborate warmth in his ragged Latin.

"Ah, Wilfred and John. Greetings to you both. It is so good to see you as I have sorely missed you both since last we talked."

I made no move. Wilfred, who had been engaged in finishing details that required intense concentration, rose deliberately. With equal deliberation he wiped his right hand on his frock to dry the inkstains and extended it toward Rashid without smiling. He spoke in Uighur.

"Greetings, Rashid. What errand brings you to our humble quarters after nearly two full years?"

Rashid ignored any rebuff that Wilfred had implied in his cool greeting.

"I have missed our talks, Wilfred. I can already see — as I have heard from others — that your facility with the Uighur tongue has grown along with the artistry you display in rendering the script. I have missed the exchanges that we had on our long journey and I have missed learning from you. You have clearly flourished without having me as your teacher. I, in contrast, have suffered in my learning for lack of exposure to your tutelage."

Wilfred withheld the appropriate rejoinder that must have flashed in his mind as it did in mine. We had agreed, particularly after the incident with Tolui, that we would do our best to give as little offense as possible to anyone.

We invited Rashid to sit and we served him tea. We sat cross-legged on cushions thrown onto a hide rug in the fashion of Mongols below the aristocratic class. The conversation wandered over a host of subjects for a half hour or more as Rashid worked up to the topic that had brought him to us. For it was plain that he had something on his mind, even as he wandered over a host of other subjects. Something furtive about the eyes gave him away. After a pause to conclude idle chatter over the signs of an early winter, he got to the point.

"I hear that you have befriended one Captain Tolui of the Imperial Guard. Is that correct?" The question was disingenuous, as he clearly knew the fact. Wilfred did not attempt to deny or diminish it.

"I am honored to count Captain Tolui as a friend, yes."

Rashid answered immediately, leaning forward as he did so.

"Are you sure that you should be so honored?" He did not wait for a reply. "Indeed, I have heard that you have helped this Captain Tolui acquire warrior skills that have brought him great approbation within the Guard. Is that not also correct?"

Wilfred shrugged. "I know not of approbation. I have taught him and many others the benefits of certain techniques of the bow that are employed by the yeomanry of England, the land whence we have come, where the bow is widely used and much favored for many purposes. The Guard has found these techniques useful. They have found them to be an improvement over the techniques used commonly here, at least in certain types of battle situations."

He paused, as though lost in thought before continuing. "In fact, I did not offer the help on my own. Tolui had heard that I was a bowman and asked for my views on Mongol technique. My longbow was taken from me during the journey as you well know, so I have no idea how he found out about my familiarity with the weapon. I did nothing but answer his question and then give him a demonstration. All that followed grew from that slender beginning.

"Besides, is it not General Subedei himself who adopts the military techniques of others whenever they can improve the army? Is it not he who employs Persians and others to construct and operate mangonels for the reduction of fortifications? These are not Mongol weapons, but the Mongols use them. My modest techniques are similar, albeit much less important."

Rashid nodded. Wilfred's references to Subedei would not deflect him. "What do you know of this Captain Tolui?"

Wilfred seemed puzzled. "How would I know, Rashid? Since we arrived in this City, we have had no one to tell us anything." If Rashid felt a rebuke, he did not show it. "Captain Tolui claims to be of aristocratic birth. I assume that he speaks the truth, as he would have no purpose in lying to us. Aside from that, I know not."

Rashid arched his eyebrows slightly, a subtle gesture betraying disbelief. "Does it not seem odd to you that an aristocrat would command only a unit of ten?"

Again Wilfred shrugged. "How would we know what is odd and what is not, Rashid? If it is odd, tell us why so."

Rashid shifted position to recline, head propped in the palm of his hand, resting on his elbow. He seemed lost in thought, as though attempting to decide whether to believe Wilfred, whether to enlighten us; and if so, to what extent. I offered him more tea from the pot we kept going over the cooking fire in the center of our ger. He took two sips before replying.

"Your friend, Tolui, has been demoted from a higher command for insubordination. Only his birthright saved him from worse punishment. His father is a close adviser to Ugedei Khan."

"What act of insubordination did he commit?"

Again, Rashid paused as though reluctant to tell us more. When he spoke, he approached his subject elliptically. "You know that Ugedei Khan is not the oldest of Ghenghis' four sons, do you not?"

We did not. Indeed, I had never given the matter any thought and doubted that Wilfred had either. Rashid continued. "Ghenghis acknowledged four sons by his principal wife, Borte; Jochi, Chaghadai, Ugedei and Tolui, who is not your friend Captain Tolui, but another of the same name. Jochi was rejected for the succession due to doubts over his fatherhood. Merkid tribesmen kidnapped Borte shortly after her marriage to Ghenghis, then known as Temuchin. They raped her before Temuchin secured her freedom. Nine months thereafter, she bore Jochi whom Ghenghis always treated as a son, except in the matter of the succession, and who served him well. Jochi did not contest Ghenghis' judgment in this regard; and in any case, he died in the same year that the Great Khan rejoined the river of life.

"Chaghadai was considered unfit to be Emperor, so the succession fell to Ugedei who rules as Great Khan to this day." Rashid lowered his voice. He approached a sensitive area and did not wish to be overheard. Before continuing, he looked carefully around the ger to make sure that we were alone. Outside, the normal evening wind began to rise, eliciting creaks and groans from the poles and felt covering of our abode. Passersby, mounted and afoot, could be heard in the street outside as the City prepared for nightfall.

"So you see, with this history, the succession does not always flow to the eldest son. Issues of judgement and choice enter the picture."

Wilfred interrupted. Quietly, respecting Rashid's tone. "Why is this an issue? Is Ugedei Khan in poor health? We have heard nothing and know nothing."

Rashid's voice was barely audible when he replied. "There are those who see Ugedei as being in poor health and who conspire against his son, Guyuk." He searched our faces for clues that we knew of these things. He found nothing, as there was nothing to find.

But Wilfred's considerable curiosity had now been aroused. "Well, what is the truth of Ugedei's health?"

Rashid could not completely hide the sneer at the corners of his mouth as he replied. "The man debauches himself with drink, food and concubines. He sickens his brain with kumiss and the liquors and fermentations brought by embassies from those who seek to curry favor with him. They know his weakness and pander to it. He was once a great warrior, but he could not now sit a horse for half a day without collapsing the horse and reducing himself to the condition of an invalid."

"Well if that be the case, who rules?"

Rashid acknowledged the edge of perception behind Wilfred's question. A man in Ugedei's condition could only be a puppet for others.

"Functionaries run the Empire as they see fit. Fortunately, they were selected with care and perform their tasks competently." Presumably, Rashid included himself within this reference. "His primary wife, Torogene, runs Ugedei." Here again, Rashid looked furtively around the ger to make sure that he was not overheard, as though expecting to see a spy. Turning back to us, he leaned close before continuing in a voice barely above a whisper. "She does not work for the good of the Empire but only in her own interest."

"And what is that?" Wilfred asked, his question and demeanor innocent. Rashid stared at him hard, as though attempting to divine hidden mendacity where none existed.

"To assure that her son, Guyuk, becomes Great Khan upon Ugedei's death."

"Why does this require effort? If he is the eldest, who are the rivals that could possibly preempt his succession?"

We had now reached the point of Rashid's visit and the crossroads of his resolve. He had to decide whether he could trust us sufficiently to continue the discussion. The decision profoundly troubled him. His demeanor left no doubt of that. There must be sedition here, of some sort. Perhaps even treason. Who could say? Wilfred might have assisted by giving him assurances of secrecy, professions of friendship and the like. He kept silent, betraying nothing by his expression. Taking my cue from him, I did the same. Wilfred apparently felt that Rashid had forfeited whatever claim he might once have had to allegiance from us.

Rashid leaned ever closer, his voice remaining low as before. "Ugedei's brother, Tolui, has four sons; Mongke, Hulegu, Khubilai and Ariq Boke. All but the latter are more fit to rule than Guyuk who has all of his father's faults and none of the redeeming energy and intelligence he displayed before he pickled his brain with fermented drink, bloated his body with rich foods and spent his energy in a harem of slave girls."

He paused, as though trying to decide whether to continue. Neither Wilfred nor I said a word, although I could feel Wilfred's growing tension as I am sure he could feel mine. After a time, Rashid proceeded with his

137

tale as before, as though imparting great secrets. "I am in communication with people who believe that Mongke should be Great Khan. Indeed, some of them believe that Ugedei should be removed now, against his will if need be, to replace him with someone of competence and energy."

Wilfred shrugged. "What does this have to do with us? We know nothing of these things."

This time, Rashid did not hesitate. "Guyuk is the commander of the Imperial Guard *tumen*. Your Captain Tolui is his supporter. Your Captain Tolui murdered a superior officer during an argument after a battle with the Sung, an offense for which any man unconnected with a Prince of the Royal House would have been executed.

"Tolui was merely demoted. Guyuk protected him and he serves Guyuk, based on some bond the details of which remain between the two of them. Now, you have not only become Tolui's friend, but you have imparted to him secrets that improve the ability of the Imperial Guard and reflect great credit upon its leader for imagination and innovation. So you have become involved in the factions of the Mongol Court at the highest level, whether you intended to become so involved or not." And we had enhanced the effectiveness of the largest military unit in the capital, commanded by he who Rashid opposed. Oh yes. We had become involved, all right.

He paused, to add emphasis to his words. "Tell me, Wilfred, everything that Tolui has said to you."

So that was it. We were being interrogated by an emissary from a claimant to the throne in opposition to the claim of the direct descendant. Or perhaps not. Who knew if this Mongke really contested the right of Guyuk? Who knew the truth of anything that Rashid told us? Why should we believe him? And even if we did believe him, why should we become involved in this lofty controversy? God knew that we had no stake in the outcome. And as ignorant as we were, it would take a miracle to keep us from getting killed if a conflict erupted between the rival factions. But it would not do simply to rebuff Rashid. We had to assume that he could cause much trouble for us himself.

Apparently Wilfred saw all this clearly and in an instant. He shrugged as he replied, his expression totally devoid of artifice. "He told us nothing of any of this, Rashid. He asks us about England and Europe. He asks us about the land of the Rus, east of the Ural Mountains. He asks us about Christ and the differences between Roman beliefs and those of the Nestorians. He takes interest in our work and tells us little. No, Rashid. Tolui is a warrior who prepares for war. He has told me of his belief that the armies will move soon to east or west, and that sooner or later, a great force under the general Batu will invade Rus and then Europe. From what he has said, that is his focus and he eagerly awaits the day. He says nothing of any issue bearing upon Imperial succession."

Whether Rashid believed Wilfred or not, he spoke the truth. No pressure could elicit more from him as there was no more to elicit. Rashid left shortly thereafter.

As soon as he left, I attempted to strike up a conversation with Wilfred on the subject that Rashid had broached. Wilfred signalled me emphatically to keep quiet. A few moments later, he came close and whispered. "Do not talk of it, Johnnie. I believe that Rashid has left spies behind to listen to us, to see if we will disclose more or that we did not tell him the truth. These are big things, Johnnie. Big and dangerous. We must take great pains now to keep out of harm's way."

So we spoke of nothing but work as we continued the final detailing of a brilliant facing page well into the night.

*   *   *   *

"We've no choice, Johnnie. We have to pick a side." The whisper came to me out of the black dark. An hour after going to bed, we both lay awake. I had heard Wilfred's restlessness, quite unusual for him. Although he had not spoken, I assumed that Rashid's visit had agitated his thoughts to a degree that drove away sleep. I, too, had felt troubled, although I could not force my mind to bring the source of worry into focus, fatigued as I was by the concentrated effort of the day.

"I don't understand, Wilfred. Why must we choose? What are we choosing?"

"Rashid castigates us for helping Tolui and thus assisting Prince Guyuk. He would not have come unless we had in fact added weight to the scale in some fashion. Even if we wished to do it, we could not withdraw

139

what we have given. So we are committed, even though we know little of the side on which we have cast our lot."

"Well, if we have already chosen, albeit without knowing, why do more? Why not just do our work and lie as low as possible?"

I could almost hear Wilfred shake his head. "Too risky, Johnnie. Too risky. We have apparently stuck our unwitting noses into a battle for succession to the Imperial Throne where no one hesitates when it comes to murder. Unless we act decisively, both sides will see us as the enemy. There is no cost to eliminating us. We have small value. We must cling to the side to which we have given what little we have to offer. Meanwhile, we are in great danger."

I felt the cold hand of fear grip my gut, not for the first time during our sojourn in Karakorum. "What should we do, Wilfred?"

"I will seek out Tolui at dawn tomorrow. I am sure that Rashid has set spies to watch our movements. So I must figure a way to leave the ger unseen."

"To what purpose?"

"To tell him that Rashid ad-Khabar has asked us to report on our conversations with him and has disparaged his commander, Prince Guyuk. I will say that Rashid has asked us to become spies for him against the Imperial Guard, using our position of friendship with Tolui and my role as instructor in archery to the other units."

I could not remember such a request by Rashid and said so.

"Don't be a fool, Johnnie. Of course, he intends to ask us to play such a role. Indeed, I expect that he will threaten us with harm if we refuse. If I am wrong, it is a tale Tolui will wish to believe in any case. It is a tale that cannot be disproved, as it is my word and yours against Rashid's. It is a tale best calculated to secure Tolui's protection for us. Therefore, it is a tale I must carry — and as soon as possible."

At first light the next morning, I threw a robe over my head to hide my identity, stepped out the door of our ger and headed for the market. Wilfred lifted the felt sidewall and crawled out the back at the same moment, to slip away down a twisting side street toward the lodgings of the Guard. As I moved briskly away, I felt rather than saw a figure detach itself from the morning shadows and follow me at a distance. Although I mingled with the crowds until midmorning before returning to begin work, I never escaped my shadow; nor did I seriously attempt to be rid of him. For I was the decoy.

Either Rashid had set only a single spy to watch us or his spies missed Wilfred, for he told me that no figure emerged from the shadows to follow him as he went swiftly toward the Guard's encampment. As we leaned over our work that afternoon, he told me of his conversation with Tolui, heads close together so that no person could overhear us from outside the walls.

"I told him of Rashid's visit and that Rashid spoke ill of Prince Guyuk, stating that he lacked the merit to succeed as Great Khan and that succession should go to Prince Mongke. I told him that Rashid had asked us to become his spies against the Imperial Guard."

"What did he reply?"

"He said that we had obviously decided to refuse the request or I would not be there telling him of it. He asked what I had said to Rashid. He hoped that I had not refused Rashid to his face. Because now he wants us to agree to be spies against Rashid and the forces that would have Mongke succeed in place of Guyuk."

"Good God. We cannot escape this sticky quagmire. What did you say to him about that?"

"I asked what possible information we might obtain that could be of help. We have no connection with the forces that support Mongke. We don't even know who they are. Rashid will not confide in us or tell us anything useful, for he is far too cunning for that. We might be of use to him as spies on the Guard because we are working with the Guard, but we are not working with the Mongke forces. So I asked Tolui to forgive me, but we could best serve the Guard as we have done, but not as spies. After a time, he understood and agreed."

Wilfred laughed softly as he regarded me, eyes twinkling. "Then Tolui told me something quite amusing. Remember that he professed mere innocent curiosity when he first began talking to us and showing an interest in our work?"

I remembered. Wilfred continued, still smiling. "Well. It turns out that Prince Guyuk sent him to find out as much as possible about us, because we arrived with Rashid in our party and Prince Guyuk had already identified Rashid ad-Khabar as a pernicious meddler in Court affairs. So Rashid asked us to spy on Tolui, who came to us as a spy himself, and who now asks us to spy on Rashid, who Tolui and his patron see as a great spy in his own right." Wilfred paused, chuckling.

"And there is more irony here, for Guyuk does not think that his cousin, Prince Mongke himself, is aware of the efforts being made supposedly on his behalf. Guyuk's mother, Torogene, believes that enemies of Ugedei and Guyuk wish to bring them down and choose Mongke as their candidate because they must choose someone and Mongke is the most worthy, the most logical and the one believed most amenable to control by those who deem Ugedei and Guyuk unfit. But they have apparently neglected to inform Mongke himself."

Wilfred laughed quietly as he rehearsed the conversation in his mind. "Tolui says, after making me promise I would not repeat it, that the whole supposed rivalry could be the result of Torogene's inflamed determination to make sure that her son, Prince Guyuk, sits on the Throne. Being jealous, vindictive, bitter over Ugedei's preference for younger and more comely women, ambition for her son has become the driving force of her life. Thus, she may have created a controversy through false accusation to justify the measures she takes to defend Guyuk's position. Her attitude has led those who disapprove of Ugedei and Guyuk to assume that her views have substance and that Mongke truly contends for power. Tolui thinks that it may all be a cruel joke."

Wilfred's expression became more thoughtful. "But joke or not, Rashid is not likely to survive this. That much is clear."

Despite his earlier observations and his decision to go against Rashid, I could tell that Wilfred did not relish the thought of the fate that his report to Tolui had set in train for Rashid ad-Khabar, his teacher, pupil and travelling companion. Hidden motives aside, the two had learned much from each other and had formed a loose bond of friendship. The connection added a layer of discomfort to the situation. Yet, as much as Wilfred might regret Rashid's fate, he would not act to mitigate it at any risk to his own. Some things could not be prevented. He could live with that, and not look back.

As for me, I cared not at all what happened to Rashid, nor did it matter to me who became Great Khan. I wished to live and work in peace.

And if peace could not be had, I wished to live. Let others create their great causes. I would keep mine small.

*   *   *   *

Tolui ushered us into the great ger of Prince Guyuk. It was night, cold and dark, many stars, no moon. We entered the enclosed space filled with men arrayed in a semicircle. Two small fires burned brightly in circular stone fireplaces on either side of the door. Four torches in stands cast their uneven light over the gathering. The fires and torches filled the space with a thick pall of acrid smoke despite the open chimney flaps, lending an unreal aspect to the setting. The night air seemed to press downward, confining the smoke as though making it loath to leave the enclosed space. The men, the walls of the ger, the vaulting reaches of the supports adorned with battle flags, pennants and yaktail standards, could be seen, but as through a fog in the flickering light. The laden air constricted breath, inflamed the eye and stung the nose.

The semicircle of men sat crosslegged on cushions of silk arrayed on an opulent floorcovering of Persian design. All the men wore the blue tunics, leather vestment and inlaid helmet of the Imperial Guard. One man sat on a cushion in the center, higher than the others. Although dressed in the same uniform, he alone wore an embroidered insignia over his heart, a red compound bow and arrow, drawn as though ready, with simulated yaktail pennants hanging off the bottom limb of the bow. Prince Guyuk himself.

Trying hard not to do so, I studied him carefully. Despite his direct descent from Temuchin, the Great Khan Ghenghis, he looked no different than most of his compatriots. Short, heavyset with powerful arms, neck and shoulders, he had the flat face, high cheekbones, slit eyes and leathery complexion typical of the northern steppe nomad of these regions. But he seemed different from his fellows in one particular, a subtle distinction that one could sense but hardly pin down at first glance. Prince Guyuk seemed slack somehow, when compared with men such as Tolui and the others in the semicircle. One sensed that he had foresworn the rigors of the saddle for the soothing environment of the harem — and that perhaps the rumors of his weakness for strong drink held a kernel of truth. Despite the imposing setting over which he presided, one did not sense that here was a man preparing for an implacable struggle to secure his birthright.

Prince Guyuk had summoned us, according to Tolui, to express his gratitude for Wilfred's instruction of his troops and for our report on the effort of some at Court to preempt his ascent to the Throne. We soon found out that gratitude alone was not the order of the day. First, we were directed to pass between the two fires as a shaman observed us, all the while waving the burned shoulderblade of a sheep over our heads. We were then ordered to advance and prostrate ourselves before the Prince and make obeisance to him and a carved wooden symbol intended to represent the God Tengri. Finally, we were compelled to drink the blood of a sacrificed animal from a pounded bronze goblet to seal our oath of allegiance. The goblet was adorned with the signs of the Zodiac and the likenesses of various pagan gods odious to contemplate, with hideous features and enormous genitals.

These rituals, of course, constituted profound blasphemy against the teachings of Christ and all profession of Christianity. It is said that when the General Batu demanded similar submissions from Duke Michael of Vladimir after the conquest of Kievan Rus, Michael refused to profane himself and his adherence to Christ. He stated that he would submit to Batu the man and the Empire he represented but would not signify his submission by acts inimical to his Christian faith. Batu thereupon put him to death without further ado, as he did all others who refused to submit in the fashion that he dictated.

We had heard of these practices, as we had heard that Batu and Prince Guyuk were close personal friends and allies, as well as cousins, Batu being Jochi's son. We did not seek martyrdom as others had sought it through conscious choice, blind faith or complacent disbelief. Wilfred and I had agreed long ago that we would do better to serve Christ in life. So despite the form of the acts required of us, we chose to view them strictly in a temporal context and performed them with sincerity — a pledge of loyalty to the person of the Prince. We had already made that choice when we reported Rashid's overture to Tolui.

After completing the acts of submission, Tolui summoned us to sit facing Guyuk on two cushions provided for that purpose. We did as ordered. After a few moments, the Prince began speaking to us in a low guttural voice, as the smoke swirled in the ger and his retainers sat stern and expressionless on either side.

"You are men of learning, so I am told. You are skilled in the crafts of books and scrolls. And you," indicating Wilfred with a casual gesture "are a man skilled in the arts of war. We are not accustomed to men of learning who are skilled in warriors' arts as well. How come you by these skills?" Wilfred looked the Prince in the eye as he responded. Before we had come in response to the summons, he had exhorted me to show deference but no fear. "I learned archery when I was but a lad of eight summers. My book learning and skills of illumination I learned later under the tutelage of experts in a monastery."

Guyuk knew of monasteries, as he had seen those of both the Buddhists and the Nestorians in his campaigns. He had participated in the destruction of centers of Islamic study. he looked hard at Wilfred, as though doubting him.

"We accept men of all beliefs within the Empire. A man's beliefs are his own concern. So any man can be a man of any god and it is neither here nor there. But you do not seem like the typical man of god to me. You did not shrink from our ritual as others of your faith have done." He paused, his face opaque as before. "Have you seen war? Have you seen the spilling of human blood?"

Wilfred did not hesitate. "I have killed, your Highness. I split the head of a man who gave me offense and I have stood with ranks of bowmen in battle." Small, peevish skirmishes by the standards of this company, hardly worth mentioning. Wilfred kept his voice calm, without bravado. "We do not shrink from your ritual because we are your guests. We have pledged our allegiance to you and would not pretend to claim superiority for our ways over yours by refusing your dictates in favor of those with which we are more familiar."

"In what wars have you fought?"

Wilfred smiled. "Wars between noblemen on the island whence we come, an island called England. It lies far, far to the west of here. Even far to the west of the most westerly lands of the Empire, west of the land of the Rus into which Prince Batu and General Subedei have conducted raids."

145

Guyuk shook his head. "I have heard of no such island. I have heard only of an island nation that lies to the east. A land variously called Nippon and Edo, with many warriors called Samurai. Are you Samurai? I have never seen or met one who calls himself by that name."

Wilfred shook his head. "No, Your Highness. Indeed, I have never heard that term before, nor have I heard of Nippon or Edo."

Prince Guyuk nodded gravely. Then he inclined his head toward me, while addressing Wilfred. "And what of that one?"

"He came to the monastery as an orphan. We took him in. He serves as my apprentice."

"Why have you come to Karakorum?" Guyuk asked.

"We came with the emissaries from the Holy Father in Rome to the Great Khan Ugedei, Your Highness. We were simply members of the party to serve and protect them. When they died, we would have returned, except that the Chancellor asked us to employ our skill assisting in the work of collecting, preserving and enhancing the literature of the conquered peoples. We have now been engaged in that project under the Chancellor's patronage for six summers."

Guyuk's expression remained impenetrable. If he had an opinion of the Chancellor's project, he kept it to himself.

It was at this point that Wilfred presented the Prince with our tribute to him, an illustrated scroll of Persian poetry by the classicist and mystic, Rumi. Wilfred had selected the piece and we had done the scroll together, necessarily in some degree of haste as we had little advance notice of the audience. The product did not measure up to the standards expected of us by the Chancellor, but we had nothing else to give, as the Prince no doubt knew.

I confess that my mind wandered as Wilfred answered the Prince's questions about the work, the author, the choices we had made for the characters and setting of the illumination. The smoke-filled air assaulted my nose, my eyes, my lungs. It made me drowsy, longing for sleep. My head ached. It seemed that the evening would never end, and yet it behooved me to act attentive, deferential, honored at being admitted to the august presence. I could only assume that some in the Prince's party studied our aspect, our every gesture, in an effort to detect any hint of insolence or disrespect.

Wilfred had answered the Prince's last question on the subject of the poet Rumi. The Prince paused, and then extended his right arm in Wilfred's direction, palm up, a common gesture by a Mongol to accompany a statement of importance.

"I thank you for your thoughtfulness. I know that it required you to take time from your assigned tasks and that you are our guests in Karakorum without independent resources." He nodded to both of us, his face wearing an expression that I took for a smile, albeit fleeting and meager, devoid of personal feeling. He continued. "I also owe you a debt of gratitude for your instruction to the men of my *tumen* in the methods of English archers. Although I believe that our methods are superior for most of the situations we face, the English method will serve us well in certain tactical settings and will add versatility to our superiority over our enemies."

He nodded again. His expression this time projected more content. Without looking at him, he held out his hand to the implacable, brooding officer sitting to his right in a posture that appeared rounded and Buddha-like in the fetid air and uneven light. The officer handed the Prince a small sack made of animal skin. The Prince leaned forward and tossed the sack so that it fell at Wilfred's feet, the clinking of coins within betraying the contents. Ten talents of silver. A bloody fortune, in our circumstances. With a subtle wave of his hand, the Prince indicated that Wilfred should take the sack. As he did so, the Prince said:

"The contents of that sack do not adequately reward you for the value you have given in the matter of archery and the matter of the Persian meddler, Rashid ad-Khabar. My grandfather built this Empire on the principal of just rewards and I would reward you justly. What more do you desire of me? Horses? Slave girls? Better quarters? Speak. Although I may not agree to all you ask, I would give you more — and of what you truly wish."

Wilfred looked the Prince in the eye and then bowed deferentially. A simple gesture that nonetheless conveyed gratitude and profound respect. I took his cue and emulated him. When he had completed his bow, he spoke. Preoccupied as I was by my discomfort, the effort to disguise it behind a facade of feigned interest, fatigue and the desire to be elsewhere, Wilfred's response struck like a thunderbolt from a cloudless sky. Indeed, my ears so rejected the significance of the words they heard that it took several moments truly to comprehend them.

"All that you offer has great value, Your Highness. I am overwhelmed with gratitude for your recognition of our modest acts as mere humble servants of the Empire. But my one great wish is to ride with the Imperial Guard when you next go to war. I realize that Brother John and I are unready to ride with your men at this time. We lack the stamina and the skill with horses that your men possess. Those skills can be acquired with training and practice. We can never be as good, of course, as men who have been born and bred to the saddle and your ways for their entire lifetimes; but I am confident that we can become proficient enough to be useful."

Plainly the Prince had not expected this answer, although it did not startle him by half as much as it startled me. Wilfred had never mentioned to me any yearning on his part to ride with the Mongol warriors on their next campaign. I had never even considered the prospect for myself. And yet, he had just volunteered the enlistment of both of us under circumstances that made the offer irrevocable. I held my breath awaiting the Prince's reply, praying that he would reject us. My prayers fell on deaf ears.

The Prince consulted none of his officers. He thought for a moment and then nodded. "I will assign Captain Tolui to train you. You will be included in the winter exercises and we will consider the matter again in the spring. If you meet the standards we expect of our men, we will include you gladly among our number. You have proved the worth of your spirits by your acts that demonstrate both competence and loyalty. You have shown great character by travelling from lands so far away to live among us while serving the Empire. Other foreigners who have done such things generally have done them to buy their lives. You, in contrast, do not perform for us under duress or as ransom, but rather by choice. You have earned the chance you seek. I will make the arrangements with the office of the Chancellor so that the time you spend in training will not be considered a shirking of your duties to him."

I was devastated. Despite the intrigues of Court, my life had become settled again in Karakorum. Stability and security, those conditions I most cherished in all the world, had been restored, at least in precarious fashion, to their rightful places at the center of my existence. I had work, shelter and food in a place free from war and unrest. This place was foreign to me in every dimension to be sure, but it was a place to which I had grown accustomed — a place that restored in me the sense of hope that Wilfred had shattered at that moment in the Papal See when he had volunteered for the Holy Father's embassy to the Court of Prester John. In that moment, he had rendered all of the solid foundations of my existence into a turbulent fluid, opaque, full of threat and foreboding.

And now, he had done it again, in even more dramatic fashion than before. I could not draw breath. The atmosphere in the ger was bad enough on its own, under the most tranquil of circumstances. But there was no tranquillity left as there seemed to be no oxygen remaining in the freighted air. My system reeled in physical shock at the implications of Wilfred's request and the Prince's acceptance.

After what seemed an eternity, we were excused to walk back to our ger. We walked in silence through the empty streets, not knowing who might be watching or who might be able to overhear through the walls of yurts and gers along our way. My fury and resentment rose with each step.

As we entered our ger and the doorflap fell shut behind us, I grabbed Wilfred by the arm and spun him around to face me in the black dark. Never before in all of our time together had I ever laid hand on him in that fashion. The gesture startled us both, but it did not deflect me from my purpose. I fairly hissed at him.

"How dare you volunteer me for military service in the ranks of these heathen barbarians. Have you totally lost your mind?"

He responded in a whisper, calm but contrite. "It is merely what I wish, Johnnie. Nothing binds you to it. You are right. I should not have volunteered you without your consent. I will speak to Tolui of your wish not to be included, first thing in the morning."

So he would go on without me. My anger and resolve collapsed, like a yurt with the support poles removed. Once again, I faced both my dependence upon him and the fact that he did not feel the tug of any obligation by reason of it. Oh, he would include me as a wayfarer in his ceremony of restlessness. But he would make no concession to my need for stability or settled circumstances. Once again, I felt injured and helpless. Even though I suspected that I might be able to go on in service to the

Mongol Court without him, I lacked the courage to risk it. In a sense, that made things even worse.

Wilfred lit a torch, placed it in a holder and signalled to me to sit. He came and sat close to me so that we could talk quietly. He began in a voice barely above a whisper.

"If God places us on earth for a purpose, then surely He intends that we seize the opportunities that the circumstances present."

"Of whose God do we speak, Wilfred? Christ? Forgive me, but I have always understood Christianity — and certainly the teachings of Francis of Assisi — to mean that one follows the way and forswears all earthly opportunity that does not strictly conform to the way." He continued, ignoring my point.

"We sit now at the center of the most powerful Empire that has ever existed among mankind. We have been given an opportunity to participate in the flow of that power, to become part of it, to see it in action, to feel it at first hand. This is an opportunity that has come to none of our country, no man of Rome, indeed no man or men of Europe. I must try it. My spirit will not allow me to do otherwise."

"Ah. So we speak no more of God, but of your spirit. Has it ever crossed your mind that perhaps you have become possessed by the Prince of Darkness?" I crossed myself quickly, praying silently for Our Lord's forgiveness of my sarcasm.

Wilfred shrugged. "Perhaps. It matters not. Whether of God or of the Devil, I cannot resist these compulsions. That much I know."

One cannot dispute with one who refuses the contest. Indeed, one can best sustain a position by offering no argument in support of it, offering no opposition to arguments opposing it. Take the position and stand on it, meeting all sallies with a shrug, a smile and silence. That was Wilfred's way in this instance as in others. It left me nothing but a sense of loss, bitter frustration, dread of an unknown future. I could not leave the matter at that.

"Isn't it enough for you to be working at the center of this great Empire, directly under the Chancellor himself? Is that not a unique enough experience? And what of our work? We are actually getting good at it, Wilfred. You can see that. Our pieces will live long after we have passed from this earth and leave a fitting spiritual legacy for those who follow after. You would forsake all that to participate in brutal wars of conquest that have no object other than plunder and subjugation for their own sakes? Please. Why, in God's name?"

I had nothing to lose. I hit him with the heaviest bludgeon that came to hand. "You must explain this to me, Wilfred. For I am the only son that you have ever had, your only true and loyal brother and the constant companion of your life for all these years. You owe me the truth."

He did not shrink from it. "I agree with all you say, Johnnie. Our position here will become more secure by the day, if Guyuk becomes Khan. If Mongke's forces overcome Guyuk, then we will be in trouble. But we were in trouble already on that score. I could give you an argument that riding with the Mongol army gives us our best chance to return home some day; but I'm not sure that is correct, nor am I sure that we have any reason to return. I certainly do not. You have no family or other ties there. Blackfriars meant more to you than it ever did to me, so perhaps you yearn to go back. If so, you have never made mention of it."

He paused, lay back and rubbed his face hard with his left hand as though attempting to clear away dust or a spider's web. "No. The real reason is the one I first gave you. A force of great unease drives me. I cannot allow this challenge to go by unanswered." He sat up, slowly rose and went to the pile of mixed parchment and paper upon which he had been working for the last several days. Searching through the sheets, he found what he was seeking and returned to sit facing me, crosslegged, with the sheets on his lap. The torchlight gave a stark cast to his features, exaggerating its points, its promontories, its depressions. Flickering shadows played over his visage, giving it a dark aspect as though from another world. He began reading from the script, voice halting as though wrestling with the translation, but choked with emotion as well.

"`There is one thing in this world that you must never forget to do. Should you forget everything else and not this, there's nothing to worry about, but if you remember all else and forget this, then you will have done nothing in your life.'

"'It's as if a king has sent you to some country to do a task, and you perform a hundred other services, but not the one he sent you to do. So human beings come to this world to do particular work. That work is the purpose, and each is specific to the person. If you don't do it, it's as though a priceless Indian sword were used to slice rotten meat. It's a golden bowl being used to cook turnips, when one filing from the bowl could buy a hundred suitable pots. It's a knife of the finest tempering nailed into a wall to hang things on.'"

He paused to look at me, to gauge my attentiveness perhaps. I recognized the text. More of Salaludin Rumi, contemporary poet and sage of Persia, born in Balck, the City of Zoroaster — he left before the Mongols destroyed it. A Sufi Moslem, his teachings transcended the dogma of Moslem, Hebrew and Christian thought, often invoking Abraham, Jacob, Moses and Jesus as well as the Prophet. It was rumored that he had even met and carried on discourse with Francis of Assisi at some point during the latter's travels in the Holy Land. I signalled for Wilfred to continue.

"'You say: But look, I'm using the dagger. It's not lying idle. Do you hear how ludicrous that sounds? For a penny, an iron nail could be bought to serve the purpose. You say: But I spend my energies on lofty enterprises. I study jurisprudence and philosophy and logic and astronomy and medicine and much more. But consider why you do these things. They are all branches of yourself.'

"'Remember the deep root of your being, the presence of your lord. Give your life to the one who already owns your breath and your moments. If you don't, you will be exactly like the man who takes a precious dagger and hammers it into his kitchen wall for a peg to hold his dipper gourd. You'll be wasting valuable keenness and foolishly ignoring your dignity and purpose.'"

He lifted his eyes again to engage mine, the torch highlighting the craggy topography of his face once again. I nodded.

"So your dignity and purpose require that you do this thing."

"Yes."

"When did this revelation come to you? During our compilations of Rumi's work?" Within the past six months, we had been given mangled fragments from that source that had been rescued from some plundering cavalryman and asked to compile, copy and illustrate them.

He paused before replying. "I have long felt it. Rumi's words crystallized for me thoughts that I could not articulate myself. He has explained my unease."

152

Anger and resentment welled within me once more, another echo of my dependency on him in all of his inconstancy. "Wilfred. Less than a year ago, you were taken with the thought of the Gautama Buddha. You espoused the belief that the highest goal of human endeavor should be the suppression of all worldly desire and ambition and the quest for an immobile, passive union with the vast, serene void of nothingness. You eagerly sought instruction at the feet of any derelict and crazed bodhisatva that we encountered.

"And now you choose instead to direct your fate — and mine, by the way — in accordance with the teachings of a man who believes in passion and the energetic fulfillment of worldly purpose as ordained by God. A man who writes glowingly of love and bread and wine and drunkenness, preaching intense emotional attachments and involvements, quests and pilgrimages. Pray God, please tell me. What do you believe? The teachings of the Buddha or those of Rumi? Who is your true seer?"

He regarded me without expression, without flinching, the light seeming to deepen the caverns where his eyes resided. "Both," he replied, his voice firm, full of conviction.

"Impossible. They are opposites."

He nodded and shrugged. "Nonetheless. Both. My mind and heart encompass both teachings simultaneously. Although opposites, I find them not in conflict. If the universe itself is filled with ambiguity, contradiction and mystery, why must belief be devoid of such?"

He paused then, as though feeling the import of what he had said, as though suddenly aware of the impact of his complex nature on me. To my surprise, tears rolled down his cheeks and he struggled a little to speak clearly. "As for the rest of it, you are right. You are son and brother to me, the only family I have in all the world. I would prefer never to do you harm, cause you worry or discomfort. I seek to protect you in all my thoughts and deeds. But I must do this thing or I will wither and die. Of that I have no doubt."

We embraced then, holding each other tight for several long moments. His tears mingled with my own. I felt his heart beating hard within him, his beard rough on my cheeks. And the thing would be done. Once again, I could only follow, for I lacked the courage to stand alone.

Thus it was that Brother Wilfred Wilcoxen of Blackfriars' Abbey,

Yorkshire, became a member of the Imperial Guard of the Mongol army, directly under the command of the man who would soon become Great Khan; and I, John Wheelwright, became a camp follower when it became clear that I could never acquire the skill and stamina to ride with Mongol warriors.

As the ancient Romans were fond of saying: "Fate leads those who will; those who won't, it drags."

CHAPTER THIRTEEN

My puny efforts to become a soldier exposed me to many details of life in the Mongol army.

In camp, the soldier wears a fur cap with ear flaps, felt stockings, boots and a vestment that reaches below the knees. For battle, he dons a leather helmet covering the nape of his neck that may be reinforced with metal ribbing on top, and a strong, flexible cuirass made of strips and layers of leather, lacquered black. Try as I might, I could never feel comfortable so attired. The protective garments encumbered me, inhibiting my movements.

I had even more difficulty with the weapons. The Mongol soldier generally carried two bows, two quivers, a curved saber, a hatchet, an iron mace suspended from his saddle, a lance furnished with a hook for unseating enemy horsemen and a horsehair rope with a running noose. Despite months of trying, I never became proficient with any of them. Indeed, I never developed the strength even to draw a Mongol bow to its full extent. The arrows I loosed at partial draw fluttered wildly, a greater threat to my companions than they ever would have been to an enemy. In contrast, Wilfred took to all the weapons as though he had been born to them, a fact that depressed me even as I admired his natural skill.

During the months in camp, Tolui painstakingly explained to us the tactics used by the Mongol hordes so successfully. Ghenghis Khan expounded the primary doctrine upon which all else was based. "In daylight, watch with the vigilance of the old wolf, at night with the eyes of the raven. In battle, fall upon the enemy like a falcon."

Patient stalking of herds of deer had taught the Mongols the skills and uses of invisible scouts. Winter hunting drives had taught coordination and encirclement. Through mobility and organization expounded by the Great Khan, they achieved surprise and the sense that they were everywhere.

155

Their light cavalry would attack the enemy and then retreat. If the enemy pursued, they would be led into a trap, attacked by heavy cavalry from all sides. Tolui drew diagrams of such encounters with a stick in dusty ground, reciting the names of victorious battles where the tactics had been employed. He told us that throughout each battle, the Mongols assailed their enemies with showers of arrows to weaken and demoralize them from a distance.

The Mongols made full use of the terror inspired by their forbidding aspect, their sudden and unexpected appearance and even their stench. They worked hard to achieve surprise, using their scouting ability to find the unexpected way — as at Bukhara where they appeared out of desert wastes considered impassable. They appeared as if out of thin air, deployed and took up widespread formations deliberately calculated to make them appear more numerous than they were.

Against an enemy in the field, they advanced at jog-trot in an awe-inspiring silence, maneuvering without shouts or commands but on signal from standard bearers. When they charged, they did so with hellish yells under a hail of arrows. Time and again, we practiced these maneuvers under the stern and watchful eye of unit commanders who were veterans of many bloody battles and who tolerated no slackness or deviation.

All of these practices applied to encounters on open ground. When faced with fortifications or walled cities, the Mongols used catapults and, in some cases, mortars that fired missiles using the Chin invention of explosive powder.

Tolui told us that the Mongols avoided hand-to-hand combat whenever possible, as the Great Khan had ordained. They did not fear it. They regarded it as inefficient when compared with the havoc that could be wrought by well-directed volleys of arrows and tactics that broke up enemy formations without frontal assault. But when a citadel could be taken only by storm, storm it they would, with murderous enthusiasm. And woe betide the defenders. For once a city or fortress refused the Mongol's demand for surrender without resistance, all the defenders were put to the sword, or worse, in almost every case. Those who attempted to surrender during the heat of a losing battle, or when the outcome became clear, usually suffered grievous and vexatious tortures before the respite of death was visited upon them.

As Tolui explained, the Mongols succeeded because their tactics and training were superior to those of their opposition, not because they were intrinsically superior as fighting men to all those that they encountered. European and Persian knights went to battle in suits of armor weighing up to one hundred pounds. They needed large, ungainly horses to carry that load, further burdening theie wretched animals with armor of their own. Horses and men so encumbered could not match the quickness or stamina of the Mongol cavalry.

With battle joined, the European or Persian knight sought a hand to hand engagement with a member of the enemy force and expected to win by the cumulative weight of victories in individual engagements. The Europeans, Persians and Turks did not train their yeomanry to maneuver or fight as a unit, relying instead upon innate skills with bow or pike. Thus it was that the Mongols confronted and decimated armies that outnumbered them, armies that could stoutly defend a prepared position, so long as they were not taken by surprise, but could not win a battle where success required movement on offense or defense.

The genius of Ghenghis Khan created this tactical advantage. He first united the Mongols themselves through bargaining, strategic alliance or force; and then he led the united tribe in victorious battles with other nomadic tribes so that in the end, the federated tribes of the Mongol Empire included Keriyat, Kira Khitai, Naiman, Uighur and many others. When the Mongols undertook a campaign to the east or west, they fielded armies as large as one hundred-fifty thousand fighting men.

Having created the alliance, the Great Khan cemented it in many ways, two being primary. He won victories, and he divided the spoils generously. Thus, the Empire purchased loyalty and the ability to command adherence to Imperial edict; and thus it was that at the time of his death in August of 1227, the Empire of Ghenghis Khan exceeded in size the empire of Alexander the Great at its highwater mark of conquest and the empire of the Romans at the apogee of its power.

*   *   *   *

As the army of Batu Khan prepared for its great western thrust even before the great quiriltai, the war council of 1235, the units intensified their training. These exercises culminated in a massive drive in the form of a hunt, conducted in the dead of winter. Part of centuries old tradition, the exercise required great discipline, stamina and coordination of a large force over great distances.

To begin, a line of horsemen was formed over a distance of as much as eighty miles, spaced five yards apart. The line began its advance at a signal, walking slowly toward a prearranged objective, a bluff at the end of a small valley, entered by means of a narrow defile. The end-point lay one hundred miles distant from the start-line. The advance did not begin until a blocking party had established itself in ambush at the end-point.

As the horsemen advanced, they drove all living things before them, deer, wolves, wild boar. Terminal disgrace befell any rider who allowed any creature to escape through the line. Thus, each was required to stay always in alignment with the others. Each must maintain the proper spacing. Each was required to coordinate with his fellows to thwart any effort by a trapped creature to escape.

The flanks of the line extended forward as the drive continued, each flank coordinated with the other, despite the length of the line, through the use of couriers, flag and smoke signals. The extending flanks drew the adjacent riders forward so that the advance, in time, came to resemble a vast semi-circle. As it approached the end-point, the center held place, the flanks constricted, entrapping all of the driven game in an ever-shrinking circle, using the chosen ground as an aid in defining the killing field. At the end, the men rode shoulder to shoulder along the shrinking perimeter. As the perimeter shrank still further, the riders formed two ranks, one behind the other at a signal.

The killing began when the drivers blocked the defile with the flanks of the driving line atop the hills that defined the valley. First the Khan himself and then his senior generals entered the circle to claim the most notable trophy. Then various warriors entered, sometimes to fight their chosen prey with nothing more than a dagger. In due course, the most senior of the warriors and the youngest would plead with the Khan for the lives of prey that remained alive within the circle and they were allowed to escape.

My brief description can hardly do justice to this exercise. For that, the reader must imagine that it is conducted during the harshest of winter conditions, when temperatures as low as thirty degrees of frost prevail. At a pace of no more than forty miles per day, the drive took at least two full days to complete. Proper deployment required several days more. All took place outdoors, without shelter other then small gers placed on carts. Maintaining the integrity of the line required that forward motion never stop, that proper pacing and spacing never be lost. Coordination of the flanks to close the circle at the preordained place required communication of a complexity unknown anywhere else in the world. The Mongols performed this exercise routinely. It formed part of their normal life as well as their preparations for war. With regular training of this sort, it was easy to see why they easily outmaneuvered the undisciplined rabble Western nations call their armies.

I myself participated in two such drives after Wilfred volunteered us to serve in the Mongol army. I particularly remember the second, as it nearly ended my life, despite several weeks of training in preparation for it. For two days and nights we moved over frozen ground, the second day in a fierce blizzard that made it impossible to see more than a few feet in any direction. The blizzard broke as we arrived at our destination.

I recall fresh snow to a depth of perhaps two feet with greater depth in the swales. The valley held no trees at all. Despite their steep faces, the hills enclosing the valley had gently rounded and sloping escarpments, poorly defined against a grey sky. I remember an indistinct and irregular horizon, suddenly emphasized by a line of black as horsemen crested the rise, closing the trap on the animals we drove before us, waving their yak-tail battle standards to exaggerate their size. The killing that quickly ensued turned the fresh snow of the valley into a trampled mosaic of blood and corpses.

In due course, I was called upon to enter the circle to kill a stag of moderate size. I performed miserably, wounding him with an awkward lance thrust that simply added to his already considerable frenzy. He charged me with antlers down, ready to inflict grievous wounds. A man known as Iglaqti from Wilfred's squad in the Guard spared me serious embarrassment by sending an arrow into the stag's neck.

I will not bother to describe the scene in greater detail as it does not further this account; but I trust that the reader can comprehend the setting and understand its implications. The hardiness, the organization and the primeval barbarity of these people placed them so far outside the norm of European behavior as to be almost beyond imagination. To this day, I cannot recall the hardship of those winter drives without shuddering in dismay. The Mongols, in contrast, enjoyed them, treating them like a protracted carnival. They revelled in the comraderie, cooperated with each other to maintain the integrity of the drive and then competed joyously in the killing at the end — all after riding for two days and nights without sleep in brutal winter conditions.

I soon discovered at first hand the purpose of these drives. They truly prepared the troops for war. For we were about to go to war, an advance of thousands of miles, almost continuously on the move, living the life of nomads as they have lived it since before time began.

And I, John Wheelwright, lover of stability, quiet and a settled life, could not but participate in it to the full.

CHAPTER FOURTEEN

Tolui seemed quite excited, particularly for one normally taciturn. "So there will soon be a new campaign. The messengers to marshall the tribes leave tonight. I have been told that the Guard will participate and we should be ready to leave Karakorum within a month."

Wilfred nodded. We sat facing each other on the floor of our ger, late on a July afternoon. The year was 1235.

I recall that the day was quite hot. A fierce sun pounded down out of a cloudless sky, as it often did during the summer months at Karakorum. We had rolled up the sides of our ger to benefit from the breeze, although it felt like the breath of an oven and was laden with dust. These handicaps were the lesser of evils when compared with the sweltering, airless tomb the ger quickly became when closed. The distant ridges that showed above the low city skyline shimmered in the heat, their cloak of grass gone tawny for lack of rain.

When Tolui did not offer any additional information, Wilfred gave vent to the curiosity that we both felt.

"What is this campaign, Tolui?"

"West. The land of Rus and beyond. We go to the limit of the steppe, and further, if rich prizes appear on the horizon."

An attack on Europe. So finally the dread promise of Subedei's raid would be redeemed. We had learned that in 1223, the great general had terrorized the eastern marches of Kievan Rus, destroying a mixed army of Russians and Turkish tribesmen at the Battle of Kalka. With all Rus in a mortal panic, he and his men had ridden away to the east, vanishing in the manner of their arrival, without rhyme or reason, without warning or omen, leaving behind only sick dread at the prospect of their return.

161

It took a moment for me to grasp the magnitude of Tolui's statement. The limits of this planned foray lay perhaps five thousand miles from where we sat. Wilfred also seemed taken aback.

"How many shall we be, Tolui?" he asked.

"Perhaps 200,000 horsemen and 50,000 thousand camp followers. There will be herds of spare horses to ride, sheep, goats and cattle to sustain the movement."

Wilfred paused a moment in thought.

"How shall we be supplied?"

"Bullock drawn carts will carry supplies and drag seige engines. We shall have our animals and, of course, the land."

"How shall we traverse the rivers and deserts and mountains along the way?"

Tolui shrugged and smiled indulgently, as though we were but children. "As we always have. The Chosen quail before no earthly obstacle, Wilfred. You shall see." I thought back on the lands through which we had passed on our way east. The enterprise seemed impossible to me.

Wilfred looked hard at Tolui. "How much time do you estimate will be required to complete such a campaign? After all, you speak of lands more than five thousand miles distant."

Tolui shrugged, holding his hands out to the side, palms up. "I make no estimate." He paused. "But General Subedei states that we should plan for an effort that will require as much as eighteen years to complete."

Eighteen years. So we stood once again at a crossroads. We could not truly expect to return to Karakorum after participating in such an exercise, even if we survived the ordeal. What of our work? Would the Chancellor consent to our going with the army when he had just delivered to us material that would require at least a year to copy? Did we really wish to become part of an army that would scourge Christian nations? Were we ready to live the lives of marauding nomads? My mind raced, filled with conflicting thoughts.

Apparently Wilfred's head teemed with questions as well.

"Tell me, Tolui, how all this comes about. I would know as many details as you can provide."

162

Tolui nodded and smiled. "You have cast your lot with us and you are entitled to know. You have heard of Batu?"

We had heard. Inheritor of the so-called Western Khanate, known as the Golden Horde. Son of Jochi.

Tolui continued.

"Batu believes that the Rus gain in strength, thus posing a risk to him and the domains entrusted to him. He also believes that their gains reflect an accretion of wealth that we should enjoy. He argues that they will pose a risk to our flank when we move against the Persians and Turks, against Baghdad and Damascus, as we inevitably must some day. So he proposed a plan to emasculate them, to subjugate them and exact tribute from them, adding their lands to his Khanate. The army will share in the rich plunder of their cities, the favors of their women and their young people whom we will take as slaves."

He paused, smiling at the thought of the plunder, both animate and inanimate. His benign expression starkly contrasted with the import of his quiet words. Wilfred had more questions.

"But Batu cannot command the armies of the entire realm. Did the Great Khan consent to this plan?"

Tolui nodded. "As you know, a quiriltai is in progress here. All of the chiefs have assembled to confer with the Great Khan. Subedei himself, venerable as he may be, has endorsed Batu's campaign. He will lead the army." I was startled at that. I had seen General Subedei from a distance on more than one occasion and I knew of his history. He had to be at least sixty years old. Yet here he was, proposing to lead the army on a campaign he projected would last eighteen years.

Tolui smiled again and shook his head in wonder. "At the conclusion of the discussions, Ugedei Khan became so enthusiastic that he proposed to lead the army himself. He embraced Subedei as a brother in arms with whom he would go to war once again. Only the Chancellor's intervention dissuaded him." Yeh Lu Chu Tsai had apparently convinced Ugedei that he was needed at the center of administration, thus sparing the army the burden of supporting his suite on the march and the legions of concubines who serviced his appetites, reputedly in relays of six per night.

Wilfred had one more question — the most important one. "So we are expected to ride with the Guard. Is that correct?"

"Yes."

"And we leave within a month?"

"Yes."

"What arrangements are required of us for horses and transport?"

"I have made all the arrangements. You will have twenty good mounts, a cart and two bullocks."

That statement took Wilfred totally by surprise. He knew enough of the local custom to know that a soldier supplied his own mounts. We would have had to spend the few talents of silver that we had hoarded to obtain ours. Tolui noted his surprise.

"You are included in this at my urging. You have no ready means of obtaining what you need. I have more than enough and am honored to share with a man of your skill, learning and energy. I have even made sure that your mounts include the particular horse on which you have trained, honing your skills as a horseman of the steppe. As a man of a seafaring nation, it is remarkable how good a rider you have become. You deserve no less."

Wilfred blushed at this. His reaction startled me as I had never seen him do so before that I could recall. It took awhile to grasp the reason, although it was simple enough. He had been accepted. Nothing proved it so much as the gesture of the horse on which he had honed his skills as a rider, a dark, stocky pony named Timur, of prodigious endurance and ill temper, quick and nasty, the mount of a true Mongol cavalryman.

I, of course, did not share in the glow of Wilfred's pleasure. For I saw that we could not decline in view of the steps Tolui had already taken. He would not have taken those steps unless he knew that the Chancellor would not stand in the way, that Tsai Chou had either given his consent or been overridden by higher authority. I knew, as well, that Tolui's respect for Wilfred did not extend to me. I was simply an appendage, like a wife or a concubine.

So we would leave Karakorum, heading back towards the west, in the general direction of England. The great quiriltai had settled at least that much for us. I found little pleasure and much dread in the prospect.

We moved slowly westward for two solid years, the great army and its supply train spread out across the steppe. In the year 1237, we crossed the lowlands of western Siberia and pushed through a pass at the southern end of the Ural Mountains. By the onset of winter, the army had reached the eastern banks of the River Volga, north of the open steppe at the margin where the great forests that extend down from the arctic meet the plain.

Much of the journey was numbing in its monotony. Day after day we rode, pushing the herds, at the pace of bullock drawn carts. The cavalry units rode on ahead but always keeping pace with the baggage train, vast numbers of carts, wagons and heavily laden camels. Many of the wagons carried mobile gers that seemed to float like galleys on the shimmering clouds of dust in the summer heat or the powdery snow that swirled in the brutal winds of the dark, cold months.

From time to time, we would stop in a particular place to wait for a reconnaissance or for lagging units to join us. We were a part of the main force that had left within a month of the quiriltai. Many of the tribes did not receive their call to join the campaign for several months thereafter as the messengers fanned out over the Mongolian plateau. So we moved at a leisurely pace to allow the others to catch up. The commanders used the time to integrate the units into a single, cohesive force, training constantly as we moved.

During the first few months of the march, I formed a loose connection with Sorghatanu, the wife of Iglaqti. She drove his wagon, his small herd of sheep and spare horses, accompanied by her daughter Setu and two young sons. We made camp next to each other on a few consecutive nights, struck up a conversation, shared a meal or two and began to travel together. As Wilfred and Iglaqti served in the same unit, a unit that also included Sorhatanu's oldest son Torluq, the arrangement worked out quite nicely. I would help with Iglaqti's herds while Sorghatanu prepared the evening meal; she or Setu would assist me with domestic chores around my camp and, in general, we pooled our resources and obligations.

We grew close as the months wore on. After a full cycle of the seasons, working and travelling in concert, seeing Wilfred, Iglaqti and

Torluq only from time to time, we had become a family. Shared travel over long distances under harsh conditions, with hard daily communal work, forges strong ties. Sorghatanu and I became like brother and sister in our companionship. At least I perceived her in that way, not being allowed by circumstance to consider any other.

*　　　　*　　　　*　　　　*

One fine autumn afternoon, I sat on a low ridge in a field of dried grass that had been pushed down by the heavy feet of continuous summer wind. Behind me, the low, rounded shapes of the Ural Mountains defined the western horizon. Tomorrow we would leave this place. And when we crossed the Urals, we would begin the war — for that's where the territory of the Rus truly began. I sat facing east, the sun warming my back against the slight chill in the breeze, a chill that foretold much worse to come over the next few months. Last night's blustery showers had swept the air clean. The ground fell away gently before me to a distant horizon sharply etched, unmarred by dust or haze, a tawny carpet of grasses, marked here and there by alders and poplars along the watercourses that seamed the uneven land, with the occasional stand of birch. An early frost had tinged the trees with the yellows, oranges and reds of autumn. The sun's slanted rays accentuated those colors as the leaves danced gently on the breeze.

The smell of dried grasses dampened by last night's rain perfumed the air. Two hawks, dark against a sky of intense blue, circled lazily on thermal currents, calling shrilly to each other. A few small white clouds hung low on the eastern horizon. Far out on the plain, I could see small bands of the Chosen moving slowly toward me, pushing their herds. Here and there, brightly colored gers bounced along on carts drawn by bullocks.

Slowly, slowly I sank into the peaceful beauty of the scene, all senses caressed by it. The silence overwhelmed the voices in my head, the heralds of anxiety that carped at me without surcease throughout day and night. I felt at one with the small clouds slowly dissolving in the ethereal blue. I felt my urgent sense of formless need dissolve, become small.

After a half hour had passed in reverie, I sensed rather than saw or heard the presence of another. Sorghatanu walked quietly up and sat

166

down beside me. She said nothing for quite awhile. Then, when the hawks called to each other again, she placed her hand gently on my shoulder.

"Do you feel it, Joh?"

"What?"

"The spirit force. One can feel it best in places of peace and beauty. Like this."

"Describe the spirit force to me, Sorghi. I know it not. I know not of what you speak."

She reached over and touched my chin, turning my head to face her. She smiled at me, an innocent expression, totally free of guile. Her bright eyes fairly danced with joy. Like most Mongol women, Sorghi was stoutly built, strong of leg, arm and back. But she was totally feminine in my eyes, and quite beautiful with finely sculpted features, dark olive skin and luxuriant black hair that she generally wore loose, as now. The breeze blew it gently across her face as she held my eye. My heart dissolved within me. We had grown very close. Without touching.

"You know it, Joh. You feel it. You have written of it as you have described your work to me. But I will tell you so that you will hear from the spirit that lives within me."

She turned to face the vista before us. "The spirit resides in all living things, in the earth, the sky, the stars, sun and moon. All life emerges from the spirit force and returns to it at the end of allotted days, to emerge again.

"So we are all kindred and we all have the same origins — the hawk and the mouse, the tiger and the deer, the Chosen and their herds. We are all kindred of the celestial bodies and of the substance of the earth — all united by the spirit force that flows through all of us like a great river." She waved her hand in a sweeping motion. "Quiet your mind, Joh. Discard the screens over your eyes, your ears, your nose to receive the sense of the spirit force in this place. For it is here — as everywhere, of course — but here most emphatically today, this afternoon." She smiled at me again. Gently beseeching. Wanting me to understand.

"Tell me, Sorghi. Is it not true that the view of the universe you have just described assumes that dogs, or sheep, or even rocks have souls?"

She paused for a moment. Then nodded. "In a sense, yes. I believe that they do."

"Are you not Christian?" I knew that she professed to be. In response to my question, she pulled from her tunic a simple wooden crucifix that she wore around her neck on a coarse cord. I had seen it before. To my shame, I had seen it while attempting furtive glances at her breasts as she bent to her work. The thought made me blush as I asked:

"How do you reconcile your views of the spirit force with Christianity? The Bible teaches that only men have souls. Only men can be saved." She smiled.

"I have asked my Christian teacher, my shaman of Christ, Joh. He tells me that the Bible says men have souls. It does not plainly say that no spirit inhabits the body of all other things. I see Christ as a prophet of the spirit force — the shaman who spoke of salvation and forgiveness as an incarnation for return to the spirit world."

She paused in thought. "You see, Joh, the Chosen, the people who live under felt tents, understand that harmony with all living things, the earth, the sky, at the level of the spirit, is essential to life and fulfillment during this allotted time. We seek the spirit level, the fundamental essence, in all things. We could not live as we do, survive and prosper in any other fashion. We could not accept our lives and find beauty in them in any other way." She paused for a moment, her eyes apparently focused on the horizon.

"Every part of this earth is sacred to us. Every shining leaf, every blade of grass, every sandy shore, every mist on the steppe, every meadow, every humming insect. All are holy in the memory and experience of the people who live under felt tents. We know the juices that course through the new grass shoots as we know the blood that courses through our veins. We are part of the earth and it is part of us. The perfumed flowers are our sisters. The bear, the deer, the great eagle, these are our brothers. The rocky crests, the waving grasses of the meadow, the body heat of the pony, and man, all belong to the same family.

"The shining water that moves in the streams and rivers is not just water but the blood of our ancestors. Each ghostly reflection in the clear waters tells of events and memories in the life of our people. The water's murmur is the voice of my father's father." She droned on quietly, without inflection, as though she spoke in a trance.

168

"This we know; the earth does not belong to man. Man belongs to the earth. All things are connected like the blood that unites us all. Man did not weave the web of life. We are all merely strands of that web. And we who live under felt tents love the earth as the newborn loves its mother's heartbeat."

I turned to look at her as she gazed off to the east, seemingly mesmerized by the shifting cloud shadows on the endless tawny plain. The wind moved her hair gently and with much grace. I have never felt closer to any human being in my life than I did to her at that moment. Her words both mystified and moved me profoundly. And I understood her not at all.

*   *   *   *

Wilfred fought his first battle as a member of the Mongol army against the Bulgars, a tribe that resided between the Urals and the Volga. He visited me in camp with the baggage train the night after the army destroyed the town of Bulgar, killing all its male inhabitants and burning the structures to the ground. Many of the soldiers who had fought in the battle came to the baggage train that night to deposit their plunder and tell their tales of glory.

I spied Wilfred as he rode into camp on Timur, still wearing his light leather armor and carrying all of his weapons, with a bag across his saddle behind him. Streaks of dried sweat marked the horse's withers. Wilfred's face, hands and legs were covered with dust and soot. It was a fine autumn evening so we sat outside and ate our dinner of mutton that we roasted over an open fire. A dozen or so men shared the meal, eating with their hands out of a large serving plate of coarse bronze. I guessed that roughly half were soldiers, the rest being men of the baggage train like myself.

Wilfred seemed content but not exuberant, not half-maniacal, like the others who had taken part in the massacre of the Bulgars. I sat next to Wilfred, waiting for the chance to converse with him when the others might be diverted. The chance came in due course.

"How was it?" I asked quietly while the others roared at some crude joke at the expense of two Bulgar woman captives tethered to a stake not far from where we sat.

He shrugged. "What you would expect. They made every mistake, charging us when they should have held, holding when they should have charged. Our arrows cut them down. Their city walls were feeble, as though put up for show and not real defense. All of their houses were of wood and burned readily." He gestured to the west where a broad column of smoke rising from the ruins tinged the glow of twilight a blood red along the rolling horizon, with the silvery grey sky of impending night above.

"Did you kill anyone?"

"Probably. I cannot be sure, but I loosed perhaps a hundred arrows at killing ranges." He shook his head at me, smiling. "No, Johnnie. I did not cut any throats or split any heads like I did that sheriff's when I was but a lad. And as I am sure that you burn with curiosity, I did not join in the general rape of the womenfolk, although all my mates urged me to do so. They even brought me a fine, young blue-eyed lass, trussed like a pig. They laid her on the ground, tied her legs to two stakes set wide apart, tore off her shift to expose her breasts and hairy parts and cheered me on."

To my shame, I felt an untoward interest in this account. "What did you do?"

He laughed. "I told them that my religion forbade me any woman taken by force. They would not have accepted the notion of celibacy, because the only Christians they know are Nestorians and Nestorians are not celibates. Indeed, from what I saw in that town, the Nestorian tribes are some of the most bloody-minded men in this bloody army."

The disturbance in my loins had not quieted. "What happened to the lass?"

He shrugged. "When I refused, they took her. Perhaps twenty of them, perhaps more. Some were most violent and cruel in the doing of it. When they had bloodied her female parts and torn her so that they derived no pleasure from it, they turned her over and rammed her up the backside. She stopped screaming after awhile." He shrugged again. "What happened to her, I cannot say as I went off to get my share of loot before the others could take it all. By that time, the fire had started as well. I had to move quickly or I would have been left out."

I knew about all these things, of course. The Mongols were well known for such behavior. Nonetheless, I found the tale most unsettling, to be so close to a place where it had actually occurred, to be listening to Wilfred describe it so coolly.

After a moment, I asked: "Were you not troubled by what you saw? Of that woman, I mean."

He paused a moment, as though surprised by the question. "No. Not really." He gestured toward the two tethered captives, wretched and trembling as they awaited their fate, examples of the point. "It is warfare, not the exclusive province of these people. Christian knights commit such deeds in their conquests." He shrugged. "At a personal level, I found it both exciting and odious at one and the same time. Exactly the same feeling I had when I saw our arrows cut down the ranks of their men like wheat before a scythe. War. That's all. I regretted only that I had no appropriate potion with which to anoint my arrows."

"But what about her screaming? Did it not unsettle you at least a little?" I shuddered to think of it. Wilfred smiled, as though my query were foolish. He clapped me on the shoulder like a father or older brother about to impart wisdom to a beloved but slightly retarded child.

"Think of the sounds you heard when the pirates attacked our galley from Venice to Constantinople. Now imagine a battle not of four hundred men but of one hundred thousand in a tightly packed area, all within hearing of each other, all participating in the making of similar sounds." He paused to make sure that I was with him, that the yells and curses and moans and clash of arms filled my head. Satisfied, he continued.

"Now imagine that perhaps twenty thousand of those men are struck by arrows. An arrow, Johnnie, is naught but a small winged dagger. It does not kill by shock or force in the manner of a mace or even a broadsword or battleax. You do not cleave a man's head in two or stave in his skull with an arrow. An arrow slips into a man's body like a burglar. It severs the tubes and strings and vessels that sustain life. The leakage is most often slow so that a man, hit thus, has ample time to feel the cold hand of death gain ascendancy within him."

He paused again, regarding me in a relaxed but intense manner I found most unnerving. I felt as though a cold-blooded demon had possessed his body, displacing the man I knew. He continued, without gesture or change of expression.

"Most men in the grip of that condition give voice to their fears with great intensity. After all, if a voiceless creature such as a rabbit in the grip of a hawk or a deer with a tiger on its back will shriek loudly enough to raise the hackles of the deaf, what would you expect from members of the human race, the most vocal of all the species?" The question did not truly invite answer. In any case, I gave none as my imagination grappled with the scene his words invoked.

"So you see, Johnnie, with that many men in their death agonies and hundreds of women enduring the same fate as the woman I have described, the cries of any particular individual lost all meaning." He shrugged. "In any case, they did for me."

At this, Wilfred turned his attention to the communal plate and withdrew a dripping shankbone. He spent the next several minutes busily denuding it of meat. He ate with much gusto.

My shock wore off after a moment or two. I noticed that he had kept the skin sack that had been tied to the back of his saddle close beside him. He observed my gaze, swallowed a last mouthful of meat and reached for the sack.

"My plunder, Johnnie. I took less than the others but I believe that I chose well." Whereupon, he reached into the sack and withdrew two large silver chalices, both elegantly designed and nearly identical, richly engraved with much detail. He set them on the ground between us within reach.

Thus displayed, I could see that the chalices were in fact identical but for the engravings. One presented the scene of the crucifixion, with the torment of Christ clearly depicted on a figure rendered in bas-relief with much sensitivity, detail and artfulness. Indeed, the figure seemed almost lifelike, as though one could imagine it writhing in agony. The rim and base of the vessel were decorated with a pattern incorporating the cross and legends written in the script of the Greeks that I could not read. I assumed them to be sacred liturgy from the manner of their presentation.

The carving on the second chalice depicted Tauroctonus, the Slayer Of The Primeval Bull, a figure of ancient Persian mythology from the cult of Mithra. Signs of the Zodiac adorned those portions of the vessel not taken up with the main carving, Scorpio the Scorpion at the autumnal, Leo the Lion within the midsummer sun, Aquarius the Water Carrier in the house of the winter solstice, and of course, Taurus the Bull in the process of being slain, as the centerpiece, his blood running as sheaves of grain down his tortured flanks.

Wilfred regarded me as I examined the pieces, awaiting my reaction. Of their great value, I had no doubt. The sheer weight of the silver gave testimony to that fact. To my untrained eye, it seemed that the engravings were of the highest quality. But as I continued to examine them, a different truth began to dawn in my brain. The same craftsman had created the chalices at roughly the same time. The styles were too similar and the degree of wear too comparable to admit of any other interpretation. An identical maker's mark on the base confirmed it.

My wonder grew as I thought of it. A sensitive Christian also a believer in astrology — a believer in the pagan mythology of Mithra?

"Where did you find these, Wilfred? They seem rendered by the same hand, although I find that hard to accept, given their expression of theologies that stand in such conflict that they could not coexist in one soul."

He nodded. "They stood side by side on the altar of a small church in the town. The church was already burning when I entered it. One of our soldiers had taken these two and was about to depart with them. I bartered for them." With what? I wondered, but dared not ask.

"What do you make of them?"

He shrugged again, a gesture that had become a staple with him. "Passing strange to have two such vessels placed with equal dignity on the altar of a Christian church, I admit. Perhaps it is the nature of this vast land to render all those who live in it shallow-rooted in their spiritual beliefs. Perhaps something in the rigors of life here renders men unwilling to gamble their souls on the selection of one true faith. Many of the Bulgars who died today wore crucifixes on chains around their necks along with other tokens and talismans I did not recognize, except that they were most assuredly not Christian. Many had similarly mixed legends on their armor, tattoos and paintings on their bodies."

These were the dead. Their reverence for multiple deities had failed to prevent an abrupt and tortured end to their temporal existences. Perhaps their diffuse theology found reward after death.

I could think of nothing to explain the objects, their surfaces dully reflecting the light of the fire as they stood on the ground between us. "Well, Wilfred. The whole thing lies beyond reach of my simple brain. Christianity as I understand it does not leave scope for companion beliefs. It is predicated upon faith in a single God, embodied in a trinity of beings. Christ and the Hebrews before him taught that on the Day of Judgment, time will end and all souls shall be judged. Mithric tradition teaches that time never ends as life forms, dissolves and reforms forever and ever. So I assume that these vessels were made by a heretic or commissioned by some heretical cult. Indeed, I believe that to be most likely. Perhaps created to be used in ceremonies of devil worship. For the sake of your soul, I urge you to have them melted down and rendered into silver talents. Those, at least, you could put to some useful purpose."

He reached forward thoughtfully and picked up the Tauroctonus piece, holding it high to catch the firelight. The flickering orange glow seemed to bring it to life. A talisman of evil. Wilfred shook his head slowly. "No, Johnnie. I would not destroy such a thing as this to convert it into common coin just because it celebrates a god in which I do not have faith. It has a value far greater than its gross weight in fine silver — if only I can divine its meaning."

I felt no such yearnings. Indeed, as Wilfred continued to hold the graceful vessel aloft in the wavering light, it's sinister aspects increased, as though a vision of the fires of hell emanated from it. A cold chill gripped my gut as I realized that there could be no greater blasphemy than to juxtapose such an object with a similar one that celebrates the most profoundly sacred event in Christian theology. Had not fire consumed the so-called church where these objects had been kept? Had not the congregants of that church been slaughtered this very day? Who could say if this were but the venal hand of man or the punishment of God? Perhaps this object itself had brought down the wrath of the Mongols on the city of Bulgar and all of its inhabitants.

My dread and horror increased when Wilfred entrusted the two chalices to me for safekeeping. They were far too heavy for him to carry, particularly with the Guard at the forefront of the advance. I carried them faithfully, despite my dread that the mere possession of such objects could condemn my soul to eternal damnation. These fears ebbed and flowed within me, prompting many prayers for understanding and forgiveness at each periodic peak of my Christian fervor.

*   *   *   *

In the spring of 1237, before the invasion, I had suffered a serious bout of the flux brought on by ingesting bad water. The Mongols believe that it offends the spirits to wash or wet their bodies in moving waters. To avoid giving offense, particularly on the eve of a massive campaign, they prefer to camp near the still waters of ponds and lakes. I took ill at one of these, perhaps due to naturally occurring contaminants, perhaps due to the residue from elements of the army that had preceded us. Who knows the true cause? In the event, I rode for two weeks with a searing gut and a raging arsehole, unable to keep food down, unable to stop shitting despite the total lack of substance in my system. The convulsions were so severe at times I thought I might shit my very guts out, leaving nothing but an empty dried husk of a body.

When the episode finally subsided, it left me in a weakened condition, lethargic and light of head, slowly recovering. Sorghatanu did what she could for me, performing some of my chores, plying me with noxious remedies, fussing and clucking over my suffering.

One day, during my recovery, we were riding at a slow pace over gently undulating ground, rich in spring grasses to the height of a horse's belly. Low, rounded hills stretched to the limits of the horizon in every direction to meet a cloudless sky, intensely blue, rising to the heavens without the slightest break in uniformity other than the occasional soaring bird. The infernal wind of the steppe had subsided to a gentle whisper, just enough to fan the soul with the scent of wildflowers and move the grasses in sedate, rippling waves. The morning sun warmed our backs as we made our way westward, dulling the memory of winter's relentless chill.

I looked around me in wonder. As far as the eye could see in every direction, the Mongol army — the Chosen —flowed like a river westward. Soldiers in their tens and hundreds rode on their dark horses in columns of twos with yak-tail standards held high. Here and there, heavily laden camels swayed along, loosely watched by their herders. Other herders

175

moved flocks of sheep numbering in the hundreds. Bullocks drew carts, some bearing fully pitched yurts and gers. As the carts descended into the folds in the land, only the moving felt tents with their colorful decorations remained visible, appearing to sail along under their own power, like galleys on the sea of grass.

Migratory animals must move in like manner, driven by an instinct that none understand. But chaotic as the movement might seem, it had a purpose; and all of the participants moved to the rhythm of that plan. Even I. In my weakened condition.

I drifted into a trancelike state, coasting effortlessly on the current of the senses — the sights of rounded hills, waving grasses, men and animals moving slowly, the warmth of the sun, the smells, the sounds. I rode an old horse with a smooth gait, hypnotic in motion, needing no guidance as he moved with the army as he had done all his life.

I felt a great sense of peace. I lifted my eyes to the vast blue void, understanding for the first time the Mongol's reverence for Tengri, the spirit of the Great Blue Sky who ordained that the Mongols should rule over all the peoples of the earth who dwelt in felt tents, their vassals and all those from whom they could exact submission. I recalled a passage from Rumi's mawkish love poems. "Close the door of words that the window of your soul may open. Abandon this world, that you may become King of all worlds. Throw away your handful of sugar that you may become a sugar field." I felt the window of my soul open as never before.

I must have ridden for hours without a thought, awake but barely, floating on the gentle stimulus of my senses. And then, as the sun crossed the top of the dome of the sky, there appeared before me a diffuse vision — a man in a dark robe and cap, sitting crosslegged. He was a Chin with white hair and thin white beard, reciting the words of Chuang-tzu I had transcribed shortly before we departed Karakorum, some of my best work by far in the employ of Tsai Chou.

"'In death, no strange fate befalls us. In the beginning we lack but life and form. We lack spirit. We are but a small part of one great indistinguishable mass. Then a time comes when the mass evolves spirit, the spirit evolves form, form evolves life. Life in its turn evolves death, a return to the great indistinguishable mass, the Great Inner Room, whence the cycle repeats itself, each time differing in some particulars than the last but not in all.'" Sorghi's spirit world echoed in the classical literature of the Chin.

The vision repeated these words over and over again before fading into the blue depths of the sky whence he had emerged. In some vague way, elusive within the torpor of my weakened state, it seemed to me that this vast westward flow of men and animals could be nothing more than a metaphor of the great indistinguishable mass, from which all spirit and form evolved and to which it would return over again to repeat the cycle.

I knew that the depth of understanding I felt at that moment, in counterpoint to the ebbs and flows of my Christian conviction, would remain with me forever.

*   *   *   *

We camped on the east bank of the River Volga in December of 1237, waiting for the freeze. For several weeks, I watched ice floes move sedately by on the slow current, with slush and skim ice near the banks. There were storms and ice fog, but most of all, there were thousands of campfires twinkling into the distance, as far as the eye could see, the sounds of laughter and shouting, the sounds of the animals.

A fierce blizzard brought a cold snap in its wake and the River finally congealed enough to allow the first patrols to cross in force. They reported that the Rus had not come forth to establish a defense line or give battle. By that time, the River had frozen sufficiently to allow the entire army to make its passage.

Tolui had told us of Subedei's plan. It was simple enough. The Mongols sought total conquest of the Rus. To achieve it, they had to prevent a joint concentration of military force by the various principalities. The most powerful Princes were Grand Duke Yuri of Suzdal and Prince Michael of Kiev. The Mongols planned a swift and decisive drive to divide Chernigov and Kiev on the south, Suzdal and Novgorod on the north. The various principalities could then be destroyed piecemeal.

Once across the Volga, we turned north into the forested lands before turning west again in the hopes that the forests would mask our approach as well as disguise our numbers. The army led the way across a broad front in the manner of the winter exercises. We of the baggage train followed close behind the army's center ranks, all kept in contact by the courier system. As the Imperial Guard held a place near the center, Wilfred and I were never far apart. Despite the heavily wooded terrain, the Mongol's communication system kept the army in cohesion as it advanced.

The going was arduous. Russian roads were few and narrow, meandering in a random fashion through dense evergreen forests. We could move fairly well through the old growth where the trees stood wide apart with branches high. But in the marshes and second-growth areas, we had to force our way. The bullock carts were the worst, often bogging down in the deep and drifted snow.

Subedei had planned the campaign to take full advantage of winter's chill — to render the rivers and bogs passable for soldiers and baggage train. That advantage, important though it may be in country dotted with marshes and bogs, comes at a price. One expects certain adverse effects from extreme cold. The conditions more than met our grimmest expectations.

Timber, leather, all manner of fabric became hard as iron. Bridles, halters, other horse tack required warming over a fire to become usable. It seemed that nothing could prevent cart axles from binding. To obtain water for man and beast, with time to drink it before it refroze, was a complex and tedious chore. To ingest snow or ice at those temperatures could be deadly. The body simply could not warm them fast enough to prevent freezing of the flesh. The weight of clothing required to stave off the cold seemed to render the most elemental movement nearly impossible, let alone the hard work we had to perform throughout the day to keep things moving. And the soldiers had to warm their bows continually to keep them in working order.

Yet, I heard no complaint, despite the hardship; and dared express none myself, although some days I wanted simply to lie down and die rather than continue. The weather was no more harsh than that which the Mongols endured most winters on the steppe. Even I had experienced such weather in the open before for short periods, while training with the army and on our progress west. But somehow, the dark and obstacles presented by the forest lands seemed to make the cold and snow much worse. Perhaps it was the pervasive gloom of it all. In the dense woods, we never saw a sunrise or a sunset, never had a clear view of the crescent moon hanging low above the horizon, never saw the full sweep of star-studded heavens. The trees muted even the howl of the wolves, distorting the long notes, rendering them small.

Although the Naiman and some of the other tribes of the north normally inhabited wooded lands for at least a part of their year, the great majority of the Mongols were not used to forested country. It lacked fodder for their animals, so they usually steered clear of it. They viewed its brooding darkness with a superstitious eye, sensing the presence of evil spirits in every shadow. Nonetheless, the woods provided ready fuel for the cooking and warming fires that sustained us. So the Mongols gave thanks for the bright flames of their fires and challenged the evil spirits with defiance as we slogged through.

I had charge of the cart and two bullocks that Tolui had commandeered for Wilfred. It carried our belongings and a small ger in which I sheltered during the nights and periods of rest. I travelled with Sorghatanu and her family, a group of camp followers of the Guard, members of soldier's families, their retainers and slaves. We were to provide support, gather and carry supplies, receive and protect plunder and shelter the fallen should they suffer wounds or sickness.

Each soldier of the Guard, it seemed, had a person or group to perform these services for him. In some cases, one person supported several members of a single family or tribe. We were perhaps a day's ride behind the army when it reached Ryazan. We caught up in time for the evening meal the next day.

Sorghatanu and I had made camp in a small clearing that we shared with perhaps three other groups when Wilfred, Tolui, Iglaqti and Torluq rode in. The night being unseasonably warm, we sat outside around a fire for the evening meal, the men close and the women in the background. Campfires flickered in the woods all around us. Dark figures moved everywhere as the entire army had concentrated here. New groups moved in continually throughout the afternoon and evening. A glow in the sky over a low ridge to the west marked the location of Ryazan, watchfires and torches burning bright as the city prepared for attack and siege.

After a few words of greeting, Tolui passed on the news to those of us of the baggage train.

179

"The City shall be destroyed. Subedei has decided to make an example for the others."

"An example?" I asked. "Could we not just demand surrender?"

Tolui shook his head. "We did. We demanded submission, a ten percent tax and five thousand young men to go with the army to march in the van when we attack Novgorod and Chernigov. The so-called Prince of Ryazan rejected our proposal with contempt." He shrugged. "So we will skin him alive over a slow fire in a few day's time."

I looked at him and then at the faces of Wilfred, Iglaqti, his three sons and other soldiers who had joined our circle. None showed any emotion as they attacked their food. Iglaqti seemed the most enigmatic and yet the most threatening to me. He was a large man for a Mongol, with broad face, a thick neck and powerful arms. His hands were large and gnarled, misshapen and menacing. His face must have been forbidding under the best of circumstances long ago. Sometime within the last ten years, he had suffered a broken jaw in battle or in an accident. The injury had knocked out several teeth and left him disfigured, giving his face a peculiarly sinister aspect. He had saved me from the wounded stag on the winter hunt. Now I spent several hours a day with his wife, helping her with his animals and other possessions. Yet we had exchanged hardly more than a word of greeting, and that devoid of warmth.

He projected no hint of friendliness tonight, nor any other emotion for that matter. He ate without expression as the women moved quietly in the shadows behind us, serving unobtrusively, making sure that the serving tray stayed full until all of the men had eaten their fill. Those served included men from the Guard whom I had never seen before. All were welcome, as we would have been at any of the countless fires in our immediate vicinity.

That evening, Wilfred and I lay close together in our robes on the floor of the ger, pitched on the bed of our cart. I was on the point of sleep when Wilfred shook me gently. It was quite late. The camp had quieted, although I could see the glimmer of campfires through the small gaps in the fabric of our shelter, and every now and then, the shadow of a form as a few soldiers and animals continued to move about.

"Johnnie. Wake Johnnie, and hear me," he whispered.

"I'm awake, Wilfred."

"We will soon have visitors, Johnnie."

"What? Who?"

"Sorghatanu, Setu and one of the two Bulgar women that Iglaqti took as a slave."

I sat up with a start. "What is this nonsense, Wilfred?"

"Shhh, Johnnie. It is serious. Iglaqti wishes to show his gratitude for your care and attention to the members of his family. He wishes to show his comraderie with me, his brother in arms. So he gives us his women for the night, keeping for himself only the eldest and scabbiest of the Bulgars."

I started to protest with rising voice. Wilfred's hand clapped over my mouth, none too gently. He held it there and pulled me close. "Shhh, Johnnie. This is serious. You will gravely insult Iglaqti if you refuse. Worse, if you refuse his wife or daughter, you will dishonor both him and her, the woman you refuse will fall out of favor and may be killed or driven away by him. So when they enter our ger, reach out and take the one who presents herself to you and give her your best."

"Good God, Wilfred. My best what? I know nothing of these things."

He chuckled quietly. "You will shortly learn, Johnnie. Fear not. They will guide you. All the women of these tribes are quite expert in such matters, from early youth." How did he know, I wondered.

I felt horror, excitement and shame by turns as I contemplated the prospect. Strange sensations rippled through my lower gut. My member began to fill and rise. So the fascinating but forbidden rite was about to be revealed from the murk of fevered conjecture, rumor and whispered tale.

I had to admit that I had looked upon both Sorghatanu and even Setu with growing fondness over the past several months. I had often sought furtive glimpses of them unclad as I moved about the camp. I had found their brown skin and long black hair quite soothing to the eye when they exposed themselves on summer afternoons. My eyes had often sought the bouncing curve of their breasts as they rode beside me, chattering endlessly about small things, always in a good humor, regardless of the weather or circumstance. Sorghatanu had become my soul's companion. But I had also assumed that they were absolutely forbidden to me despite their growing friendliness and occasionally suggestive behavior. In my mind's eye, I pictured Iglaqti disemboweling me with his scimitar if ever I should lie with either of them, as if I would know how to do so. It never occurred to me that he would offer them to me in that way, despite my dim knowledge of local custom in matters of hospitality and gratitude.

The younger of the two Bulgar women was far from repulsive either, although her condition of sexual servitude had rendered her nearly catatonic with fear and depression. It seemed as though she expected death or worse at any moment, without hope of redemption and with no relief in sight. She whimpered like a whipped dog while refusing to speak. Perhaps she knew not the language, or perhaps the shock of her circumstances had paralyzed her tongue. In any case, I could not help but note her rich female attributes that the Mongols ruthlessly exposed whenever the whim struck them. In spite of myself, I found the sight and thought of her exciting in a most carnal sense.

The three women quietly entered the ger shortly thereafter. Without preliminaries, they stepped out of their shifts and slipped into our sleeping robes unclad, Sorghatanu and the Bulgar woman attending to Wilfred and Setu with me. She was smooth, firm, muscular and totally adept, slipping under me, spreading her beautiful thighs and putting me inside her so quickly that I hardly knew what had happened.

I could not believe that human flesh could be so sweet. I became totally self absorbed in the feeling she elicited from my body; and yet, at the same time, acutely attuned to every beat of her heart, every pulse of her hips, her abdomen, the rise and fall of her breasts as she moved beneath me, as though our systems were joined throughout and not just where I held place inside her. Although we occasionally brushed against them in their gyrations, Wilfred and his companions might as well have been on another planet. When the rite ended in an explosion of sensation that left me gasping, she extricated herself from beneath me and began to knead every muscle in my body with her powerful hands, expertly tracing every cord and tendon from connection to connection, immobilizing me with transcendent ecstasy that slid inexorably into a deep and dreamless sleep.

I awoke as Wilfred prepared to leave for the coming battle. Night still held sway, although it remained dark at these latitudes well into the morning. I could hear the sounds of sheep restlessly foraging near the camp, the sound of our bullocks lowing as they awaited their ration of grain. The women were gone. Only a slight essence remained to assure me that the events of the night had not been a dream.

*   *   *   *

Snow began to fall shortly after dawn. It turned into a full blizzard by noon, with heavy snow through the following night and well into the next day. I left the ger only to gather wood for the fire and make sure that our animals had water. The trees took on a heavy burden, weighing down their branches and softening their profiles. The ground, the sky and all in between had a dull white aspect with objects and creatures alike indistinct, their outlines blurred, merging into a background that seemed both near and far at one and the same time.

I encountered Sorghatanu and Setu during the course of the day as we went about our chores. They were cordial and friendly, moving briskly as was their wont. Neither more nor less friendly than before the events of the night. As it was not in their nature to dissemble, I could only assume that they attributed little significance to what had happened. I, on the other hand, felt that my life had altered profoundly, in a way both ominous and exciting.

The storm seemed to grow in its intensity throughout the day. The army moved through it, investing Ryazan, surrounding the town to cut off all chance of escape or succor. By late afternoon, we knew that Wilfred, Iglaqti and Torluq would not be returning for the night. The soldiers would spend the night on the line in shelters improvised from tree boughs. The Imperial Guard took its position opposite the main gate that led onto the road to Kolumna, Suzdal, Vladimir and Novgorod.

I ate the evening meal in Sorghatanu's ger with Setu, the two boys and the two Bulgar women. No one said much as storm winds began to blow with great ferocity, dumping the snow load from the trees and setting up a great howl and roar through the branches. The walls of the ger billowed and rocked, riling the smoke from the cooking fire until the air within became thick with it, dimming the light of the fire and torches as though the storm sought to soften with smoke the vision within as it had softened with snow the vision without.

183

When the meal ended I returned the short distance to my ger. Neither Sorghatanu nor Setu had had much to say to me. They had chores to complete before I took my leave. In the close quarters of the crowded ger, I could neither help nor stay out of the way. The storm clouds had lowered almost to the ground by that point, shutting out all light from the sky. Were it not for the campfires scattered about in the woods and gers, the night would have been pitch black. I doubt that I could have found our ger but for those fires.

I considered the prospect of lighting a torch and attempting to read but lacked the heart for it. The word had come down that we would be working with the army on the morrow in the construction of siege works. So it would be wise to get as much rest as possible. Sleep should be easy this night as the storm kept movement of soldiers and animals to a minimum and blotted out intrusive sounds. Early as it was, I stepped out of my felt boots, took off my padded winter garments and slipped into the sleeping robes. Bitter cold at first, they warmed quickly and I relaxed into them, listening to the storm, feeling the ger rock with it. A pang of longing moved through me as I thought of the women in the next ger. But I assumed from what Wilfred had said that they had come last night solely as Iglaqti's special gift — a gift otherwise forbidden to me.

I tried to turn my mind away from Setu's smooth body by resorting to prayer, starting with those in which I had been trained. When that did not work particularly well, I tried others that I had transcribed over the years from the teachings of Tao, Buddha, even Islam. Nothing served to banish the warmth of those muscular thighs from the shadowy edges of my consciousness. They hovered there as the robes warmed and I descended toward sleep.

I had lain suspended on the fulcrum between sleep and wakefulness for perhaps an hour when Sorghatanu entered the ger. She moved with such stealth that I sensed her presence in a general, indistinct way before hearing or touching her. For an instant, I thought that she might have come to cut my throat in revenge for my coupling with her daughter. But that could not be as she had lain without complaint under an adjoining robe at the time, albeit occupied with Wilfred.

She moved quickly in the dark cold of the ger. By the time I had become fully aware of her presence, she lay beside me naked, her rich hair pungent with pine smoke and mutton spread over my face, holding me tight against her for warmth, shivering ever so slightly. She spoke in a whisper.

"Joh. Please allow me to share your bed tonight. Setu tells me that you are an innocent and gentle man. She said that you touched her with great reverence as though she were made of gold or precious gems. That you caressed her with tenderness, the way a man might caress a favored horse, unlike the men of our tribes. I wish to know such a man as that." She pulled me even closer to whisper directly in my ear. "I wish to know you." She giggled for an instant and then slipped down into the robe so that her head lay now against my chest, holding me tight, touching me with an extended, furtive tongue, quickly moving down my body.

I was surprised at the strength of her arms, the agility of her movements, startled by my own confusion. Was she mocking me? I must have been ridiculously inept with Setu. The women must have talked of it. No doubt, I had been the butt of many jokes this day. But my delight at her presence overpowered any perceived insults to my rising manhood. In any case, the symphony of sensation she created within me was compensation enough.

That was but the beginning. For she took charge of me and had her way for the better part of the next two hours. We did the best we could to create a storm within, every bit the equal of the raging night without. At the end of it, as we lay bathed in each other's sweat and the effluvium of our joinder, I knew that I had passed a threshold of experience through which there could be no return. I would never be the same, either as a man or in the sight of God. And, God forgive me, I did not care.

We kicked off the robe covering us to let the chill night air cool our steaming bodies. She lay next to me as we had begun, with her rich hair spread over my chest, her breathe gentle on my skin. I seemed to float weightless on a current of quiet euphoria with only one note of discord hovering in the shadows.

"Sorghi, will not Iglaqti wish to kill me for this?"

She laughed, propped herself up on an elbow, tossed her head to swing her hair behind her and smiled impishly from a distance of but a few inches from my face. Dark as it was, I could still make her out in the dim and uneven reflected light of a nearby campfire that somehow leaked through rents in the wall of our ger. Her eyes danced with mirth, crinkled at the corners, shining as though they caught every speck of light afoot in that turbulent darkness. "He would be pleased. He has noted your interest and wishes to sell me to you to be rid of me. He will be angry only if you do not find me satisfying, as that would depress the price. In that case, he will vent his wrath upon me, not you."

"But how can he feel that way? Are you not man and wife? Were you not married in Christian sacrament?" Iglaqti and Sorghatanu were of the Keriyat people, a people that had embraced Christ — albeit of the Nestorian heresy — shortly after the turn of the century.

Her voice grew solemn. The mirth subsided. "Yes, Joh. We were properly married. A priest invoked the blessing of the Father, the Son and the Holy Spirit upon our union. My parents had arranged the wedding with the chief of Iglaqti's clan when I was but three summers under the Great Blue Sky. I was married at thirteen summers and bore Torluq, who fights beside Iglaqti and your Wilfred, less than one year thereafter."

Her voice resumed its normally cheerful tone. "In truth, Iglaqti never cared for me. He was never enthusiastic when he lay with me. For the last several cycles of the seasons, he has lain with me rarely. I believe he does it only to avoid ridicule from the men of the tribe and the Guard. In these camps, you know, everyone knows what everyone else is doing."

"Doesn't that bother you?" I couldn't imagine how one so wanton and lustful as Sorghi could deal with an indifferent man. But then, I could not imagine a man who knew her nature being indifferent to her. The whole arrangement was incomprehensible. I assumed that my naivete in such matters led to my bewilderment. No other explanation offered itself.

"It did at first. I felt worthless. But I soon learned that our honored guests enjoyed me and I them. So then I understood that Iglaqti had the problem, not I."

"Why do you stay with him?"

"Where would I go? He is my husband. I help tend his animals, maintain his belongings, make and mend his clothes, raise the children, who may or may not be his, although he accepts them as such." She chuckled again before continuing. "He protects me and preserves my status as wife and not concubine. Although he can be rough, he does not hit me as other men hit their women."

She paused. Although her tone did not change, I felt a hint of subdued anguish in her next statement. "And because he is good in all these ways, I make room for the concubines and slave women he takes from time to time. I make them welcome. I try to ease their pain. Particularly with the slave women. For if he cannot sell them when he tires of them, he either kills them or turns them out so he will no longer bear the burden of their upkeep. In most cases, they starve or freeze when that happens."

I had nothing to say to all this. My mind could not encompass the dimensions of such a picture. As I felt affection for this vital woman mushroom within me, my confusion grew apace. Were these human beings? Were these the same human beings who made such a project of preserving the most elevated spiritual thought of all mankind? If they were indeed not human, why did I feel a bond of shared joy with this being that transcended all similar feelings in my entire life for any other human being I had ever known?

Without warning, I found myself shedding hot tears for her, holding her close. My sobs and hug made her uneasy. After a short time, she squirmed to free herself, wiping away my tears with her fingertips. She whispered: "What's wrong, Johnnie? Do you want me to go?"

"No, no Sorghi. Please stay. I will try to control myself better. It's just that right now, I yearn so much to be close to you that I cannot manage the feeling. It throws me like a wild horse."

We lay still again in silence for quite awhile, brushed by the uneasy breath of the storm. We pulled the robe up and moved close to each other, the icy chill of the air having cooled the residuum of our ardor. Her hands moved restlessly over my body, kneading my muscles with a firm, expert touch. Some of her movements made clear an intent to arouse me again. I took her hands in mine.

"Before we couple again, Sorghi, please tell me of your life. I would know you better. It is a matter of importance to me."

She laughed, an unrestrained expression of joy. "Why should you care about such things, Joh? I am nothing. A mere possession. It is my joy to be your possession for the remainder of this night and for many nights to come. Beyond that, I am not significant."

Sorghatanu had an obstinate streak of epic proportions. I had witnessed it, experienced it often on our journey, sometimes in frustration, sometimes in admiration, always in awe. Once set upon a task, no difficulty would deter her. If she felt that her place allowed her to participate in an argument, she could not be moved from any position once firmly taken. So I knew better than to quarrel.

"Perhaps you are indeed of no account, Sorghi. But I am not a man of Mongol predisposition. I yearn to know all there is to know of my possession. My curiosity goes far beyond the dark wet place between your legs and the shapely flesh of your breasts. If I am indeed to possess you, I must know your spirit — and to know that, I must know how your life has forged that spirit."

Once again she laughed with delight. "Are you a follower of St. Benedict, Johnnie? The priest who spoke to me of Jesus when I was a young girl told me of false priests he called `Benedictines' who were dangerous because of their exceptional cleverness in argument. He warned me to beware of such men, to avoid them, to shun their teachings. Above all, he warned me not to couple with them unless I wished to have children born with red eyes, a pointed tail and the horns of a yak. Are you Benedictine, Johnnie? Have I unwittingly doomed myself to such a bizarre motherhood?"

"No. I am Franciscan. Not a follower of St. Benedict."

"I know nothing good or bad of Franciscans. The priest made no mention of them. So I will tell you what you seek to know. If you were a follower of St. Benedict, I would instead argue with you to test your skills." She lay back, chuckling. I could not see but dimly, in outline only. My mind's eye imagined her staring up at the dark ceiling, marshalling her memories. After a moment, she began her tale. Despite the noise of the storm and her calm tone, the sound of her voice filled the ger.

"I am of the Keriyat people. My father and mother were simple herders, not of noble birth. Our clan followed the grasses as did most of the tribes and clans. Mostly we used the grasslands in the valley of the Orkhon River, to the north and west of where Karakorum lies today, moving upriver to the highlands in the spring, downriver in autumn, near to where the River flows into Lake Baikal. We shared the area with other tribes and clans, the Ungarrids, the Merkid, the Bjorjin. The land of a woodland people called the Naiman lay to the north. Temuchin, he who became leader and called himself Ghenghis Khan, was of the Bjorjin clan of the Qiyat tribe and an ally of my grandfather. That would be thirty-five, perhaps forty summers ago.

"I remember riding, strapped tightly to my mother's back as an infant. I recall her hair in my face. I recall the smoke of many fires, the cold of many winters, the heat of many summers. When I was but eight summers under the Great Blue Sky, my parents put me in charge of a herd of nine goats. I stayed with them all summer long, sleeping among them under the stars, finding the ones that got lost or wandered off. That first year, I did not go inside a yurt or ger at any time for five months. My parents or brothers would bring food to me so I could eat with the animals in my charge. I rarely, if ever, left them whatever the weather, cold or hot, wet or dry. I was supposed to drive off any wolves that might come, although I had no idea how to do that and I had no weapon other than a staff. To my good fortune, no wolves came. As I was small and smelled like a goat, they might have eaten me for one. I was sure my father would kill me if I lost any of those animals, so my summer was uneasy although I recall it with fondness."

She paused as though sorting through memories. I felt her shift in the robes, moving closer so that our bodies touched from shoulder to foot. She turned her head so that I could feel her breath gentle on my neck, see her features, the light of her eyes. When she continued, her voice was low, barely above a whisper.

"I remember many battles between the tribes and clans. I remember the men riding off to do battle countless times. At first, I did not understand why the men fought. Then, I would hear that this or that family or this or that tribe wanted our grasslands, or we wanted theirs. Sometimes animals would disappear and the men would fight because of their belief that the animals had been stolen. Sometimes, the men would hold big meetings and join together to fight the Naiman or the Tangut peoples. I was a child and did not understand these things."

Her voice seemed to catch. She stopped for just a moment. "I remember an afternoon during my tenth summer under the Great Blue Sky when the men of our clan were off fighting. A band of Merkid rode into our camp. There may have been ten or twenty, I could not say. They asked for a drink of kumiss. When one of the women brought some, they took it. Then they grabbed her and threw her on the ground. Three men held her while the others ripped off her clothes and mounted her. They tortured her with objects. They used a knife point to increase her pain, although they did not give injury from which the body could not heal. They laughed while they did it — the way drunk men laugh when they are cruel. Then they went through the camp and did the same to all the other women they could catch.

"I hid. They did not find me. From my hiding place, I watched them as they did the same things to my mother and sister. After a time, they took a few things and rode away. They took a few of the young women. They probably would have taken me if I had been found."

She rolled over and pushed close so that her back touched me from shoulder to waist, her firm bottom pressed against my manhood. Her hair brushed my face, neck and shoulders. I could barely hear her above the wind as she spoke quietly with her head turned away. Her voice seemed devoid of feeling, as before.

"When our men returned, they decided to seek vengeance on the Merkid. So they rode off again, leaving us to tend the animals, fearful that the Merkid or men of some other tribe might find us. Our men came back in a few days. They had recovered the girls the Merkid had taken and they had a few of the Merkid women, tethered by the neck with their hands bound tightly behind them.

"They counted the raid a success, with revenge fully exacted. I saw the matter differently as my father had been sorely wounded in the encounter and all could see that he would soon die. That meant that I, my mother, my sister and brother, would be required to go live with my uncle where my mother would become his concubine and I would be subject to his pleasure."

She readjusted her position to face me, a short distance now between us. She propped her head on her right hand with her elbow on the robe, her face close to mine.

"My father was distant and severe. He demanded much of me as he did of my brother and sister. But he was fair in his judgments, affectionate in his fashion. I felt a great void open within me as I watched him die. I hated my uncle. My heart filled with dread at the thought of falling under his dominion. He was a loud man. A cruel man. His soul knew not how to smile. He had the face of a storm on the horizon, always a storm bearing down."

At this, she stopped, as though an unseen hand had been clapped over her mouth. After a time, she lay down with her torso on me, her lovely breasts pressing into my chest, her hair enshrouding us both, mouth seeking mine. Then she whispered. "Let us speak no more of somber things tonight, dear Johnnie. Hear the storm die?" I had not detected it, but listening now I could tell that she was right. The wind had subsided to fitful gusts. "Tomorrow will be a day of much hard work. Lie still now and let me fill the vessel of your body with the joys of earth and sky. And then we shall rest. If you insist, I will complete my tale some other time so that you will know of your possession." My possession. What treasure had been bestowed upon me.

I gave in to her. She left no room for argument.

*   *   *   *

The frozen forest rang with the shouts of working men, the sounds of axes, the crash of falling timber. In every direction, teams of men struggled to fell trees, to strip branches with teams of bullocks dragging the denuded trunks toward Ryazan.

I caught glimpses of the town itself through the woods off to my left. It stood behind an earthen wall with a defensive structure on top made of wood and stone, all but the steepest inclines covered with fresh snow. The wall had angles and towers to create defensive strong points, with towers on each side of the main gate positioned to assail attackers from the sides and above. Bright pennants and flags stood out from poles atop the walls in the stiff breeze. Behind the walls, I could see the snow-clad roofs of buildings and the occasional onion dome of a church with gold cross on top, glinting in the winter sunlight. From this distance, it appeared that most of the structures in the town were of wood.

The day had dawned clear, bright and cold with only a few ragged wisps of cloud against the blue of the winter sky. The low angle of the sun gave texture to the light in a manner that highlighted the nuances of the scene in a pleasing way. A strong northwest breeze gave bite to air already cold in the aftermath of the blizzard. Two feet of new snow covered everything with white powder, softening outlines, deadening sound.

And yet, the woods reverberated with noise. The sounds of preliminary skirmishing could be heard from the direction of the town as regiments of Mongol horsemen showered the top of the wall and the towers with arrows. But it was the woodcutting that generated the most noise. Subedei had determined to surround the town with a stockade, erected as close as possible to the town walls. His troops could then maneuver from behind the log barricade while the defenders remained ignorant of their location. His siege engines could approach the town walls with impunity to launch their projectiles from short range.

I had been assigned to drag logs from the woods to the stockade site, using our two bullocks. Sorghatanu had received the same order for herself. We had decided to work together during the course of the day, dragging logs from the same cutting location to the same stockade segment. I followed her as we moved through the snow, using the frozen course already laid down by those who had gone before. The woods teemed with activity, seemingly chaotic but in fact well organized.

I had a taste of the coming battle as I dragged the first log toward the short section of stockade in place opposite the main gate. Arrows and other projectiles launched from the walls fell around me. The snow was littered with them. In one spot, a pool of bright blood proved that not all arrows fell harmlessly.

As I came close, a squad of horsemen rode from the shelter of the nearby woods to shower the ramparts with arrows in an effort to put down the defenders. The tactic appeared to work. The flow of missiles loosed in my direction all but ceased as I drove the last fifty yards or so to take shelter behind the few logs that had been put in place. A squad of soldiers on foot quickly unhitched the log my bullocks had been dragging and maneuvered it into place to extend the growing stockade. I waited for Sorghatanu to drag her log in so that we could go back together. A squad of horseman rode in, as they had done for me, to provide cover for her progress. We received similar protection as we departed.

All the while, the defenders and the horsemen traded shouts and insults most vile and obscene. The men building the stockade kept silent.

Even so, it sounded as though thousands of men were bellowing curses at each other, punctuated every now and then by the shriek of an unlucky one found by an arrow.

Back and forth we went, from woods to stockade, all day long in the cold and din. By mid afternoon, the snow from the town walls out to a distance of a half mile or more had been trampled by man and beast, scoured by dragged tree trunks. Thick stands of trees had simply disappeared, the ground littered with the debris of their severed branches. The stockade of tree trunks lashed together stood opposite perhaps one-third of the town walls with openings and overlaps through which the Mongols could pour when the time came for the assault.

The steady creak, rattle and thump of Persian mangonels could be heard. No sooner did the Mongols complete a section of stockade than they assembled a catapult behind it to commence the bombardment of the defending ramparts. I watched the huge boulders fly through the air to thunder against the main gate and the towers. The Mongols had devoted dozens of carts to the transport of boulders best suited by size and shape for their catapults. I could now see at first hand the wisdom behind such an effort. Within hours, even my untrained eye detected signs that the defenses were beginning to fail under the onslaught. A timber knocked loose here, a tower shaking violently after a direct hit there, all foretold an early and bloody end to the siege.

I returned to our ger at dusk, bone weary from the hard work, the cold and the tension. Sorghatanu had returned shortly before to prepare the evening meal at her ger perhaps fifty feet from mine. Camp and cooking fires crackled throughout the woods sending plumes of smoke straight to the heavens in the still air. No clouds marked the night sky, with a rising moon in the first quarter almost directly overhead surrounded by a carpet of stars. The cold descended from the heavens, attacking all exposed flesh, searing the lungs.

Setu came to invite me to the evening meal at her family's ger shortly after I attended to our animals. There was no way to shelter them from the cold. But unlike me, they were born to it. None of them seemed to suffer distress as I spread hay for them and tried to give them a few drops of water before it refroze.

Wilfred, Iglaqti and two other men of the Guard rode in to partake of the meal shortly after I entered Sorghatanu's ger, shivering. We sat in the usual circle around the cooking pot, mostly in silence. After a time, the men began to talk of the coming battle.

"Do you think that we will attack tomorrow?" Wilfred asked. Iglaqti shook his head.

"We will attack when the catapults breach the walls. Subedei builds stockades to provide cover. He will not sacrifice the benefits of cover until the time is ripe."

"When will that be, do you think?"

One of the men I did not know responded. "Those walls won't hold for more than a few days." The man smiled. He had an innocent, youthful face with twinkling eyes. "My guess is that we will be drinking their blood and fucking their women to death in a few days' time. I hope that the town holds young beauties and riches. The pickings were pretty thin in Bulgar."

I glanced at Sorghatanu to see if such talk affected her in light of her experiences as a youth. If it did, she gave no sign, working cheerfully in service to her man and her guests despite the fatigue of the day.

"It will be an interesting time, all right," Iglaqti said. "According to Tolui, Subedei has ordered that we make an example of Ryazan. We will kill all but a hundred men and the women we take as slaves. The men will be made to watch the execution of the others. If we catch the Prince of this place and his family, we will torture them to death and make the men watch that, too. They will then be sent ahead to the other towns of this region as heralds of our coming."

"To what end?" I could not contain the question.

The smiling, friendly man I did not know replied: "To bring terror. Some may surrender without battle and agree to become vassals rather than be flayed alive after watching their children impaled on sharp stakes. Who knows to what end? Subedei and Batu cannot accept too many surrenders. This army lives on plunder. How can we both plunder and spare a city at one and the same time?"

He laughed, a cheerful uplifting sound. The others joined in, as did Sorghatanu and Setu, even Wilfred a little. Even the Bulgar women who understood not a word. As no one had bothered them for at least two days, perhaps they had started to believe in the possibility of survival.

So whatever the end, the Mongols would make an example of Ryazan. To my shame, I confess that I felt a morbid interest in observing what that might mean in practical terms.

The men had no duties to perform that night. Wilfred spent the night in our ger as Iglaqti did in his. I could not but wonder whose robe he shared and what might be occurring within it. In spite of myself, I felt an aching void in my gut at the thought of Sorghatanu or even Setu in that man's embrace. I could only hope that he slaked his loins on the Bulgar women. Despite my fatigue, uncertainty and jealous demons so exercised me that I remained awake well into the night, while Wilfred slept like an angel.

*   *   *   *

"We will take the city by storm tomorrow." Wilfred spoke the words as though describing a mundane chore. Only three days had passed since the stockade had taken sufficient shape to shelter siege engines. The walls had not survived even such a short bombardment. He looked at me hard. "I suggest that you stay away."

"Should I not bring the wagon?" I had received no orders. But somehow, it seemed vaguely to be expected that I would assist men of the Guard with their plunder. Wilfred shook his head.

"Find a task that keeps you in camp unless you receive a direct order."

"Why? Will it be dangerous?"

"There is always some danger. You could be mistaken for a Rus. You could be struck by a stray arrow or other missile. You could become trapped by fire." He shrugged. "But I suggest that you stay away because of what you might see."

"What?"

"You heard it described last night. It will be that bad or worse. But no words can do justice to such a scene. Believe me. I know. You are strong, Johnnie. But even so, you should avoid such displays unless you are given no choice. They inject poison into the spirit, whether perpetrated by Christian, pagan or those who profess no religion at all."

He left several hours before dawn the next morning. Shortly after first light, I could hear the din of the assault, the war cry of the charging horsemen, the shouts and howls of the combatants. The noise faded quickly. I could not tell whether this signified a change in the wind or a shift in the battlefront as the defenders retreated before the rampage. I busied myself about the camp, tending animals, mending felt panels of the ger and generally trying to ignore the battle for survival in progress less than a half mile away. I saw Sorghatanu engaged in similar tasks around her own camp. We waved to each other, but did not speak.

Shortly after noon, a rider came through camp announcing that Ryazan had fallen, summoning all those within earshot to the town square a short distance inside the main gate. I decided to ignore the invitation as Wilfred had suggested, hanging back even though I saw Sorghatanu and her family ride off toward the town.

Perhaps an hour passed without incident as I busied myself with various chores. But at some point, I became aware of shouting and cheering of the type one might hear at a tournament of knights or a coronation or a carnival. The cheers came in waves, at intervals, as though in response to a speech or spectacle. My curiosity grew as I paid closer attention. I began to detect an additional sound interjected between the cheers, a sound that seemed to call forth the cheers as though in response, a sound of banshee wailing, a sound that seemed divorced from human or animal origin as though the very soul of the earth cried out in anguish. Horror and fascination fueled a curiosity I could not resist. I hitched the bullocks to the wagon and went toward the city, as though to help in the collection of Guardsmen's loot. The noise grew, as I approached. Nearing the main gate in a bustle of soldiers and camp followers, I could hear continuous yelling punctuated from time to time by the roar of a crowd, thousands of human voices shouting in unison, interspersed with the wailing noise, point and counterpoint. I still could not identify it although it raised the hackles on the back of my neck.

I entered Ryazan through what was left of the main gate. The buttresses on both sides of the earthen bulwarks had been knocked askew. One tower leaned crazily over a bearing column fractured by a boulder from a catapult. The tilt of it exposed the rampart at the top where several defenders lay, some perforated by arrows, some with their throats cut.

Blood oozed down the side of the structure to feed a vermilion pool in the snow at the base. Dead and dying Rus lay about at random. Some appeared to have died from arrow or sword wounds while fighting. Some were plainly civilians or prisoners who had been beheaded or trussed and then stabbed. Crowds of Mongols moved through the gate in both directions on some business or other, ignoring the carnage that surrounded them.

A cavalryman on horseback led a group of women captives out of the city tethered by the neck in single file, their hands tied behind them. The clothes of some were in disarray. The rest were naked altogether, despite the fierce cold. Mongol men and women jeered them, jabbed at them, handled them rudely as they passed by. I still recall the anguish and fear etched on their faces. I did not expect many of them to survive the night.

Fires had started in the town. Perhaps the defenders had sought to use fire as a desperate, last-ditch tactic. Perhaps the Mongols had started the fires deliberately, to carry out their plan of destruction. Or perhaps it was an accident. Whatever the cause, smoke lay low over the rooftops, tinting the sky, the scent of distant burning ominous on the evening breeze.

The roaring and wailing filled the air now, overpowering all other noise as I pushed through the crowd. It reverberated in the narrow streets, rebounding off the structures like a physical force pounding against my head and chest. All around me, soldiers and camp followers were looting the buildings in a veritable orgy of unbridled theft and desecration, a revel that bordered on manic insanity. All of my senses were assailed by alien stimuli as though I had been cast into the netherworld.

I soon reached the town square, stepping directly into the cauldron of noise that had reached me in camp, one half mile away. The scene was simple enough.

Mongol soldiers and many camp followers stood watching the Prince of Ryazan being flayed alive on a rack placed above a fire on the elevated steps of a church that faced the square. Into the ground at the foot of the steps, the Mongols had driven four sharp stakes on which they had impaled the naked Princess and their three children who still writhed in their death agony. Presumably, the Prince had seen that and other horrors done before his own ordeal began. Off to the right, the Mongols held a large group of trembling Rus on their knees, trussed by the neck, forcing them to

197

watch the spectacle. I assumed that these were the witnesses who would be sent forth to testify as to the fate that awaited any town or city that refused to submit to Subedei's terms.

The banshee wails came from the Prince himself, although I would never have guessed that any human voice could make such a terrible sound. Each time the Mongols tending to the Prince ripped skin from his tortured body the way a huntsman would skin a deer, his explosive shriek would elicit a responding cheer of delight from the crowd, a cheer of taunt and triumphant derision. The faces in the crowd were filled with frenzy, excitement, an orgiastic pleasure at the spectacle.

It took several minutes of frantic effort to turn my bullocks around. Panic constricted my belly, depriving me of breath. I felt the walls of the city close in. My mind's eye saw them filled with flame, running with blood. I felt that I would be drowned, suffocated, burned alive if I did not escape immediately.

It was then that I saw Sorghatanu in the crowd, transported by the spectacle as the rest of them were. She exploded with shouts, her arms waving wildly, with each unearthly howl from the Prince. Despite the cold, sweat ran down her face. She had taken off her felt coat, and sweat stained her jerkin. I looked at her hard to make sure that I had not mistaken a stranger for my possession. I had not. So taken was she by the spectacle that she did not see me though I struggled for several minutes with my team almost directly in front of her.

Yea though I walk through the valley of the shadow of death, I shall fear no evil. For Thou art with me. Oh dear God, please be with me now. A voice screamed in my head, beseeching divine guidance as a drowning man clutches at straws. My plea echoed like a solitary cry in the dark cavern of loneliness. I rode back through the gate to camp utterly undone.

I could not separate and describe the emotions that rampaged through me. I could not comprehend how such a hardy people, such a cheerful people, a people with such spiritual connection to the earth, the heavens, the currents of nature, a people respectful of all spiritual beliefs, could be capable of what I had just witnessed. The most vicious animals in all creation would never commit such acts or enjoy them so absolutely.

I had learned by then that men fresh from battle are filled with a demonic excitement. Often they cannot sit still regardless of fatigue. They yell. They gyrate around, waving their arms. They are prone to violence on almost any provocation, no matter how slight. They have an explosive urge to fornicate as though the mortal danger of battle engenders a great urge to breed and thus leave an heir before the next encounter can bring an abrupt end to their line.

Apparently, those who witness and enjoy rituals of torture experience a similar excitement. Sorghatanu came to me that night and would not be denied. She overwhelmed me, annihilating my sense of abhorrence in a torrent of fevered passion. Finally sensing a troubled reserve on my part, she cried piteously, professing her love, her willingness to do all and be all I could ever want on this earth. Her tears ran down my cheeks as she lay on me sobbing over the very possibility that she might have displeased me in some way.

I never told her that I had seen her in the city. I never told her of my reaction to seeing her. I tried to banish the memory for both our sakes. But the vision of her frenzied face in that awful crowd flashed before my eyes unbidden, at random, sometimes at the peak of our coupling.

For it was often at those very moments that her face took on the aspect that I had observed in the Ryazan town square.

*   *   *   *

After Ryazan, the army moved north to Kolumna and thence into Suzdalia where it invested and captured the town of Moscow. It then veered back east to take Vladimir, using a stockade to create cover for the assault as at Ryazan. We of the camp stayed close to the army through all these travels and battles, pushing with great effort to keep up through the bleak winter landscape.

After the battle of Vladimir, the army divided into groups, the better to move about the country in an effort to track down and flush out an army assembled by the Grand Duke of Suzdalia. By February, 1238, scouts had located the Grand Duke's force while remaining undetected by the Suzdalians. Called in through their system of communications, the Mongol army converged upon the Grand Duke from every side, caught his force by surprise and annihilated it in a shower of arrows.

In the meantime, Batu had taken a contingent north to capture Novgorod. A sudden thaw frustrated his efforts when it turned the country into an impassable quagmire. Batu abandoned Novgorod and turned south to rejoin Subedei. The entire army then headed south, intending to spend the summer in the rich, grassland steppes known as the Don Basin, defined on the east by the tranquil Don River. The defenders of the town of Kozelsk caused a delay by advancing unexpectedly to confront the vanguard of the Mongol army and inflicting heavy losses. Subedei responded by besieging the town and killing everyone in it. The defenders fought bravely. In the end, they held us up for two months.

When the army had divided for the effort to catch the Grand Duke of Suzdalia, we of the camp and baggage train halted in the region of Kolumna near Vladimir. We moved too slowly to keep up with the war of rapid movement then being conducted by Subedei and Batu. The commanders concluded that the camp should stop and take a defensive position. So we established a fortified redoubt on a low, forested ridge above a frozen plain of swamp and grasslands to await the army's move south.

We stayed in that place for nearly two months. Wilfred, Iglaqti and Torluq were away with the Guard in Subedei's force. The men who guarded the camp were of different units, from different tribes — men we did not know and who did not know us. In most cases, they were men with whom we did not share a common language.

Sorghatanu and I kept together the entire time, living the daily routine of husband and wife but in the first blush of union. Although I could not banish the visions of Ryazan entirely, they receded into the deep inner corridors of consciousness. Common and cooperative work filled our days, passion our nights. We gathered wood together, repaired harnesses and carts together, tended our flocks together, ate together and then lay in the same robes at night.

She brought Setu to me when the monthlies gripped her, lying with us to instruct her daughter. When she felt that union might leave her with child, she would not allow me entry into her body but relieved me in other ways. She told me often that any night without such release was bad for my health and spirit, stultifying to my creativity. She seemed motivated in these matters solely by the aim of giving me pleasure. She showered me with tears of joy whenever she felt that her efforts had succeeded particularly well. After our coupling, she would lie awake for long hours expertly caressing and massaging my body with unbounded tenderness. I cannot imagine that one could experience any greater pleasures of the body on this earth.

We never argued or disagreed on any subject. I was filled with a sense of continuous joy, of revitalization, of wonder at my capacity for pleasure, a pleasure rooted in closeness with another being. My mind simply could not encompass the notion that such exalted feelings were sinful, sufficient to condemn one's soul to eternal damnation.

Still, the vision of Ryazan would not fade. I cursed it often as it leapt to mind unbidden, unexpected, at moments most uncongenial to its presence.

*　　　　*　　　　*　　　　*

The Mongol army stayed encamped on the Don for a full year, gathering its strength. Reinforcements arrived from the vassal tribes, along with herds of horses driven from Mongolia. Small detachments rode out in all directions to conduct raids and to capture Turkic nomads to be pressed into service as slave soldiers. Circassians, Kipchaks, Alans and Cumans all became minions of the Mongol Khan in this fashion. So successful were these raids that they gathered up more slave soldiers than the Mongol army could employ. So Batu sold the excess for gold to the new Sultan of Egypt.

As all these events took place, our camp took on the look and feel of a permanent settlement. The Guard rode out from time to time on its various raids, in one instance chasing the leader of the Kipchaks, Khan Kotian, all the way to the passes of the Carpathian Mountains on the Hungarian border. But I had no occasion to move and no interest in doing so. Sorghatanu stayed close and our connection did not diminish. Indeed, it seemed to intensify amid the hustle and bustle of that busy camp. Wilfred, Iglaqti and Torluq resided with us from time to time, but they also left for long periods, leaving us to explore each other and grow closer without restraint.

At some point during that sojourn, I rejected Setu when Sorghatanu brought her to me. She reacted as though I had rejected her, rather than her daughter.

201

"What's wrong, Joh? Why do you not wish it?"

"Because you are the only woman on earth for me now. I want no other."

I recall that Setu let out a wail of anguish at this. I knew that she did not care for me particularly. I am sure she resented submitting to me on her mother's orders. But a rejection of this sort deeply offended a Mongol woman's honor. I took her face firmly in my hands and held it close to mine.

"Shhh, Setu. Hear me. You are beautiful. You are a gift. I do not reject you when I choose to await Sorghi. I choose to wait for her because of regard for her, not through lack of regard for you."

Setu was not mollified. Her culture did not admit of these concepts. She maintained her resentment — and I suspect that she began to carry tales to Iglaqti. For it is from that point forward that I commenced to have increasing difficulties with him.

CHAPTER FIFTEEN

The campaign resumed in the Spring, after our year of sojourn in the bend of the Don. The start was delayed by a dispute between Guyuk and Batu over the extent of the realms that each would control and from which each could derive tribute.

I know no details other than that the Princes of the Imperial Mongolian Empire contested with each other in the manner of Princes everywhere, regardless of their power and wealth, as though nothing on earth or in heaven could ever be enough for either of them. At least, they resolved the matter without killing each other, as would have been the case among contending princes of Byzantium.

The Mongol attack began against Chernigov and then Pereislav, the latter lying east of the Dnieper River not far from Kiev. Both cities fell quickly with the usual carnage. Observing these events and deeming the Mongols invincible, Prince Michael of Kiev abandoned the City and fled west, leaving its defense in the hands of his governor, one Dmitri.

Kiev was then the political and religious capital of the land of Rus, much larger than the other cities destroyed by the Mongols, containing more than four hundred churches within its walls. Aware of its importance, Batu entrusted the assault to his cousin Mongke, a great warrior and future Great Khan, a man less bloody-minded than Subedei. Mongke sought to preserve the City by seeking its surrender without battle. Dmitri murdered Mongke's envoys, thus sealing the fate of both the City and the citizens under his charge.

*   *   *   *

I entered Iglaqti's ger in response to his summons, delivered by Torluq. Wilfred was there when I arrived. He appeared somber and did not engage my eye when I entered. I felt tension rise within me. The aspect of the situation did not bode well.

The army was poised for assault on the east bank of the Dnieper River, opposite Kiev, visible in the distance on its high bluff. We awaited the winter's freeze so we could cross and destroy the City. No one on either bank doubted that that would happen, except perhaps, those few Rus who still believed in miracles. The sun stood low in the southwest, dropping quickly in its early winter trajectory. Its bright, slanting rays cast long shadows and conveyed little heat. The night would be cold, of that there could be no doubt.

I greeted Iglaqti, Wilfred and Torluq and took my seat on the floor opposite Iglaqti, facing him. Iglaqti's visage was as forbidding as ever, worse tonight because of the cold rage I could see in his hooded eyes.

He wasted no time. As soon as I was seated, he leaned forward, extended his right arm to point a crooked index finger directly into my face. "You, Johnnie, continue to fuck my wife and daughter behind my back. I conferred the privilege of their bodies upon you as a host to an honored guest for one night. Instead, you took the privilege without my leave the next night and the next. From the rumors that abound in this camp, it is clear to me that you now take them for your own, whenever and however you wish. What do you have to say to this?"

I summoned all the courage I could muster and looked him in the eye. "It is true, honorable Iglaqti. I apologize for any offense I have given you."

He fairly exploded, bellowing. "Offense? Offense, you say? You have defiled my honor among the men of this camp. You have made me look the fool."

I knew that I must try to remain calm and above all, show no fear. "I apologize once more, honorable Iglaqti. I stupidly and wrongly assumed that you would not care as you spend all the time that you are in camp dallying with the slave women you have captured."

"Did Sorghatanu tell you that?" He did not raise his voice, but it took on an edge like a butcher's knife. My heart leapt in fear for her at this menace. She had assured me that he did not beat her as many Mongols did their wives. But it was also true that the custom would have allowed him to kill or disfigure her for what she had done with me.

"No, honorable Iglaqti. That too is a rumor widely circulated among the men of this camp."

Iglaqti glanced at Wilfred. I thought that I detected a fleeting smile pass between them. His face was stern as before when he returned his gaze to me — but his anger had subsided.

"You will buy her from me, then. She will be yours. I will solace myself in my loss with my slave women and the price that you shall pay me."

My heart leapt within me. Could this be? "I would buy her gladly, honorable Iglaqti. As you know, however, I am not a man of means, but tell me the price and I will make every effort to raise it."

He did not hesitate. There would be no more effort to disguise this exercise as a matter of honor. "Forty sheep of good quality — two rams, thirty-eight ewes."

I feigned shock. "A fine woman she is, honorable Iglaqti. But worth no more than twelve sheep of good quality." He expressed shock and indignation in his turn at my insult to his wife. So it went, for twenty or more minutes. We arrived at a final price of twenty sheep, two rams and eighteen ewes, or four cavalry grade horses, my choice. By the end of the haggling, it had become a silly game. There was no chance on God's good earth that I could ever raise such a price, even the price that I finally offered. Nonetheless, we touched hands on it to seal the bargain. Somehow, I had lost the note on which the discussion had begun, the purpose of Iglaqti's summons. His reminder left no room for doubt.

"As you are an honorable man, Johnnie, you have made a gentleman's bargain. In that bargain, you recognize that the woman is mine until you have paid her price. So long as she is mine, you will have no liaison with her without my leave. If you do not respect me in this, I will cut off your balls and feed them to you before I split your head with my battleax." He paused, looking at Wilfred, before turning back to me. "Your friend and protector agrees that I am in the right in this."

I looked at Wilfred. He nodded. I searched for a sign of reassurance from him and found none. I departed Iglaqti's ger at the first opportunity, leaving them to share their meal. Wilfred stayed. I ate unheated mutton alone, outside in the cold, watching the winter sky. A few scattered clouds intervened between me and the stars, ghostly white in the reflected light of the slender moon. They seemed close enough to touch but offered no solace in my forlorn state.

We had been told that the army would ride north to cross the River just above its confluence with the Desna the next morning. The ice was thick enough on both Rivers at that point to carry the weight of horsemen. The army would invest the City and prepare for the attack from the west side, through the main gate. We of the camp would follow in a few days time, as soon as ice formed on the Dnieper of sufficient thickness.

At some point during the night, Wilfred, Iglaqti and Torluq rode away to join the Guard in preparation for the dawn crossing. I lay down in my sleeping robes, leaving the flap of my ger open to admit the night sky despite the cold, feeling melancholy and alone. The lustre of the heavens failed to soothe me in my loss. Now that she was forbidden to me, I realized how much in thrall I had become to Sorghi's company. I missed her body and her skills with mine, to be sure. Most of all, I missed her warmth and her enormous heart. I missed her good humor. I missed the sounds she made while asleep. I missed even her blasphemous but challenging observations concerning the spirit force.

Many hours passed before sleep overtook me in my loneliness. I awoke in the pre-dawn hours to find her beside me. So stealthy was she that I had not heard her approach, nor had I sensed her presence until her naked body lay against mine. She placed her hand gently over my mouth to quiet me as she whispered with mouth pressed against my ear.

"Say not a word, Joh. I have come to thee of my own will. I care not what he thinks or says." She kissed me then, a powerful, possessive thing, and whispered again. "It is my ripe time so you must not enter me. Lie back. Restrain all movement and I will bring you the sunburst in my own way." Her hand over my mouth silenced my protest. Then with her fingers, her lips, her tongue, all expertly applied, she produced a tidal wave of carnal ecstasy that rolled from my loins, up my spine to explode in my head in a manner that I had never experienced before, leaving me breathless and spent.

I finally regained my voice after several moments. "Sorghi, please show me how to give you the same pleasure. I yearn to do it." She resisted for a time, urging me to rest, then finally relented. With her hand on my wrist she guided me to the places outside and inside her body, the hotbeds from which carnal delight grows. She taught me the rhythms and pressures that nourished that growth in the most fruitful way, leading to an explosive convulsion of feeling and movement, leaving her gasping. I could not believe the joy I felt at producing such ecstasy for her. Under what amounted to a sentence of death, we clung to each other the whole night through, alternately crying, professing our love and fervently pleasuring each other.

Thus passed the next three days and nights before the River Dnieper formed a surface of ice sufficient in thickness so that we of the baggage train could cross and join the battle for Kiev. By that point, Iglaqti must have known that we had violated his injunction. For as Sorghi had said, there were no secrets in that camp. And little Setu had yet to exact her full revenge.

*   *   *   *

The Mongol army moved close for the assault. By that point, we had received so many reinforcements, so many fresh mounts that the multitude seemed twice as large as that with which we had first crossed the Urals. We invested the City in clouds, our thundering wagons, bellowing herds, the hooves of thousands of horses, war cries and shouts drowning out all other sounds.

Terrified citizens of Kiev probably felt deafened by the noise. As a member of that vast throng, I can state that the Mongols made no more and no less noise than they had made on past occasions. Approaching doom created a sound novel to the Kievan ear. I, on the other hand, had heard it often.

The assault began at the western or Polish gate and quickly broke into the City. Sorghatanu and I were assigned to follow a contingent of Guardsmen closely with our wagon to help in the collection of plunder. I would have preferred to wait beyond the walls as I had on other occasions, but Kiev was simply too vast for that.

The looting and murder began almost at once as the defenders fled before the onslaught. Kiev contained no citadel so Dmitri sought to make a last stand at the Church of the Virgin in the heart of the City. He had attempted to fortify the Church at the last moment. But so many terrified citizens sought sanctuary within its upper reaches to escape the wrath of the invaders that the Church collapsed under the weight of them. Although I did not witness this event or its aftermath, the systematic slaughter of all those not killed in the fall, I do not feel that I missed anything unique. Similar scenes unfolded on every side wherever we went.

After entering the City in our cart, an officer of the Guard directed us to follow a narrow street between wooden buildings toward a square that we could see a short distance away. The Cathedral of St. Sophia stood on the opposite side. As soon as we started toward it, we could see that the square was being used as a killing ground.

Despite that horror in the foreground, I could not take my eyes off the Cathedral itself, a masonry structure of imposing size with thirteen domes, stepped to reflect the varying naves and ambulatories within. Several of the highest domes rested on extended drumlike structures that added to their height, with a two-story triple arcade facing the square. Clad in white-washed stucco with golden domes, the Cathedral caught the light in a manner completely incongruous to the setting. Sorghatanu tugged at my sleeve to point at the structure. I could barely hear her above the din of battle and pillage surrounding us on all sides.

"How beautiful it is, Joh. A House of Christ such as I have never seen. What will become of it?"

The question jarred me almost as much as the scene at Ryazan. To see the Cathedral, one had to elevate the eye above a foreground in which, at that very moment, squads of Mongol soldiers wielding scimitars were energetically beheading captives, civilian and soldier alike. Decapitated corpses and disembodied heads lay about at random in pools of gore. The screams of captives awaiting their fate filled the air along with the stench of blood and excrement.

I looked at her, trying to recognize the only woman on earth for me, fairly shouting to be heard.

"We will defile it, of course. We will attempt to destroy it. Even now, I suspect that soldiers are urinating on the altar, beating captives to death with the scepter, raping women in the main nave. Is that not what this army does in all such structures?"

A great moan echoed in the square as another group of hapless Rus were selected for beheading. Sorghatanu did not take her eyes from mine in her concern for the Cathedral.

"Must it be so? After that, what will happen?" She turned to look at the gleaming domes surmounted by their ornate crosses of the Orthodox form. The sound of swords striking flesh, heads striking pavement, the liquid sound of blood flowing unrestrained went without apparent notice by her. I could speak, but only with great effort.

"Our men will seek to destroy it somehow. They may not succeed. It has a masonry composition that may resist fire."

Sorghatanu remained unmoved by the fate of the Kievans, almost as though she could not see or sense that part of our surroundings. She worked enthusiastically to help in the collection of the loot. We had filled our wagon within a short time and left to take the load to a collection point near our camp. She then went back to her ger and I returned to the city with my cart as the first fires began to consume the City and the remains of its inhabitants.

Once again, I passed through a City gate congested with bustling military traffic that included the usual trussed slave women, being led away in desolation. It was late in the battle with the defenders overcome except for a few doomed and desperate men. I was ordered to return to the square in front of the Cathedral of St. Sophia, there to assist members of the Guard with their plunder.

As I reentered the square paved with cobblestones covered with dried and drying blood, I could see fires burning in many structures in the neighborhood. Several columns of black smoke boiled fiercely into the winter air, partially obscuring the gold onion domes of the Cathedral and its ornate balustrade.

The air bore an acrid burden of smoke, tinged with the stench of burning flesh. Dozens of bodies lay at random on the red-stained snow in the contorted postures of violent death. From various side streets I could hear the din of ongoing skirmishes, the shouts and curses of men engaged in mortal combat, the screams of the stricken all against the background of wood crackling in the burgeoning firestorm.

I looked about for a member of the Guard who might need assistance. It would be gross understatement to say that the situation filled me with anxiety. I was poised for flight, expecting disaster from every quarter. My normally placid bullocks were on the point of panic from the fires, barely controllable.

Just as I had decided that I should flee the flames before they surrounded and consumed me, a dark Mongol figure emerged from the Cathedral bearing a heavy sack and the shield of a Guardsman. I started forward to assist him, stopping suddenly when I recognized Iglaqti. At that moment, he pitched forward onto his face, thrashing convulsively, the sack falling behind. I ran to him. There he lay, his life's blood pumping onto the snow, grasping futilely at the arrow through his neck that had killed him. A Mongol arrow that had been loosed from a dark, smoke-filled alley to Iglaqti's left as he had emerged from the Cathedral.

My shock and incomprehension paralyzed me for a moment as I stood over him. Wilfred suddenly appeared, where I know not. He kicked at Iglaqti with his boot. When the man did not respond with any movement, Wilfred picked up the sack, glanced within and withdrew an ornate silver crucifix of the type that the Orthodox use as an altar piece. He stuck the crucifix in his belt and thrust the sack at me, his voice loud and commanding. "Here Johnnie. Take this sack to Sorghatanu. The contents belong to her now. Tell no one what you have seen here. No one. Do you understand?" His eyes pierced me like the wrath of God.

"But who will report his death, Wilfred?"

"His failure to return alive will be report enough. Tell no one, not even your precious fucking partner. Do you understand me, Johnnie?" Shouting above the din, he grabbed my arm. The fever of battle possessed him. He had the grip of an iron man. I nodded hurriedly.

"Then go and do not tarry. These flames will soon build to a heat that will roast your lustful arse like a leg of mutton." He pushed me away, bent down and grabbed Iglaqti's remains by the armpits and began dragging his burden toward the alley where the flames burned most brightly. I stood watching until he hissed at me to leave in a tone I dared not disobey. As I left the square, I looked over my shoulder in time to see him push Iglaqti's body through a doorway into a building that would shortly be engulfed in flames. Nothing would remain of the man within the hour but ashes. The

210

dark pony Timur stood to one side, prancing nervously at the smoke and flame.

That was the last I saw of Wilfred until he returned to the camp on the second night thereafter, exhausted, covered with soot and dried blood, reeking of woodsmoke and other less recognizable odors.

I quickly drove clear of the City and headed back toward camp in the turmoil of soldiers, supply wagons and captives. Despite the cauldron of atrocity behind me, my mind raced with the soaring prospects that now gleamed brightly on my horizon. Iglaqti was dead. Sorghatanu was now free to be mine as I could be hers. To my discredit, I did not mourn him in the slightest or feel guilt for his death. He had threatened my life for taking what he did not want.

My hopes disappeared quickly, as surely as the wooden buildings of Kiev. I had not been back in camp more than an hour when Sorghatanu told me that if Iglaqti died, she would be obliged to go to his brother. He tended communal herds in the Valley of the Orkhon, nine month's steady ride to the east by bullock cart, a short distance from where we had commenced the campaign.

*   *   *   *

"She cannot leave like that." I shouted in anguish. Wilfred looked up calmly.

"She has no choice. Her husband was killed. She must go to his brother in accordance with their tradition. He tends the flocks of the tribe in the Keriyat homeland."

"Where she will become his concubine. I cannot allow that to happen."

"And how will you stop it?"

"Iglaqti offered her to me for twenty sheep or four horses. I must get them somehow."

"Iglaqti is dead. You must deal with his brother now. He is a long ride from here. He is not bound by his brother's price. Indeed, I expect that he will ask much more. After all, your Sorghi was old stuff to Iglaqti.

211

She will be a novelty to the brother, although I suspect that he has had her often enough given the custom of these people."

Wilfred's voice and expression remained calm and noncommittal, maddening. I felt as though I would suffocate. Never in my life have I felt such frustration. My voice rose against my will to a level of pleading, as though for my life.

"Wilfred please. Do you not understand that I love this woman?"

At this he laughed. "So it's love, is it? The first woman in your life who fondled your manhood. The first woman in your life who slipped under you and pulled you into her. The first woman in your life who pressed her breasts into you while she made your seed flow. For you, that's love."

He laughed again, shaking his head. "Tell me, oh beloved, of what else your love encompasses? Do you discuss religion or philosophy with this woman? Does she fill your head with marvelous insights into the qualities of God, the universe, nature, the spirit world? Of what profound subjects does she speak while she pulls your pud?"

My voice took on a tone of pout, against my will. "She speaks of her childhood and the heritage of her people. She speaks of the spirit world as well."

Wilfred's eyebrows elevated. "Ah. The glories of the goatherding life in the Valley of the Orkhon, where the summers are unbearably hot, the winters unspeakably cold, the mosquitoes as large as buzzards and as numerous as the lice on the heads of the human inhabitants. Where nobody reads nor writes nor cares and everyone fucks their brothers' wives, their sisters and all the local sheep. Ah, the bucolic pastoral life under the shelter of Tengri, he the spirit of the Great Blue Sky."

"Damn you, Wilfred. God damn you to hell."

He shrugged and returned his attention to the dinner pot. "Go with her, if you wish it so profoundly. At least you will have dalliance with the daughter every month when the mother is in her monthlies. That is, until you find Iglaqti's brother who will probably insist on the privileges of the daughter as well. At least the daughter will keep her shape and smooth skin for a few years longer, although she too is no better than a dog between the ears, albeit a finer piece of firm meat between the thighs." He spoke casually, his tone adding edge to the insult.

Wilfred had never attacked me like this. I knew not what to say to him, so I kept my peace. But he did not let up.

"Are you blind, Johnnie? Do you not see all the stout, toothless, slack-breasted hags around this camp? Do you not hear their carping? Does it not occur to you that the women of these people become thus at an early age due to the life they must lead? How long do you suppose it shall be before your beloved Sorghi turns into a frog-faced harridan who touches you not and yells at you non-stop?" His voice remained calm as before, in stark contrast to the words he uttered. I felt as though I had been battered, so profoundly did his onslaught wound me.

We sat for several moments in silence. Wilfred ate slowly in his fashion. I sat still, not moving, shrouded in misery. Unable to eat, on the verge of nausea. After a time he spoke, his voice more calm and measured. More sympathetic.

"Look, go with her if you must. Contrary to my resolve, I will give you objects from my plunder that should fetch half the price that Iglaqti demanded. You will have to raise the rest yourself. You must expect the brother to demand more at first." He paused, then continued. "And there is one other thing you must weigh in the balance."

"What is that?" I could barely speak above a whisper.

"If you go, you will be making a commitment to the Keriyat life from which you may never escape. How would you ever manage to come this far west again on your own? How will you sustain yourself, let alone your possession and your possession's children? You have no animals, no horses, none of the things you must have in that life. Think hard on these things before you choose."

I felt a dark hole open in my chest as my heart broke, leaving an aching void. He was right. I knew that I could never make that choice, particularly after what I had seen and experienced on this campaign. In my heart, I knew that the great bulk of my pain derived from these very considerations. She was of one people — I of another. The gulf between us could be bridged but only for a short time. As despair rose up to swallow me like a vast wave, I could not suppress the question I had vowed never to ask.

"It was you that killed Iglaqti, was it not?"

His expression never changed nor did the tone of his voice. He did not shift his gaze from his food. "Who knows? It makes no difference. He was a soldier and he died a soldier's death. Fortunate for you it was, as he had vowed to kill you as soon as he returned to camp for dishonoring him and abusing his hospitality. He would have done it, too. He has killed many, and thought nothing of it. He would kill as readily as scratch his arse after a flea bite." Wilfred shrugged. "So he died. You live."

Sorghatanu left within a week, travelling with a caravan taking plunder back to the heartland of the Empire. Her young children, Setu, Iglaqti's small herds and a wagonload of Iglaqti's booty accompanied her. We spent the night before her departure entwined, in tears, pledging undying love and a commitment to find each other again that neither of us believed. We vowed to pray for reunion, a vow that I actually kept for a time.

Her departure severed my last tie with the Mongol people. From that point forward, I was a fellow traveller only, looking for a way out, bound once again to Wilfred and to no other — as he had ordained by the arrow he had sent through Iglaqti's throat.

*   *   *   *

After my last night with Sorghatanu, I reaffirmed my vows of celibacy to which I have been true ever since. I have confessed the sins of fornication and adultery, performed acts of contrition as prescribed by my confessor and received absolution. Even so, Sorghi visits me often in my dreams and arouses me so that I waken with the echoes of lust in my loins. Each time, I confess again, perform acts of contrition and receive absolution, to the growing exasperation of my confessor.

Despite fervent prayer for respite, her memory remains with me after all these years. From time to time I wonder if she still lives, and if so, whether I remain with her as well, a troubling presence in the dark of night.

CHAPTER SIXTEEN

Enough of massacre, torture, rape and pillage. Understand only that these things attended the Mongols, wherever they went on this campaign, with only few exceptions.

From his comrades in arms, from my own fleeting observations, I knew that Wilfred fought with energy and bravery in the battles. His stamina on the march equalled or exceeded that of his fellows. His unit was often in the vanguard. He was often with the first men to burst into a city, the first men to spring out of hiding during an ambush.

He must have killed many men in these encounters and he suffered several wounds himself, all of them minor and quickly healed. I also heard that Wilfred never killed a prisoner, never harmed women or children, never joined in the orgies of torture that so often punctuated the fall of a town or city; and never participated in the general rape of the womenfolk. He plundered with discrimination, taking only small objects of value from churches on the verge of destruction. He never sought to collect piles of booty from the homes or palaces of the conquered, and he enslaved no one to serve him.

At first, some of the men in his unit badgered him, and even threatened him, over his abstention from these activities. They soon stopped. The stature he gained through valor and skill in battle quickly overshadowed his peculiar scruples. By the time we reached Cracow, the men of the entire Guard unit viewed him with respect. Many men told me that they owed their lives to his quick ruthlessness on the battleground, his unerring aim and rapid fire.

To my knowledge, Wilfred never took any woman by force. He observed his vows except in circumstances where to do so would risk offense to a gracious host. In those circumstances, however, he took the offered womenfolk with enthusiasm and apparent skill that could only be the product of experience. I know these things well, as we often occupied the same ger during these encounters. Often the same or adjacent sleeping robes.

Thus we advanced after Kiev, through a succession of weeks and months, inexorably and unstoppable, through the forests and plains of Poland, Hungary, Austria. Although the terrain changed, the routine of the days on the march, the days of battle, did not. Chmielnik, Breslau, Liegnitz, Buda, Pest, Weiner Neustadt — all felt the searing wrath of the Mongols.

It was said that sixty-thousand Christian knights died under King Bela on the Hungarian Plain after the disaster at Cracow. I did not count the dead, but I rode among them after the battle with those who followed the army. To my undying shame, I even participated to a small degree in the plunder of the corpses and their horses, opulently comparisoned and bedecked as they lay in their individual pools of congealing blood.

It was Mongol custom to take everything of potential value from enemy dead — weapons, of course, even though not the sort of weapons that they might use. Armor, jewelry, pennants, harnesses — all were wrenched from the stiffening remains and spirited away. Many had gone into battle wearing elegant finery. Many of the Teutonic Knights, had worn crosses heavy with precious gems. All were taken. In most cases, the Mongols preserved the crosses as well as the gems. Even the pagans among them did not harbor revulsion against the symbols of Christ or Christian belief, but only against those adherents who resisted them.

I could see that many of the knights had died by stab wound to the throat or face, often through the eye. Detachments of Mongol cavalry known as mangudai, or suicide troops, had trained to unhorse European knights with rope nooses thrown over their heads while speeding by on their agile ponies. Laden with armor, a knight could not quickly regain his feet after such a setback. The Mongols would leap from their horses, lift the visor of the prostrate wretch and despatch him with a dagger. Many others had gone down and died similarly after Mongol arrows had taken their mounts from under them.

I recall the scene and blush still with shame.

CHAPTER JEVENTEEN

The ruin of Weiner Neustadt smoldered in the distance to our rear, smoke rising from the burning City a gray smudge on the southeastern horizon. We rode with a tumen, a unit of ten thousand horsemen led by a recently promoted Tolui, on the southern flank of the invasion. Southern Poland, the Hungarian Plain lay in our wake as our force swept up the flat lands along both banks of the River Danube. Terror spread before us, a giant tidal wave racing ahead on the impetus of slaughter and destruction that attended our progress through the countryside.

Following the usual practice, Tolui had set one hundred citizens of Wiener Neustadt on the road to Vienna after forcing them to witness the most refined, protracted and hideous tortures inflicted on some of their fellow citizens. Several riders herded at least a thousand captive elderly, women and children along the road ahead of us. Tolui could use them as human shields for a frontal assault; or perhaps he could trick the Viennese defenders into opening the gates of the City by driving the sorry wretches forward under the lash in the hopes that their pleading cries might confuse the gatekeepers.

Our force pushed forward slowly through cultivated fields bordered by small forest patches on gently rolling ground. Peasant cottages and small villages lay about, here and there, all deserted, all soon to be consumed in flames. A clear, bright day under cloudless sky, we could see the foothills that rose to the Alps all along the western and northwestern horizons. I rode with a small group of camp followers at the rear of the force.

Each rise gave me a full view of our party, the ranks of soldiers on their horses with pennants fluttering in the breeze, the sweep of the countryside, the outriders ahead and on each flank, the herders pushing

217

bands of spare horses, wagons with supplies and booty, strings of captives, mostly young women and boys, hands tied behind them and strung in line by the neck. I had seen it all so many times before. In recent days, the sight had come to fill me with helpless gloom — a discomfort of the abdomen rather than the heart — no matter how beautiful the setting.

We heard the pealing church-bells of the City before we crested the last rise. No one could mistake the sound of alarm and panic. We knew the situation in Austria and in the City quite well from the tales told by prisoners under interrogation. When the Mongol armies first pushed west across the frontiers of the land of Rus, the fatuous Duke of Austria saw the attack as an opportunity to extract concessions from the stricken Hungarians. A massive Mongol incursion into Germany to the north with Leignitz sacked, several other cities destroyed, their populations decimated, did not stir him from his complacency.

Then, Batu despatched our tumen into Austria to lay waste the Duke's own lands. As the incursion engulfed Weiner Neustadt and other Austrian towns on the approaches to Vienna, the Duke had pleaded for help from other European monarchs. None had been forthcoming, we were told. After the destruction of the armies that had rushed to the aid of King Bela on the Hungarian Plain, perhaps no crowned head anywhere in Europe had men to spare for the defense of the Duke's possessions.

From my vantage point on a little knoll at the rear, I saw Tolui issue a series of orders. Our column stopped. Most of the soldiers dismounted and spread out, loosening saddles and tethering their mounts. We would rest here awhile. The morning was not far advanced and, by all appearances, the day would be a fine one. The light would persist quite late at this time of year. We had ample time to attack, if that were Tolui's decision. I saw him select two patrols of ten, despatching one to the west and the other straight over the crest ahead toward the City itself. I thought I saw Wilfred in the second patrol, although I could not be sure, given the distance.

I tethered the two bullocks that carried our possessions, Wilfred's and mine, and stretched out in the grass. Who knew how long we might tarry at this place? I had learned to pass the long periods of travel, the interminable and unexplained delays of this campaign, mostly in solitude, introspection and prayer. For me, the company of barbarian strangers had become barren, devoid of all attributes that raised human life above that of the beasts. Sorghatanu was gone. That was the end of it.

I must have slept — for when I became aware of commotion in our camp, the sun had already passed its zenith, standing high and bright in the western sky. I quickly found a herder of casual acquaintance with whom I had shared a meal or two on campaign.

"What news, Torluken?"

"We go back."

"How so?"

"The Great Khan Ugedei has rejoined Tengri. Prince Batu is summoned to Karakorum for a Grand Quiriltai to choose a successor. We are to retire to the valley of the Volga in the land of the Rus and await his return."

Another death at Karakorum, another sudden deflection of life's currents. Already the soldiers had resaddled their horses, and reassembled their belongings. Several had mounted, preparing to ride off to the east. Where was Wilfred? I moved hurriedly through the camp looking for him. The day had become quite warm. The sudden activity had torn the damp ground creating ruts that tripped me. Frustration and anxiety weighed me down, impeding my movements. Breathless and on the verge of panic, I ran into the first patrol returned from the west as they changed their lathered mounts for new ones. I knew one of them, one of Wilfred's friends, a man with Mongol father and Russian mother who retained vestige of both origins as well as two names, Laqtu and Ilarion. He saw me before I saw him.

"Whoa, Johnnie. Why the frantic look?"

"I cannot find Wilfred."

"He went with the second patrol to test the defenses at the eastern gate. They should return shortly."

I looked toward the low crest in that direction, hoping to see him ride in at that moment. I could not disguise my panic.

Laqtu laughed, his broad, dark face a mass of creases that moved like the waves of a windblown sea.

"Fear not, Johnnie. The citizens of that City either run for their lives or prostrate themselves in their churches. We saw them streaming out of the City on the western roads, trampling each other in their haste, mothers casting aside babies, men thrusting aside women to be first across bridges and culverts." He laughed again.

"We rode in to take a prisoner. He confirmed that the City has few defenders, fewer still not prostrate with fear, quivering in their own shit. They had all heard of the happenings at Weiner Neustadt. All feel themselves being skinned alive over a slow fire."

"Where is this prisoner, Laqtu?" I looked about in puzzlement.

He turned, took a hide bag off the back of his horse and withdrew a human head, still oozing, eyes still wide with terror, mouth open, silently shrieking. The head of a priest by the look of the haircut as well as the crucifix that Laqtu said had hung around the man's neck. I did not ask why Laqtu had kept this man's head from among all the others he had severed. I did not need to ask why he had killed someone who plainly posed no threat.

I turned away, feeling my panic subside, looking in the direction of the City from which Wilfred would return. Nothing. A slow resolve formed and then possessed me. A great calm seemed to descend upon me like a blanket, soothing away my panic. After a few moments, I walked back to my tethered bullocks, carefully selected the most important of our belongings, loaded up the strongest of the animals and set off for the City. When questioned, I stated that I sought Wilfred with provisions in case he or any member of the patrol had suffered mishap. No one stopped me. I waved an informal salute at Tolui as I passed him. He waved and smiled back at me before turning away.

By the time I reached the crest, I could hear the shrieks of the captives driven up from Wiener Neustadt. As they would not be needed to aid an assault on Vienna, the Mongols had no further use for them. They were now being killed at this place. I muttered a silent prayer for the salvation of their souls and quick passage to the next world.

*   *   *   *

Green fields and open ground lay before me, sloping in uneven but gentle folds to the wide River Danube, perhaps a mile distant. Here and there, small groves marked the location of peasant huts and a few richer dwellings. Lines of trees marked country lanes. I could see the walls of the City on the near bank of the River, the spires of its churches and the roofs of other buildings rising above the ramparts in an irregular, crowded jumble. With care and method, I studied every fold in the country, every crest and defile for signs of the patrol. I saw nothing. The country appeared deserted, devoid of all life. Neither man nor beast could be seen.

I decided to continue all the way to the City gates, if necessary. The risk seemed slight. Even a garrison rendered hysterical by fear could not possibly mistake me for a Mongol invasion force. The Mongols themselves had sent many civilians on ahead. At least a few of them must have found their way to Vienna. I would be seen as but one among many, a victim, a refugee, possibly a man with important information. I walked on, leading the bullock, studying the ground before me intently.

After a time, I became aware of several dark shapes lying scattered about in the tall grass perhaps a quarter of a mile away, near the River. I could not make them out at first. I soon identified them as downed horses as I approached. Within one hundred yards, it was clear that I had arrived at the scene of a sharp skirmish. A myriad of hoofprints had ripped the sodden ground. Mongol arrows were scattered in great numbers where they had fallen. Articles of clothing, helmets both Mongol and European, lay partly obscured in the trampled grass. Dark pools of blood congealed in the depressions here and there.

The remains of perhaps thirty horses dotted the small depression where the battle had reached its climax, the tortured carcasses in various postures of death, some pierced by arrows, others showing hideous sword slashes. Several of these were Mongol ponies. I looked carefully but in vain for Timur, Wilfred's favorite. As the carcasses had been stripped of all saddlery and tack, I had no means by which to identify any of those killed or captured. There were no human remains. If men had died here, someone had removed the corpses.

I am not a good tracker — but anyone could have followed the trail leading away from that killing ground back toward the City. Anyone could discern that the patrol had come to grief, all of its members killed or captured by a force of nearly one hundred assailants, judging by the hoof prints.

221

My mind simply rejected all possibility that Wilfred might not have survived. He was a captive. As Christians, as men of God, having consecrated our lives to His service, Wilfred and I would convince the men of Vienna that we had been impressed into the Mongol army against our wills. As good Christian men themselves, as Catholics and loyal followers of Rome, how could they not believe us? How could they not set him free? After all, I would be the bearer of the best possible news — the Mongols had called off the invasion. Even now their legions streamed back toward the east.

I resumed my push for the City gates, trying in vain to speed the bullock along, all the while feeling like a sleep-walker struggling vainly to hold reality at a distance. My sense of hope did not survive many steps. The impact of what I had seen finally struck me like the blow of a mace. I stumbled, fell to the ground, unable to see or breathe, my stomach and chest filled with the most overpowering pain, a pain both dull and sharp, a presence yet a void, burning fire but cold as the coldest ice. Spasms of grief and torment forced the breath from my body.

I know not how long I lay stricken. When I sat up, the sun hung low in the western sky. I had no time to proceed further in daylight and too much danger lurked here for one moving at night.

So it came to pass that I, the most fearful of men, a man who values safety, security and stability above all of life's possible conditions, lay down that night under the stars in the company of a bullock, in the midst of a battle ground, not far from the spot where I believed that my mentor, my protector, my beloved companion, the only family I had in the entire world had met a violent end. It would not have been possible for anyone to be more bereft than I at that moment. Desperate prayers brought neither relief nor solace. Convulsive sobs wracked me, contorting my body, driving all hope from my soul.

In the tortured pauses between them I prayed in vain for the courage and dispensation to end my own life as I writhed in anguish, crushing the sweet-smelling grasses of an Austrian springtime.

*　　　　*　　　　*　　　　*

I must have lost consciousness, for I was awakened by a gentle rain. Night still held sway over the melancholy meadow. Low clouds cut off all light. Darkness reigned supreme over the entire world. Only the torches at the City gates dispelled the notion that grief had struck me blind.

The rain increased in its intensity. I did not know the whereabouts of the bullock and could not hope to find him before dawn dissipated the opaque night. My grief had so distracted me that I had failed to tether him or take the bag of our belongings off his back. So I had no access to the garment that I had packed for shelter from foul weather. Perhaps it was gone for good, along with the meager treasures that Wilfred had kept and that I had packed so as not to be devoid of all resources. What more pernicious twist of fate could be imagined than to be left in such state by the random wanderings of one of the dumbest beasts in God's creation?

I shivered violently in the dark under pelting skies, filled with despair and hopelessness. My God, why hast Thou forsaken me? Fresh bursts of rain riding a cold wind answered my plea.

When the light of a somber dawn pushed away the dark after an interminable night, I found the bullock standing almost exactly where I had last seen him at dusk. His back to the windblown rain, he stolidly cropped the rich grass at his feet. He allowed me to approach him without argument, seeming not even to notice. I removed the bag from his back, throwing the hide robe over my shoulders. Warming slightly, I began to think more rationally.

Clearly, I could not leave this place without making sure of Wilfred's fate. Unless I found the truth of the matter, I would never know a moment's peace all the days of my life. Thus, I must enter the City. But in the bleak light of dawn I saw things more clearly than I had the afternoon before. I could not enter the City carrying any vestige of my time with the Mongols. The Viennese would instantly despatch such a one in their panic. The bullock must remain behind as he was of the steppe, a smaller breed unknown in Europe. Worse, his halter was composed of woven horsehair, his pack supports typical of plains nomads.

In the end, I discarded the great bulk of our belongings, including the hide robe that sheltered me from the rain, the felt boots that protected my feet. Had it not been for a pair of decrepit sandals that I had retained for an unknown reason, I would have been forced to approach the City unshod.

The guards opened a door in the eastern gate to admit me without much hesitation. The men in the towers and those on the ramparts showed little interest in me, a small, forlorn figure, unarmed and wet to the bone, hungry and shivering, devoid of menace. The captain of the guard detained me for a few moments for questioning. It took a while for us to find a common language. Ultimately he found a priest with whom I had discourse in halting Latin.

"Whence do you come?"

"Weiner Neustadt. Cracow before that." The truth. I prayed that I would not be forced to lie to a priest.

"What of the barbarians? Have you seen them?"

"I have. They turned back to the east yesterday."

The priest's eyebrows raised in disbelief, in hope. He conversed with the captain in a guttural tongue, both animated.

"Where did you see this?"

"Just over the crest of the low ridge to the southeast. Come. Let us climb the ramparts and I will point it out to you."

We did so. I told them of the massacre that had taken place there. They showed neither anger nor surprise. In time, the shock of even the most heinous events subsides with monotonous repetition.

After further heated discourse with the captain, the priest asked: "Did they leave for good or was it just a feint to draw the defenders away?"

I shrugged. "Who can say? I know not. Who can predict what barbarians will do?" I looked up and crossed myself as though praying for Christ's intervention on behalf of the City. The interview finished, they gave me a hunk of stale black bread, half a sausage, wished me well and dismissed me.

A main street ran directly from the eastern gate toward the City center, roughly parallel to the River Danube. Gabled buildings composed of dark wood and clay crowded close to the edge of the street for a short distance, extended roof overhangs creating a dark, tunnel effect.

The City was silent and deserted, most of the inhabitants having fled in panic before the feared onslaught of the Mongol tempest. The slap of my sandals on the cobblestones echoed eerily in the void. After a distance of perhaps one hundred feet, the street entered a large, open area, paved with cobblestones, roughly circular with an austere structure — an official building of some sort — directly opposite. A heavy wooden balustrade projected from the second level of the building under a steeply pitched roof and a gabled front. And there, on the left side of the balustrade as one faced the building, hung the bodies of ten men in a line, as from an improvised gibbet, their arms lashed in outstretched posture against the front of the balustrade support, a caricature of crucifixion, their heads bound to the uprights by coarse rope pulled tight around their necks, their bodies hanging down in unnatural postures contorted by death.

My knees buckled at the sight. It took the greatest effort of will I have ever deployed to retain a semblance of composure, knowing that any show of sympathy for the men or consternation over their fate could lead quickly to my demise. Although I prayed that God might kill me, I somehow feared death at the hands of the Austrians, a grim paradox that I have never comprehended. I wished to run from that place but could not. Instead, I found myself drawn ever closer until I stood almost beneath them. Wilfred's remains hung third from the left.

For as long as God grants me life, the vision of that startling and gruesome scene will not depart my mind's eye, torturing me and bringing me low at odd moments. The body was plainly his — yet no vestige of him remained. All remnant of his vitality, his power, his relentless energy had departed with his spirit, leaving behind a leaking, obscene ruin. His mouth hung open, a blackened, swollen tongue protruding unnaturally. The brilliant piercing eyes had been replaced by dark holes. A dried bloodstain of imposing size trailed down from the left side of his chest.

The wreck before me had nothing to do with him, the man I revered beyond all others on this earth. Yet that wreck was clearly all that remained of him. I could not help but wonder how he died, whether he still had the breath of life in him when the Austrians strung him up. My mind recoiled from the thought of it as the hand recoils from a rock too hot to hold.

It took a few moments before I noticed crude, handwritten signs that the Austrians had pinned to each of the corpses. The translator priest entered the open area at that instant, hurrying on some errand or other. He stopped when he saw me. I asked him to read the signs for me.

"Barbarian dog," indicating the Mongols. "English pig," pointing to Wilfred.

"An Englishman? How could that be? How do you know?"

"We took him alive. One of the priests here recognized his tongue."

"So he was alive, then?"

"Barely. Babbling. Out of his head. He did not last long. We saw to that." The priest glanced up and spat. "The worst of the lot, he was. A so-called Christian riding with the forces of Anti-Christ. What could be more vile and disgusting? Well, he roasts in the fires of Hell now. We refused him the absolution for which he pleaded with his last breath." He spat again and hurried away on his errand.

I raised my eyes once again, once again overwhelmed by the gruesome distortion of he who had stood as the rock at the center of my universe all my life as boy and man, now an empty vessel, broken forever. I prayed with all my power for his soul, invoking every blessing and imprecation within my memory. His image swam out of focus. My eyes filled with hot tears. Once again, my chest convulsed with wracking sobs. I hurried away before my grief brought me to ruin.

Once away from the gibbet, my anguish did not betray me. Most of the wretched citizens of Vienna who remained, who had not already bolted in fevered panic, were so consumed by anxiety that none of them seemed to notice my condition, let alone question its cause. I walked through the City, out the western gate, following the River Road toward Linz, in solitude despite the many others proceeding in the same direction. Only one point of dim light shone in the sea of grief that suffused my entire being. Blackfriars Abbey. I knew only that it lay to the west — far distant, perhaps beyond reach in this life.

A few miles west of Vienna, the River Road to Linz swung to the north, close to the River itself. A dense grove of hardwoods stood along the riverbank. Unable to go further under my burden of bereavement, I turned off the road into the wood, working may way into its dark, clammy fastness until I reached a tiny clearing within a few feet of the water's edge. There I lay down and surrendered to the madness of uncontrolled lamentation. For one full day, a complete cycle of light and dark, I languished there in an abyss of my own creation, praying for a death that would not come.

CHAPTER EIGHTEEN

I made my way west slowly, up the Valley of the Danube — Linz, Passau, Deggendorf, towns and villages riven with terror of the Mongols. The squabbles of the petty nobles and princelings that normally tormented the lives of commonfolk in these parts shrunk to triviality under the looming threat of the Anti-Christ, the mythical forces of Gog and Magog unleashed upon the populace by a vengeful God in punishment for its sins. Only I knew the truth. The Mongols were headed for a camp a thousand miles to the east. If ever they came this way again, at least three years must pass, just by virtue of the distances that I alone knew.

I sheltered in monasteries along the way, partaking of their provenance, assisting with the chores, praying with all my power for relief from the fog of gloom that enshrouded me. To no avail. The vision of Wilfred's remains came to me every night in the post midnight hours, his death mask jarring me awake. I often cried out to the discomfiture of those with whom I shared a cell. Often he appeared as a Christlike figure, a blasphemy, despite my love for him, sowing confusion and despair. His memory, his death, the void in my life his absence created, the loss of his protection in dealing with the hostile forces of this life, left me bewildered, weak, defenseless, a leaf helplessly careening on the gusts of a winter storm.

Slowly, throughout the summer and fall, I made my way across the Germanic Provinces of the Holy Roman Empire. Nurnburg, Heidelburg, the ancient Roman city of Trier. From time to time, I suffered delay caused by unrest among the local noblemen.

Despite my efforts at Christian tolerance, I viewed them all with disdain. It is almost as though the noblemen of any Christian nation cannot tolerate peace. They cannot abide the tranquil stability that men need to raise crops, maintain herds, nurture their families, engage in productive commerce and serve Christ.

Let such conditions exist for a time and some nobleman or collection of noblemen will be rendered insane by it, driven to pick a fight with another nobleman or collection of noblemen over a contrived point of honor or a claim of title to property that neither needs. On each such occasion, they will gather a small rabble of ignorant, untrained yeoman who put their lives at risk for a cause that none understand, call it an army and contrive a battle, destroying fields and villages, sucking the blood of those in whose name they claim to be fighting; and above all, destroying the peace essential to productive work in service to God and mankind. It is said — and truly — when nobles fight, it is the peasants' thatch that burns.

I am no lover of the Mongols nor of their ways, but the landed gentry of these benighted provinces are nothing but vandals when compared to them. Who among these dwarfs truly knows of warfare? Who among them knows of sixty-thousand mounted men charging in perfect order, maneuvering without a misstep as they destroy an even more numerous enemy? Who among them knows of pyramids of human heads forty-feet high, piled to mark the place where the gates of a proud city once stood and where now there stands nothing but ash heaps?

Most of these fatheaded, strutting worthies would soil their bodkins at the mere sight of what I have seen countless times. They would run squealing in fright from the battles in which Brother Wilfred was a heroic, eager and victorious participant. They know only ways to inflict small miseries, to upset the fragile balance on which civilized life depends. They are heroes only in the tales they tell of themselves or that they pay bards to sing in their honor.

To my shame, the fervor of thoughts such as these provided the only respite from the despondent haze through which I travelled.

*   *   *   *

I fell ill at Trier, a wasting sickness that I could not shake. Most food would not stay down, yet I suffered from severe and persistent flux. On the worst days, the spasms of my bowel produced only a bloody discharge. These debilitations robbed me of my strength. I could hardly stand erect. I lost the will to live. I could not pray with sincerity. My mind wandered of its own like an unruly dog.

Fretting over my deteriorating condition, the Brothers of the small monastery where I lay decided to move me to the larger one founded by St. Bernard at the village of Clervaux, across the River Moselle in the Forest of Ardennes. They had heard that the physicians in residence there possessed extraordinary skill and learning, the Brothers adept at facilitating convalescence. Indeed, St. Bernard had been known for performing miraculous cures. In their solicitude for me, the Brothers of Trier hoped that the atmosphere of miracle in the aura of St. Bernard would save my life.

I rode from Trier to Clervaux on the back of a donkey, swathed in torpor, slipping in and out of delirium. I barely noted the autumn chill, the groups of peasants scything grain in the fields, collecting apples from trees heavy laden, filling baskets with grapes from bountiful vineyards.

When we crossed the River near the village of Echternacht, a strange event took place within me, as though a torch had flared in the abyss of my despair, rekindling purpose, resolve, illuminating an object for my life. Where were we? I shook my head vigorously in an effort to clear it. I saw hardwoods, a dense forest turning, bright yellow and red leaves shaking before the breeze in the slanting rays of an autumn sun. We splashed through a small creek rushing over a stony bed at the bottom of the first hill, the same size and sound as the creek along the northern cloister wall at Blackfriars.

In my weakened and desperate state, the Ardennes could have been the wood in which Blackfriars lay. The look of it, the smell, the sounds, all identical. St. Bernard's monastery made the picture complete, resting in the same sort of dark, wooded copse, similar in construction.

The very arrival at that place — indeed, the very crossing of the River Moselle — commenced both the cure for my physical ailment and the process of transcending Wilfred's death. It also reinforced an earthly desire, to resume a sheltered, safe, monastic life of service in that place whence I had begun my great journey.

The Brothers at Clervaux took me in, showing me care and kindness. I recovered slowly. My affliction had shriveled me to nothing but skin and bones. By the time that I regained a semblance of my former self and a modicum of strength, the first snows had fallen. Winters can be quite severe in the Ardennes and the lands to the west. This one bid fair to be among the worst in memory. Abbot Francis persuaded me to stay on to await the advent of spring.

"You lack the strength to travel in the cold season, even with the help of Christ and all of our prayers," he said.

"But how shall I earn my keep?" The monastery had few resources, an air of austerity of which Wilfred would have approved. No fat monks here. I was not comfortable simply to be a dependent when the Brothers had so little to spare.

The Abbot smiled and shrugged. "I know not. In good time, God will guide us."

Whether by divine guidance or not, who could say? Within a fortnight, I was assisting the Brothers engaged in illumination. Without consciously intending to do so, I incorporated flowing Arabic and Uighur characters into my border work and the embellishments. I did not form words, but rather used the figures for their intrinsic, rounded beauty, their exquisite flow that had always captivated me.

The Brothers thought my work divinely inspired, an extraordinary tribute to the saints and martyrs to whom the pages were dedicated. They marvelled at my skill, the beauty of creation of which they had never seen the like, the product of an unknown and mysterious school in an otherwise structured discipline. Wilfred's adventurous example, exposure to eastern figures unknown in the west, years of practice away from the strictures of established forms all combined to give my product a unique aspect in their eyes. They found it most pleasing.

I worked as an assistant to a Brother Benedict from the land of the Swiss. An austere and distant man, he soon became curious to know where I had learned my craft. His hand was square, heavy, uninspired, traditional and lifeless. I sensed in him a most un-Christian jealousy and resentment of my skill. Only the discipline of silence that prevailed during most of the day at Clervaux kept him from pressing me in ways that would have been hard to avoid. And I could not ever forget that these were lands in which the Inquisition held sway. I treated Brother Benedict with obsequious respect in an effort to forestall any motivation on his part to detect the hand of the Prince of Darkness in my work and denounce me.

The fullness of my modest strength and energy returned with the warming weather of springtime. The trees budded and began to leaf out in luminous greens against the bright sky. Wildflowers bloomed in every glade, the pristine streams and springs that flow everywhere in the Ardennes, numerous as the veins in the hands of a craftsman, gushed with the bounty of melted snow, lending the sights, sounds and smells of rushing water to the healing air.

I became restless to resume my journey. Clervaux had saved my earthly life, restored my strength, succored me in my hour of need. I would always be grateful and pray for the well-being of the Brothers here. But I belonged at Blackfriars. Only there could I be safe. Only there could I serve God as He intended.

I have little to tell of my journey to Calais, the trip across the Channel and my passage through London. I had sold the chalices and other items Wilfred's death had left to me. The last few coins I paid to the boatman, living on the charity of monasteries and churches from that point forward. I needed little. My travels had taught me much, not least that we all require less than we believe we need to survive. Who better to teach austerity than the Mongols, after all? I had, perforce, become a keen student.

Contrary to my memory, the overawed impressions of a country youth, London seemed small to me — slovenly and undistinguished, unkempt and rowdy but in a peevish and trivial way. Despite the comfort I derived from hearing everyone speaking a tongue known to me, the City had the aspect of a graceless, overgrown country town, no match for the faded grandeur of Rome, the defiled magnificence of Constantinople, the exotic architectural diversity of Samarkand.

I did not tarry to ponder these matters. The greening countryside of England quickened my step in pace with my lifting heart. Soon I would reach the ivy-covered walls of stone that marked the outer limits of my sanctuary. By God's good grace, I would not depart again until the beginning of new life in the next world.

231

I stood on the crest of the last gentle rise to peer down into the forest where Blackfriars lay. The trees, newly leafed and rocking gently in the morning breeze, obscured the Abbey entirely. Smoke rising from the cooking fires gave away the location. The road continued down the gentle slope to the edge of the wood and disappeared behind the trees as it curved to the left. One-half mile more and I would be home. Birdsong and the smells of spring filled the air.

Off to the right, a peasant slowly plowed his field behind an elderly horse. Behind him, a short distance further away, I saw the hut in which he lived, made of mud wattle and thatch. A family named Hardesty had lived there many years before, cheerful while constantly staving off starvation, good friends of Wilfred's and the other monks.

The scene, the proximity to my goal, should have filled my heart with boundless joy. It did not. I had dreamed for the last two nights that the Abbot would turn me away. Did Abbot Harold still live on this earth? Would any new Abbot — or Abbot Harold himself for that matter — care enough to take me in? Who was I anyway? Nothing but an orphan, an apprentice, not even a fully fledged lay brother. Why would the Abbot even remember me, so unremarkable was I? What reason would he have to grant me residence?

The night before as I tried to sleep on open ground, I had clearly seen Wilfred's death mask against the starry sky. With sightless eyes and bloated tongue, I swear that he spoke to me. I could not make out his meaning no matter how hard I tried, although at the end I imagined that his shade cried out in a tone of gurgling horror: "Hide, Johnnie. For the love of Christ, hide," only to disappear in a flash of pink as though jerked away by an unseen hand. I awoke sweating, in a sitting position, facing the rosy light of a peaceful dawn sky.

I stood on that rise in a welter of indecision and fear for at least an hour. Sounds of the day's activities came from the Abbey, the clang of a smith's hammer, the creaking of the mill wheel. I finally bestirred myself and approached the gate to confront the same rough wood entry structure set in the stone wall, the same ragged bell rope. I hesitated a moment before pulling it.

A small, bent figure in brown robe and sandals stood before me — Abbott Harold himself, much aged, his hair gone all white, his face a sea of creases, his jaw sunken from the loss of teeth.

"Yes, my son?" I recalled the voice. Higher in tone, thinner in quality, but the same nonetheless.

"Do you not recognize me, Abbot Harold?"

He leaned forward, squinting in the bright morning light, his face close to mine. He shook his head, smiling sheepishly. "Forgive me, my son. These old eyes fade with each passing day. Your voice and aspect seem vaguely familiar, but I cannot place them."

The moment had come. I could not risk the truth despite the enormity of the lie, an outright fraud on a loyal servant of Christ, a grave sin. "I am Brother Wilfred, Abbot Harold. Brother Wilfred who left this Abbey many years ago to accompany Bishop Michael on his mission to the Holy Father in Rome where I joined the Holy Father's mission to Prester John in the vast lands east of Constantinople, beyond Persia."

Abbot Harold's jaw fell open in shock. He squinted hard at me again. A slow smile lit up the broken landscape of his face.

"Brother Wilfred."

"Yes, Abbot Harold."

"We have sorely missed thee, Brother. We are fewer in number now, elderly and infirm. The chores of this place remain as insistent as before. We fall behind in our illuminations. Despite our prayers, we suffer from despondency that you always dispelled with your energy and uplifted spirits. I hope that you return to stay on."

My heart soared. "Yes, Abbot Harold. I have returned to resume life and prayer here for the rest of this life, if you will have me."

So it was that I gained sanctuary within the cloistered walls of Blackfriars Abbey as an imposter. No one ever questioned my identity. Only two brothers remained of those once close to Brother Wilfred who might have exposed me, Hieronymus and Bartholomew — the former gone blind and the latter beset by the demons that reside in the wine jug.

233

In a lucid moment one morning, Brother Bartholomew squinted at me suddenly as though troubled by a discordant note rising from the deepest recesses of memory.

"Brother Wilfred, where is thy longbow? Dost thou still practice the warrior's art of archery?"

I shook my head. "Lost, Brother Bartholomew. Lost in my travels." He nodded, dropping the matter.

*   *   *   *

Within a few months of my return, I became responsible for the work of illumination that took place at Blackfriars Abbey. Three apprentices worked and studied diligently under my tutelage. The work of the Abbey quickly acquired a reputation for inspired devotional beauty. People spoke of its rounded and flowing qualities, the use of forms in the scrolling and embellishment unlike those used in any other holy manuscripts. It is said that our work is uniquely spiritual and uplifting, a fitting complement to the sacred texts so adorned.

I responded to all queries concerning the origins of my craft and the details of its technical aspects with generalities. "It is the inspiration of God, insights from on high. I am but a humble implement in His hands."

Who is to say where the truth lies in such matters?

CHAPTER NINETEEN

Christmas night, anno Domini 1275. It is quiet in the Abbey save for the snoring of a few of the Brothers in nearby cells. The night air carries a heavy freight of chill and damp, the sky clear, suffused with the beauty of God's light, stars without number to the limits of view in every direction, screened only by the bare branches of the trees in the Abbey yard. There is no moon. Although no breeze stirs the night air outside, a draft gently agitates the single candle flame in my cell.

A sense of winter overpowers all other sensations, as though the cold has become a solid thing, an oppressive, torturing inescapable presence. Blackfriars' setting nurtures chill at all seasons, never more so than during the dark months. It's stone walls magnify the cold. Moss and moisture stains on the inner surface of the stone testify to the infernal dampness. The fire in the grate is impotent in the face of such an onslaught, its dancing flame nothing but fraud, promising warmth, delivering only a wavering, mirthless light.

I have lived here at Blackfriars as Brother Wilfred. My assumption of his identity has never been questioned to this day, thirty-two years on. No one remains alive that could question it now — except me. My question may be the most imperative of all. For my life, my place and all of the work that I have performed in diligent service, have all been done on the foundation of a lie. And not just a small falsehood, crafted to smooth the mundane flow of daily life in a matter of little consequence, but a willful lie as to my very identity to Abbot Harold, my temporal father and superior in the Church — for the purpose of gaining my place here.

In the early years, I could not bring myself to confess my sin for fear of exposure, unable to trust in the confidence of the confessional. After I had proven my worth through work and service, I could not bring myself to confess out of an overpowering sense of shame. When Abbot Harold passed into the next world, it seemed that confession would be inadequate, as though the sin had passed beyond the reach of remission.

Roughly two years ago, I began to pray that my Lord and Savior free me from the travails of this life and gather me to his bosom in the next. As my eyesight failed and my hand became unsteady, I lost my craft. The ability to teach was all that remained to me, and that I could no longer do by example. I believed that my life of useful service had ended, that my life lacked further purpose. My prayers went unanswered.

Instead, as my eyes grew dim, bowels and bladder became unruly, I began to dream vivid images of Brother Wilfred on our journey, his restless energy, his spiritual curiosity, his intelligence and strength. The darker scenes visited me as well, all the blood and the horror again, visions that had not troubled my waking or sleeping hours for thirty years. I had deliberately banished all thoughts of these events to avoid the inner discords they spawned. The walls of banishment broke under the onslaught. All the tension, all the horrors came to me nightly in tableaux of vivid detail, as though the events they depicted had occurred yesterday.

Then one night, the horror of a particular dream rousted me from my slumbers with racing heart, gripped by mortal terror, bathed in sweat in this dank place forsaken of all warmth. In the gloom, my eyes lit upon the quills and parchment that lay before me on a crude bench in my cell, as though the Lord had placed them there to demand my attention. At that moment, I realized what I must do. I would not be granted my release from the agony of this life and admitted to Heaven — full remission of my sin — until I had performed one last task that only I could perform.

I must first chronicle Brother Wilfred's tale in its entirety. For he was, above all, a man of God — but truly a man created in the image of God, with all the noble virtues and faults of humanity. God simply could not abide that such a man, a man who had lived an adventure of breadth and dimension beyond that of all but a handful of men, would pass from this vale of tears unknown, unremembered, unheralded. Brother Wilfred's tale was mine alone to tell. God ordained that I tell it.

And thus, I commenced the writing of these chronicles two years ago,

236

every word true to the last detail. Much more remains to be written, but I have faith that the hand of God will guide me in the writing of it. As will the shade of Brother Wilfred who continues to inhabit my dreams, night after night.

CHAPTER TWENTY

It is an hour or so past midnight and the storm's fury does not abate. I can hear branches rattle in the moaning gusts, tortured by their icy burden. Surely the orchard will suffer grievously from this storm. Although the well-being of our trees has mainly fallen to me of late, I am detached from such concerns. A larger matter troubles my heart, submerging me in a sink of gloom and confusion, a perfect accompaniment to the weather and the decline of my temporal powers.

I have just reread my manuscript, an uneven collection of parchment sheets that stands in two stacks in a corner of my cell. I have no shame for its quality as a literary product. Exposed as I have been to the fine works I have illuminated throughout the decades of my life, I have absorbed the structure and cadence of writing. As a competent but unremarkable musician can hear a great work and play it back, albeit without the flair of the master, I can see that I have completed a lively, informative and even profound work in many respects. Yet I have failed in my purpose.

Wilfred undertook the great journey that I have chronicled — on which I accompanied him against my nature — as part of the Pope's effort to make alliance with a chimera, the Kingdom of Prester John, a myth constructed on the thin air of hope. Desperate for a potent ally against Moslem power, prepared to believe that any enemy of the Moslems must be Christian, the Pope sent us to create a holy compact with an Empire that turned out to be that of Ghenghis Khan. That empire was neither Christian nor Anti-Christ, but rather a cataclysmic force of nature, like an earthquake or erupting volcano, naked power wherever the motivations intrinsic to its essence directed, destroying all that stood in the way.

None of that matters now, except for the depressing conclusion that one can draw from it, a constant human failing. In the absence of hard facts or the ability to face those we find uncongenial to our cherished beliefs, we create wishdreams, burnish them with our hopes until they gain the patina of immutable truth, and then we sacrifice our lives to them. A celebration of futility, the perfect accompaniment to the completion of my writing, recounting futility and senseless waste, above all else.

I began my manuscript to create an account of an epic journey through space, time, the spirit, and above all, a range of unprecedented human experience, believing that God ordained the effort. In these particulars, I have succeeded. The story contains those elements, truly. I sought to reflect credit upon Brother Wilfred — to bring fame to his memory, as I loved and revered him, to record a hero's progress. His energy and manifold gifts come through in the manuscript, as well. It could not be otherwise.

But my readers will see him as a murderer disguised as a man of God. He will be seen as an apostate, a man who strayed from his vocation to devote his considerable skills at holy illumination to the enhancement of heathen works. He will be seen as a skillful and energetic warrior in the service of a pagan power, brutal, barbarous and without soul. His essence will be lost in a storm of conventional disapproval.

As I have assumed Wilfred's identity over these past decades, even those who read and understand the tale — as I would have them read and understand it — will see in it nothing but a deranged paean of self-praise. They will see nothing but the delusions of a warped senility, a frantic quest for immortality through self-serving fable. I cannot abide the prospect. It profanes my love for him, a love that I alone can understand. And my tale cannot absolve me from the sin I committed when I assumed his identity in this holy place by a lie to the keeper of it.

How could I have failed to see all this before? Working in a dark cell with quill and parchment, grappling with the turgid recall of events long ago — struggling to be as precise in detail as possible — I lost the larger view. That view strikes me full as I reread the product whole.

Dull, pervasive pain is now my constant companion. Movement of any kind requires effort. I seem to need more and more sleep, but my sleep is troubled, rarely restful. I sense the constriction of my vision, as though I see all things through a dark tunnel that grows more attenuated, smaller in diameter, more dimly lit with each passing day. A shroud darkens my mood and numbs my mind as I struggle against the chill. Tonight's storm can hardly serve as a point of climax, for winter has just begun. It can only be a grim forerunner of more to come. I have no will to face the onslaught of yet one more season of dark and cold.

The light in the grate flares as I feed the first page to the fire. The parchment oil adds bright vigor to the flame. The light becomes the focal point of the room, casting ephemeral illumination into the dark corners of my cell, dancing shadows on the stone ceiling. I feel far away, not sure whether I inhabit a dream or my earthly quarters. The flame dies down, only to revive with each sheet. The rank odor of burning parchment fills the air. Tendrils of oily smoke trace the vagrant wind currents that the stone walls cannot hold at bay. I see all through a film, as though under water.

My vision grows ever dimmer, my limbs weightier with the passing hours. The minor effort required to feed sheets to the flame exhausts me. The sheets appear to dance just out of reach as though to mock me — as in a state of suspended consciousness. But just as the chronicle itself had to be written, I feel that I must complete this work also, as though the tasks possessed wills of their own and selected me as their instrument. I near the end at last. The flame's unquenched appetite rises eagerly to feast on the last sheet, delivered to the grate with trembling hand, barely visible to my failing eye as it recedes in a tunnel of darkness.

I lie back in relief with nothing before my eyes or consciousness but the flame. As it subsides, I feel myself rise slowly to meet the cold, the dark of this unsettled night. No vision of the Blessed Virgin or of the Savior comes to meet me as I travel to rejoin the great river of life that flows through a winter landscape.

EPILOGUE

When Brother Wilfred had not been seen by mid-morning, two of the Brothers went to his cell.   There they found his earthly remains in a position of repose on the rough shelf that served as his bed.   Eyes closed, face starkly white, it appeared to all that he had passed away in serene peace, secure in the protection of his Lord and Savior.

Sheets of parchment lay about.   Several of the sheets had been partially consumed by the flame of the grate. The air reeked with the stink of their burning.   Two large stacks of unburned sheets remained, ragged and uneven in the corner of the cell.

Examining the sheets, the Brothers discovered that they were filled with neat columns of graceful, rounded figures rendered in Wilfred's hand - figures familiar to those who had closely examined Brother Wilfred's works of illumination.   But the parchments presented the figures in regimented order, not intertwined as a component of delicate scroll-work or embroidery.

In agitated consultation, the Brothers concluded that the figures on the parchment had to be writing of some sort, but of a sort that none of them had ever see. The work of the Devil? Brother Archibald contended that Brother Wilfred had become possessed and a medium for evil from the netherworld. Brother Bertram scoffed, declaring that Brother Wilfred had merely fallen into the dementia that overtook all mortal men at a certain age.   Indeed, Brother Wilfred had been observed of late speaking with passion and vigorous gesticulation to unseen interlocutors.

It was well known in the Abbey that nightmares often interrupted his sleep.   As he had lost his skill at illumination with dimming eyesight and unsteady hand, he became withdrawn, introverted, prone to long periods of silence behind an opaque and mournful visage. It had been rumored for at least two years that he labored in his cell on a weighty project that he would discuss with no one.

After several weeks of rancor and indecision, Abbot Anselm decided that the disposition and meaning of the parchments should be determined by the Archbishop of Canterbury. Whether of God or the Devil, only higher authority, more learned and scholarly men, could decide. The Archbishop himself passed the question - and the manuscript - on to the Holy See at Rome after protracted examination, deliberation and ultimate bewilderment.

There the matter languished for some fifty years. By a miracle of happenstance, the manuscript survived the various agitation's and incivilities that beset the Papacy until a scholar, steeped in the languages of the East, could take up the task of translation. His work, when completed, rekindled dilemma and agonized inquiry among senior Cardinals, particularly those attuned to the temporal and political considerations of the Pope's position.

After much debate, the Cardinals decided to retain the manuscript, as it provided the sole record of the fate that had befallen the members of Pope Gregory's mission sent in search of Prester John. They had vanished without a trace, as though into thin air — a mystery that had spawned much rumor and speculation, a mystery unmasked by John's parchments. But the Cardinals also determined to keep the existence of the work a secret. The Holy See could not afford possible offense to wealthy benefactors, the Venetian family Polo, whose pride it was that their illustrious forebears, Marco and his brother, had been the first Roman Catholics to penetrate to the heart of the Empire, though their journey to the East did not even begin until more than two decades after Wilfred's and John's had ended.

BILBLOGRAPHY

Alexander, Johnathan J.G.; Medival Illuminators and their Methods of Work, (Yale University Press, 1992).

Anderson, G.L., (Editor), Masterpieces of the Orient, (Norton, 1961).

Barker, Hazel; Russia and Central Asia By Road, (Brandt Publications, 1997).

Barks and Green, The Illuminated Rumi, (Broadway Books, 1997).

Bishop, Morris; The Middle Ages, (Houghton Mifflin Co., 1968).

Cantor, Norman F., (Editor); The Encyclopedia of the Middle Ages, (Viking Press, 1999).

Campbell, Joseph; Occidental Mythology: The Masks of God, (Penguin Books, 1976).

Campbell, Joseph: Oriental Mythology: The Masks of God, (Penguin Books, 1976).

Campbell, Joseph; The Power of Myth, (Anchor Books Doubleday, 1988).

Campbell, Joseph; Primitive Mythology: The Masks of God, (Penguin Books, 1976).

Encyclopedia Brittanica, (William Benton Publisher, 1967).

Fletcher, Sir Bannister; A History of Architecture, (20th ed., Architectural Press, 1996).

Goode's World Atlas, (19th ed., Rand McNally, 1995).

Grousset, Rene; The Empire of the Steppes, A History of Central Asia, (Rutgers University Press, 1970).

Halperin, Charles J.; Russia and the Golden Horde; The Mongol Impact on Medieval Russian History, (Indiana University Press, 1985).

King, John, et al.; Central Asia: Lonely Planet Travel Survival Kit, (Lonely Planet Publications, 1996).

Le Guin, Ursula K.; Lao Tzu Tao Te Ching: A Book About the Way and the Power of the Way, (Shambhala, 1998).

Marshall, Robert; Storm From the East: From Genghis Khan to Khubilai Khan, (University of California Press, 1993).

McCullough, David Willis (editor); Chronicles of the Barbarians, (History Book Clun, 1998).

Morgan, David; The Mongols, (Basil Blackwell Ltd., 1986).

Norwich, John Julius; Byzantium; The Decline and Fall, (Alfred A. Knopf, Inc., 1995).

Ratchnevsy, Paul; Genghis Khan, His Life and Legacy, (Basil Blackwell Ltd., 1991).

Rumi, In the Arms of the Beloved, Translation by Johnathan Star, (Penguin Putnam, Inc., 1997).

Strayer, Joseph R.; The Albigensian Crusades, (Ann Arbor Paperback, 1992).

The Wayfarers is part of our series *Another Great American First Novel*.

To Order Call Toll Free
1-877-990-1299

Other titles in the series are:

An Offer of Truth – Taylor Daigneault, ISBN: 0 947993 89 4

Buddha's War – Dean Krystek, ISBN: 0 947993 87 8

Going Away Party – Laura Pedersen, ISBN: 0 947993 77 0

L.A. Breakdown – Lou Mathews, ISBN: 0 947993 80 0

Making It – Ira Skutch, ISBN: 0 947993 84 3

The Munich Sabbatical – Pat-Ann Morgan, ISBN: 0 947993 67 3

OverUnder Sideways Down – Gordon Skene, ISBN 0 947993 79 9

Searching for Grace – Cynthia Kear, ISBN: 0 947993 75 4

For further informtion, please visit our web site:

Http://www.malvernfirst.com

Or contact:

The Malvern Publishing Company, Ltd.

32 Old Street

Upton-upon-Severn, Worcestershire

WR8 0HW, England

Tel: (44) 01684 592430

Fax: (44) 01684 594480

We are represented in the United States by;

The British Book Company, Inc.

149 Palos Verdes Blvd., Ste. B

Redondo Beach, CA

Tel: (310) 373-5917

Fax: (310) 373-7342